AN OFFICE ROMANCE NOVEL

RUTHLESS

NEW YORK TIMES BESTSELLING AUTHOR
DEBORAH BLADON

Also by Deborah Bladon

Chapter 1

Bella

"What are you wearing?"

Rolling my eyes, I press the phone closer to my ear. "That's creepy as fuck. Why would you ask me that?"

"Duh." My best friend, Max Polley, drags that one syllable out as I cross the street headed toward a restaurant in the West Village that I've never been to.

"Maxwell," I snap back, weaving my way through the early evening pedestrian traffic. "Focus."

I'm finally done work for the week. That should bring a sense of relief, but it feels as though half of Manhattan has converged on this block. It's swarming with people. I escaped my crowded office only to dive into this mess.

"I'm focused." He clears his throat. "The guy you're meeting for dinner is named Dale Simpson or Smithson. Maybe it's Samson. All I remember is that there's a son in his surname."

I inch my way past a group of five women who have come to a dead stop in front of a hotel. Rolling suitcases sit at their heels.

Tourists.

I toss them a smile as I pass them by. "What does he look like, Max?"

He heaves a sigh. "I asked Tiffany to send me a picture of him, but so far there's nothing incoming from her."

I slow, anxiety dictating my movements. "Remind me again why I'm going on this date. You know I'd much rather come down to the store and hang out with you."

Max ignores my request to join him. "Remember a few months ago when I was Tiff's plus one at her friend's wedding? I saw Dale that night for a split second. You know that I save every face to memory. I'll describe him to you."

I agreed to this blind date less than an hour ago as a favor to Max.

He arranged it as a favor to his friend. Tiffany Alesso met Max a year ago when she walked into the shoe store his family owns. She bought a dozen pair of stilettoes from him. The commission on the sale paid his rent for a month.

It also funded our joint twenty-third birthday getaway to Atlantic City.

Max covered the bus tickets and the hotel. I sprang for the food and one hundred dollars each for gambling.

We didn't win a dime, but we created memories that will last us forever.

"If you weren't my best friend, I would bail on this," I point out.

"Stop walking and talking." Max laughs. "You sound breathy, Bella. You need to tone that down before you meet Dale or he's going to think you're panting for him."

"What does he look like?" I repeat, stopping to lean against the exterior wall of a cell phone store.

"He's taller than me." He pauses for a moment. "Dark brown hair, blue eyes, no beard when I met him. He's a good-looking guy. I'd give him a solid nine-and-a-half out of ten."

I know his type, so picking Dale out in a crowded restaurant should be a breeze.

"The reservation was for seven," Max goes on, "It's almost seven fifteen. Tiff said Dale's early to everything, so he's probably already seated and waiting for you."

I set off again toward the restaurant. "He can't fault me for being late, Max. An hour ago I didn't even know he existed."

"What are you wearing?" He bounces back to the first thing he asked when I called him.

"Why does that matter?" I ask as I round the corner.

"Isabella Calvetti." My name comes out like a warning. "I'm trying to find you a husband. Work with me here."

"A husband?" I laugh. "I'm twenty-four-years-old. I'm not looking for a life partner."

"I know, I know," he says, his voice edged with fake exasperation. "You're looking for a good time."

I hang my head. "I need to go. I'm almost there."

"The outfit, Bella," he presses. "Tell me what you're wearing."
I look down. "The black heels you gave me for my birthday last year and…"

"Killer, so fucking killer," he interrupts in a rush. "Go on."

"That short sleeve white sweater I bought last month."

"Your boobs are perky melons in that thing."

"Creepy as fuck, again, Max."

"Tell me you're not wearing your grandma's pants."

"My grandma sometimes wears black dress pants, and I sometimes wear black dress pants. It's a coincidence." I stop just short of the entrance to Atlas 22, one of the best seafood restaurants in the city. "I'm wearing my black leather skirt if you must know."

"Damn." I hear the smile in his tone. "The one that makes your ass look like a million bucks?"

I glance at my reflection in one of the panes of glass with the Atlas 22 logo etched on them. "As much as I appreciate the compliment, I need to go."

"Hair and makeup?"

I take a step closer to the glass and study myself. "My hair is just past my shoulders and dark brown, and yes, I wear makeup."

"You're so not funny," he drawls. "You know how to answer the question."

I bite back a laugh. "My hair is on point. That conditioner you recommended works like a charm. The curls are loose, and my makeup is at least an eight out of ten."

"You're ready to knock Dale's pants off."

"No," I answer with a smile. "I'm ready to see if his pants are worth knocking off. I need to go inside and meet him."

"Remember that he's Tiffany's friend's cousin and he's visiting from Philly."

"Cousin from Philly," I repeat back. "I've got it."

I peer through the windows, but the place is packed. I can't see past the bar crowd to the dining area.

"Call me after you've had your way with him."

"You mean after he's bought me dessert?"

"Thanks again for doing this." His voice softens. "Tiffany's stuck at work, so you're doing her a huge favor by filling her seat at dinner."

"I'm happy to do it," I say, trying to mask the nervous energy racing through me. "I'll call you later."

"Love you, Bella."

"Love you," I repeat back.

Ending the call, I drop my phone in my black leather purse and yank open the door to Atlas 22, so I can get this blind date over and done with.

Chapter 2

Bella

"Can I help you, Miss?" A female voice hisses in my left ear as I stare into the packed dining room of the restaurant.

I turn to the sight of a tall, blonde-haired woman. She's wearing a black dress and an earpiece. She has to be the hostess.

"I'm meeting someone."

"Who?" Her question may be directed at me, but her gaze is stuck on something to the left of us.

I sigh, wishing Max had been more confident about Dale's surname. "I believe his name is Dale…"

"Right," she says in a clipped tone. "When he arrived, he mentioned someone would be joining him. He's over there waiting for you."

She points a finger at a man glancing in our direction.

If this is what a nine-and-a-half looks like on Max's scale of hotness, I don't know what the hell a ten would look like.

Dale checks every single one of my boxes. His brown hair is tousled just enough to look sexy, not messy. Dark lashes frame his brilliant blue eyes. His square, smooth jawline complements the rest of his picture perfect face.

He looks like every fantasy I've ever had wrapped in an expensive suit.

Custom made.

I'm not just talking about the dark blue suit or gray tie.

If I were to place an order for a perfect man, Dale would drop from the sky and land in my bed.

A vision of what he must look like naked flashes in front of me.

I blink my eyes shut twice.

The woman next to me whispers something in her earpiece. Her expression morphs into a scowl. "If you'll excuse me, there's a situation I need to address. Wait right here, and someone will seat you momentarily."

"I'll seat myself," I tell her even though she's already expertly navigating her way through the crowded dining room. She's headed straight toward a gray-haired man wearing a chef's jacket. His left hand is waving frantically in the air.

Sucking in a deep breath, I smooth a hand over my hair.

I set off on shaky legs toward Dale's table. I hurry past a waitress carrying a full tray of food that smells incredible.

I take two steps to the left to avoid a woman who is taking a seat at a long, rectangular table where at least a dozen people are already enjoying cocktails.

Just as I'm about to tap Dale on the shoulder, he glances back.

"Hello," I say nervously, my hand stuck in mid-air.

I go for it because there are no guarantees in life and I may never get another chance to touch this man.

I pat his shoulder with my hand. The contact is minimal, but he's solid as stone under that suit jacket.

"I'm Bella," I sigh. "Or Isabella. You can call me either."

He moves to stand, but I skirt around him and plop myself in the wooden chair opposite him.

"There's no need to get up." I shake my head. "I appreciate that you wanted to. My grandma Marti would say you are a true gentleman."

I try and mimic my grandma's slight Italian accent on that last word, but it comes out more like a bad impersonation of a Parisian.

"I'm sorry I'm late," I go on because that's exactly what I do when I'm flustered. I talk too much. "I hope you weren't waiting long."

Picking up the glass of water in front of him, Dale leans back and takes a sip.

"Is this your first time here?" I ask through a grin. "It's mine. The food smells delicious."

Dale's gaze floats up when a waiter approaches us with a tray in his hand.

He sets a half-filled glass tumbler in front of Dale. "Whiskey neat for you, sir."

His hand moves to grab the stem of the other glass on the tray, but he stops when he glances at me.

"Is that a cosmopolitan?" I say, clapping my hands lightly together. "How did you know it's my favorite?"

The waiter's gaze shifts to my date. "Sir, should I bring an…"

"This is fine." Dale's rich baritone voice is more intoxicating than the drink could ever be. "Thank you."

The waiter slides the glass across the white linen tablecloth.

After the day I had at work, this is going to hit the spot, and if all goes well, Dale will be hitting the spot later back at his hotel.

The spot being my ever-elusive G-spot.

He looks like the kind of man who knows exactly where it is.

I've never had sex on a first date, or a second date, but with Dale I'd happily make an exception.

I take a sip of the drink. Pleasure ripples through me.

"Is it to your liking, Isabella?"

I glance across the table at him. He's shifted in his seat. He's leaning forward now, his index finger circling the rim of his glass.

"Very much so." I nod. "Are you going to try your drink?"

"In time." A smile ghosts his mouth.

I have no problem drinking alone, so I take another taste of my cosmopolitan. Lowering the glass to the table, I tilt my head. "What's Philadelphia like? I've never been there."

That perks one of his dark brows. "Are you considering visiting Philadelphia?"

"Are you offering to show me around?" I volley back.

It's bold, but if I don't take the bull by the horns, I'll need to get a new vibrator because mine is wearing out fast.

Dale finally takes a long sip of his whiskey.

I watch his Adam's apple bob on a swallow. Everything about him is so masculine, right down to the size of his hands and the scent of his cologne.

"I haven't gone on many blind dates," I confess, not bothering to add this week to the end of that sentence.

My sister, Gina, set me up with the brother of one of her friends four nights ago. That date lasted ten minutes because he misunderstood and thought he was meeting Gina for dinner, not me.

"Is that so?" Dale studies my face.

"I usually meet men at the regular places." I tuck a strand of hair behind my ear. "Dating apps, clubs, the library."

"The library?" He laughs, and oh my God, what was that?

How can a man's laugh be that sexy?

I snap back to the conversation at hand. "I like men who read."

He drinks again, and I stare like it's the first time I've ever witnessed a human being quench their thirst.

I tear my eyes away from his face. "Maybe I should say I like men who can read."

I wait for the laugh that never comes from him.

Dammit. I want to hear it again.

I go on, "I'm not that picky. To be honest, I've dated all types of men."

"And that means what?" His eyes search mine. "Tell me about the men you've dated, Isabella."

Chapter 3

Bella

"Where, oh where, do I start?" I bark out a laugh.

"The beginning generally works." Dale takes a sip of water.

I should follow his lead, but I need something stronger, so I go for the cosmo. I swallow a large enough gulp to fuel my courage.

"Does the beginning matter when the end looks like you?" I whisper under my breath.

Dale leans closer. "I missed that. What did you say?"

"I said," I pause for a beat to come up with something. "I said that the beginning doesn't matter. What matters is that the last few men I've dated have all been one and done."

"One. And. Done," he pauses for a beat after each word. "So one date and they're done?"

"For the most part." I laugh. "I can tell very early if there's a connection or not. If I don't feel a spark, I don't see a reason to agree to a second date."

"Ah." He tilts his head. "You're a woman who values her time."

"Precisely," I say as though it's the truth.

I devote entirely too much time to binge-watching shows on the weekends. If I add in how much time I spend debating what to eat for dinner each night, I'd have to admit that I value indecision more than anything.

"Take the last guy I dated." I can't resist, so I go for the joke. "Please, take him."

That doesn't warrant a laugh from Dale, or even a smile.

"He was one of those men who always has to be right." I roll my eyes. "You know the type."

Dale nods. "Very well."

Does that mean he's that type? Did I just put my foot in my mouth?

I keep talking because I'm committed to finishing any story I start, especially if I can squeeze a compliment in. "If I would have told him that your eyes are iridescent blue like a sea in Greece, he would have told me that they're yellow."

"My eyes in particular?" He arches a brow.

I'm jealous. I have to apply eyeliner and two coats of mascara every morning to rim my eyes so they look just the way I like.

Dale has to exist.

Not fair.

"You have nice eyes," I offer.

"As do you, Isabella." He stares into my eyes. "Your eyes are the color of the sky when an intense storm is approaching. Countless shades of blue with specks of gray."

I part my lips, but there are no words.

Literally. I sit and stare at him.

"So there was the argumentative one and done." He swallows another mouthful of whiskey. "Who else couldn't keep your attention?"

"There have been a few that fall squarely in the boring one and done category." I wiggle my fingers in the air. 'Too many to count."

His eyes follow the movement of my hand. "They were banished immediately, were they?"

"I cut them loose quickly." I laugh. "Out of fear of falling asleep in my dinner, of course."

"Naturally," he drawls. "Argumentative and boring men don't cut it in Isabella's world."

"Or married men." I shrug a shoulder. "That's happened."

His gaze skims over my face. "You've gone on a date with a married man?"

"No." I shake my head. "I realized before I agreed to a date. So technically those men weren't one and done. They were none and done."

"As they should be," he comments with a curve of his lips.

I sip the last remaining luscious drops of my cosmo. I glance around wondering why the waiter hasn't brought us menus.

I should be grateful that he's slow. I'm good with this date lasting all weekend.

"I'm having a great time." I grin. "I'm glad I took a chance on this blind date."

I catch sight of a pretty redheaded woman approaching from the left. Her gaze is trained on Dale. A smile plays on her ruby red lips. It grows wider with each step she takes toward us.

She's expertly navigating her way through the crowded restaurant as if it's a runway and she's a supermodel.

I can't help but stare.

I'm not alone.

People sitting at the tables near us glance at her as she breezes past. Her low cut black dress is clinging to her body. The lace bra she's wearing peeks out with every forward step she takes.

I wait for Dale to notice her, but he's focused on me.

Out of the corner of my eye, I see her slowing as she nears us. She comes to a complete stop when she's almost in Dale's lap.

Her hand leaps to his shoulder, but her touch isn't tentative. She runs her fingers over the fabric of his suit jacket until they leisurely tangle in the hair on the back of his head.

"Forgive me, lover," she purrs. "I saw an old friend on my way to the ladies' room. I had to stop to catch up with her."

What the hell?

Her gaze slides from Dale to me before finally settling on the empty glass on the table in front of me. "Who are you and where's the cosmo I ordered?"

Chapter 4

Bella

I skid my chair back so quickly that it bumps into a waitress.

The tray in her hand wobbles precariously close to the head of a man sitting directly behind me.

Dammit.

Not only am I completely humiliated, but I'm about to knock someone out cold.

"Look out," I scream as I jump to my feet.

The man sitting behind me ducks just as the tray glides past his head. It doesn't hit him, but a small silver spoon that tumbles from it bounces off his shoulder.

Everything else on the tray crashes to the floor.

Taking a step to the side, I reach for my purse. I slung it over the back of the chair I was sitting in. I tug on the strap so hard that the chair falls over at my feet.

Near silence settles over the restaurant.

I don't look up because I know that every eye in the place is on me, including not-Dale and his girlfriend.

"Bella? Are you Bella?"

I nod softly before I turn and face the man asking the question.

He's good-looking in an ordinary kind of way. His brown hair is cut short to his head. A five o'clock shadow peppers his jaw.

Concern knits his brow. His blue eyes rake me over from head-to-toe. "Tiffany told me I'd be having dinner with the most beautiful woman in the restaurant. She was right. I'm Dale Samuelson."

Two waiters descend on us as they move to clear the broken plates and glasses.

"Let's get you out of the way of the glass." Dale rests a hand on my elbow. "Come join me at my table. It's over there."

I turn in the direction he's pointing. There's an empty table less than ten feet from where we are. If I had just looked beyond not-Dale, I might have seen real Dale when I arrived.

As embarrassed as I am, I glance at the man I just shared a drink with. I can't read the expression on his face, but I'm sure he can read what's written all over mine.

Horror.

I flirted with a stranger, stole his girlfriend's drink, and told him all about my string of dating flops.

"Can I get a cosmopolitan?" The redhead asks the waitress who is trying to wipe smashed peas from the front of her white button-down shirt. "Mine seems to have disappeared into thin air."

She snaps her fingers next to my ear.

I should apologize, but where the hell would I start?

This is Manhattan. I can duck out of here, disappear into the crowds of the city, and never see these people again.

I'll become a funny story to them, and they'll become a reminder to me why I'll never go on another blind date again.

I turn to real Dale. "Can I get a rain check on dinner?"

"I'm in New York until the end of the month," he says softly. "If you're up to it, we can plan something while I'm here."

I nod.

"I'll see you out." He slides a hand around my waist.

I don't resist because I could use his kind touch to get me past the people who are still throwing looks at me.

I know I caused an unwanted distraction.

We start across the quiet restaurant toward the exit. I steal a fleeting glance over my shoulder.

Not-Dale is still on his feet. His eyes lock on mine for a split second.

Our short date may have been unintended, but I know I'll never forget it. I know I'll never forget him.

***

Tapping my foot on the hardwood floor in his living room, I wait for Max to stop laughing.

This is the very reason why I've avoided him for the past two days. I tried to avoid everyone, but I live with my sister. I moved in with her three months ago when my former roommate decided she was moving to Minneapolis.

When I got home after my disastrous blind date on Friday, Gina wasn't around so I went straight to my bedroom. That solace lasted until yesterday afternoon when she dragged me out of bed and down to our grandmother's Italian restaurant.

Helping in the kitchen was a good distraction, but my grandma Marti knew something was up with me. She kept shooting me questioning looks as we made ravioli together. I told her I was thinking about a work issue.

It wasn't a complete lie.

I have to work on my issues; in particular, my issues with dating. A break is in order.

I'll follow through with my dinner with the real Dale, but that's it. After that, dating is taking a back seat to everything else in my life.

"I still can't believe that you sat at the wrong table." Max shakes his head, sending the front of his blond hair tumbling onto his forehead. "You didn't call him Dale even once? Did you do all the talking?"

"No," I lie. "He said a few things."

"Not one of those things was his name?"

Braiding the end of my ponytail, I shrug. "It doesn't matter at this point. What matters is that I can't go back to Atlas 22."

"Sure, you can." He pats my shoulder, picking a small piece of lint from my blue sweater. "A week from now, no one will remember that you trashed the place."

I hide my face in my hands. "I'm trying to forget it ever happened."

Max tugs my hands down. His hazel eyes lock on my frown. "Cheer up, Bella. You still have your date with Dale to look forward to."

I wish I were meeting non-Dale for dinner instead.

Max places another picture in the photo album on his lap.

One Sunday a month, Max and I convene at his apartment for pasta night and pictures on his couch.

I bring the pasta from Calvetti's, my grandma's restaurant. Max drags a cardboard box filled with pictures out of his front closet. While we eat whatever my grandma packed for dinner, Max tells me stories about his family while he sorts through the old photographs.

One or two pictures make the cut each week. Tonight a baby photo of Max and a weathered, yellowing photograph of his great-grandfather took their rightful place on the tenth page of the album.

Genealogy is all the rage in Max's world at the moment.

I stretch out my legs. "I need to get home. It's back to the grind tomorrow."

Max skims a hand over the knee of my leggings. "Do you want to go to a movie this week?"

"Wednesday works for me." I punctuate my answer with a nod of my head.

"It's a date unless Dale asks you out for dinner that night." He narrows his gaze. "By Dale, I mean the real Dale and not some random in a restaurant."

That random in the restaurant hasn't left my thoughts all weekend.

I may have enjoyed some alone time in bed while thinking about what could have been after our date if only it were a real date.

I tug on the hood of Max's gray sweatshirt. "I'm going home. I'll text you when I'm done work tomorrow."

"You better." He kisses my cheek. "I hope it's as boring as a Monday should be."

Chapter 5

Bella

I peer around the corner into Duke Garent's office, expecting to see my boss's smiling face.

The gray-haired man in a black suit standing with his back to me, staring out at the morning view of midtown Manhattan shouldn't be here.

Ivan Garent, Duke's father, works out of the Chicago office of Garent Industries. Whenever he plans a trip to New York, I'm on the list of people who need to know about it.

I had no clue that he'd be here today.

If I had known, I would have chosen something other than the red sheath dress I'm wearing. I paired it with a pair of red heels and matching lipstick.

Duke doesn't subscribe to a dress code. I wore a dark blue suit to my interview with him. He told me that day that he doesn't follow the same rules as his dad and I could wear whatever I wanted to the office if I landed the position of his executive assistant.

I take my job seriously, but a pop of color never hurt anyone.

I glance at the watch on my wrist. It's ten minutes before nine. I'm early.

Duke is late. He's usually in his office by eight-thirty or so he tells me.

I clear my throat. "Mr. Garent?"

That turns him on his heel. A soft smile crosses his lips. The man is as handsome as he is distinguished.

He started the company when he was in his early twenties. Fifty years later, he stands at the helm of an international conglomerate that manages hundreds of subsidiaries.

"Isabella Calvetti." He approaches me with open arms.

I go in for the hug because I've known Ivan since I was seventeen and an intern in the summer program that Garent hosted.

That internship turned into a part-time college job and ultimately, a full-time position after I graduated from NYU with dual degrees in economics and marketing.

I've worked my way up the ranks, finally landing this coveted position six months ago.

It's not my end goal, but I love the work. I learn new things daily, and I can't complain about my compensation package.

Ivan takes a step back, looking me over. "You look as lovely as ever. Tell me, how is life treating you?"

Other than that bump in the road on Friday night at Atlas 22 I can't complain.

I'm determined to put that behind me. That's why this morning I responded to the text message that Dale sent me last night asking if I'd be interested in having dinner with him tomorrow.

I accepted.

He's good-looking, kind, and leaving town in a few days, so it won't turn into anything more than a fun evening.

"Life is good." I cross my arms over my chest. "How are you?"

"I'm alright." His gaze drops.

Curiosity nips at me.

The last time I spoke with Duke was Friday before I left the office. He was excited about the weekend since he was planning on heading to Fire Island to visit with friends.

He would have let me know via text if he was going to be out of the office today. He should be here by now. His dad shouldn't be here.

I clear my throat. "I'm surprised to see you. Duke didn't mention that you'd be visiting New York."

"It was a last minute decision. Duke didn't have time to fill you in." Ivan scratches his chin. "We need to talk."

Fear bubbles inside of me. Duke and I are friends outside of the office. He once told me that if he ever had to fire me, he'd fly his dad in to handle it.

I can recite every line in my employment contract from memory.

I haven't done anything wrong, other than a handful of lunches that ran a few minutes over. Duke always looks the other way when that happens because he's often out of the office for two or three hours at a time for lunch.

"About?" I ask tentatively.

"Have a seat." He gestures toward the two ornate leather chairs that sit in front of Duke's massive desk.

My boss spared no expense when he had this space redecorated three months ago.

My desk sits outside this office. I was grateful when Duke didn't ask his interior designer to extend his vision to my area. I prefer sleek minimalism to what's going on in here.

Lowering myself into one of the chairs, I smooth the skirt of my dress.

Ivan rounds the desk and plops himself in Duke's chair.

Throne is a better way to describe it. The seat is brown leather. The back and arms are crafted from what looks like gold.

Duke works hard to live up to his name. I'm surprised he doesn't parade around the office with a crown atop his head.

"You've been working for my son for a few months." Ivan rests both hands on a blue file folder.

I'm the one who puts every file, paper, and receipt on Duke's desk and I don't recognize the folder.

"Six months," I affirm with a nod of my head.

I pick at the chipped red nail polish on my thumb. It's no match for my anxiety.

Ivan's next move is all silence and seriousness. He twists the folder around, slides it across the desk, and leans back in his son's chair.

I stare at the nondescript folder. There's no label. I don't see a clue about what is inside. All I spot is the corner of a white piece of paper sticking out.

"What's this?" I ask, studying Ivan's face for a hint.

"Open it."

His expression gives nothing away, so I look down and flip open the folder. There are two copies of an employment contract inside with my name on them.

I run my index finger under each word on the first page, reading slowly. When I reach the six-figure a year salary, I stop. That has to be a misprint. I make mid-five figures now.

I move on to the bullet points about a monthly commuting allowance, an expense account, and three weeks paid vacation a year.

Every item listed is a huge step up from the contract I signed a half a year ago.

I skim the other four pages. All the information looks identical to my current contract. I skip over the details about performance reviews, confidentiality, and everything else that I read carefully before I accepted the job.

I finally look up at Ivan and repeat my question. "What is this?"

"Your future." He slides a silver pen across the desk. "You've done remarkable work. I need you to agree to stay with Garent for the next year. Sign on the dotted line, Isabella, and everything listed is yours."

Chapter 6

Bella

"You never bring me lunch on Mondays." Max reaches for the sandwich in my hand. "You're all about getting your week in order."

That sounds like me.

Typically, I do spend most of the day Monday lining up Duke's week. I schedule his meetings and go over what he has to accomplish before six p.m. on Friday.

Today is different.

After I signed my new contract, Ivan had to leave Duke's office to take a call. When he finally came back an hour later, I was at my desk, working on a proposal for a company that Duke wants to buy out.

Ivan apologized for having to leave the building, but he assured me that he'd be back by mid-afternoon. He told me that I could take an extended lunch break if I wanted to celebrate my new contract.

There is no one I'd rather celebrate with than my best friend.

I yank a mini bottle of champagne out of my purse.

Max's gaze falls to the bottle before it lands back on my face. "Bella?"

Since the bottle was in the discount bin at the liquor store, I have no trouble unscrewing the cap.

"No cork?" He chuckles. "Am I right to assume that this celebratory lunch is low-key since you invested in the cheap stuff?"

I examine the label of the bottle in my hand. "You're wrong to assume that."

He brings the parchment paper wrapped roasted vegetable sandwich in his hand to his nose. Inhaling deeply, he leans back in his chair. "This smells incredible. I win for best lunch today."

I look around, but Max and I are the only two people in the break room in the back of Polleys, the shoe store Max's mom owns.

I pick at the corner of my grilled chicken and arugula wrap. "Something happened this morning."

"I'm going to learn what that is at some point, right?" Max tilts his head. "My lunch break is only thirty minutes. We're barreling toward the five-minute mark so spit it out so I can eat my sandwich."

Teasing Max is one of my favorite things to do. It started when we were kids. Max, his mom, and his grandparents lived in the same building as my family. Max would have dinner with us at least a couple of times a week.

When we ended up in the same class in third grade, we made a vow to be best friends until the end of time.

Time is still moving forward, and we're closer than ever.

"It has to do with work."

He takes a large bite of the ciabatta bun and vegetables. Red pepper sauce drips from the corner of his mouth.

I reach for a paper napkin, but he beats me to it, gliding it along his lips.

I wait for him to finish chewing because I know he'll have questions.

"If you don't tell me what's going on, Bella, I'll call Duke myself."

I slide a piece of arugula from my wrap and pop it in my mouth. "This is about Ivan. He was waiting for me this morning."

"Ivan Garent?" He straightens in his chair. "Mr. Money himself is in Manhattan?"

"He's here because he had a morning meeting with Ms. Money herself." I brush a hand over my shoulder.

His eyes don't leave my face. "Ms. Money? You?"

"You're looking at someone who just signed a new contract with Garent Industries. Let me count the ways this benefits me. A six-figure a year salary, an expense account, an allowance for commuting, and three weeks of vacation this year."

Max's jaw drops.

I cup my hand over my ear. "Is that Maui I hear calling my name? Our names?"

Max tugs on the collar of the light green polo shirt he's wearing. "Excuse me? Repeat, please. Repeat."

I laugh. "You heard me. I got a raise this morning. A very big raise."

"I'm not a mathematician, but it sounds like your pay doubled." He pushes back from the table. He moves across the break room to grab two paper cups that are next to the coffee maker.

I didn't think of it that way, until now. "Doubled plus an extra ten grand on top of that."

Sitting back down, Max narrows his eyes. "That's a huge raise. Plus the perks. What the hell do you have to do to earn that?"

"Nothing." I shrug it off. "Mr. Garent said that they want to keep me for the next year."

"There's keeping, and then there's keeping." He drawls out the last word. He studies me as he pours a splash of champagne into each cup. "Did you help Duke bury a body? Are you his alibi but not really his alibi? What the hell is going on?"

I tug on the bottom of a strand of my hair. "It's nothing like that. I'm worth it. They see the value in what I have to offer, and they don't want to lose me."

He picks up the cup in front of him. "Here's to whatever the hell you're going to have to do to earn that extra money. Cheers!"

I raise my cup and tap it against the side of his. "You're wrong, Max. All I have to do is continue to be the best assistant Duke Garent has ever had."

"Mark my words, Bella." He points a finger at me. "There was some fine print in that contract you signed that you didn't bother to read. I, for one, can't wait to find out what it is."

***

I get back to my desk shortly after one to find Duke's office door closed.

I breathe a sigh of relief. As soon as it opens it, I'll ask my boss about the new contract.

Max planted seeds of doubt in my mind.

I know I'm great at my job. Duke has told me often that I'm irreplaceable. It makes perfect sense that he'd want to keep me here at Garent Industries.

What doesn't make sense is that I signed a contract six months ago that guaranteed I'd remain in my position for a full year.

I wasn't going anywhere. I couldn't go anywhere without facing the board of Garent to plead my case to leave the company.

Duke and Ivan didn't have to give me a raise, so why did they?

The phone on my desk rings. The flashing red light that accompanies the sound is a sure sign that Duke needs something from me.

I debate opening his door to see what it is, but I pick up the call instead.

"Hi, Duke," I say cheerily. "What do you need?"

"A moment of your time, Ms. Calvetti."

It takes my brain a few seconds to catch up to what's going on. That's not Duke's voice. This voice is too deep and rough. It's too something…

"Who is this?" I question.

"Come into my office, Ms. Calvetti."

What the hell is going on?

I glance down at the phone. I was sure that the call was coming from inside Duke's office, but if that were true, I'd be talking to my boss.

"Who are you, and where is your office?" I ask as politely as I can.

"My office is ten feet from where you're standing," he snaps.

I spin to face Duke's door. "You're in Duke's office?"

"Ms. Calvetti." His tone lowers. "Get in here now."

Frustrated, I slam the phone down, stalk across the floor, and swing open Duke's door.

I shake my head twice when I see the man standing in the middle of my boss's office.

"What the hell?" I mutter under my breath.

He smirks. "Well, well, well, what do we have here?"

There's no way this is real.

It's him.

The gorgeous man less than two feet away from me is the same man I mistakenly thought was Dale on Friday night.

I thought I'd never see him again.

My stomach quivers in excitement or maybe confusion. "How did you find me?"

"Find you?" he questions.

"We met at Atlas 22," I say quietly. "How did you know that I work here? I never mentioned Garent Industries."

Clearing his throat he looks me dead in the eyes. "Our run-in at the restaurant was purely coincidental."

My brow furrows as I take in what he said. "I don't understand."

"I'll make it crystal clear." He takes a step closer to me. "I'm Barrett Adler. I'm your new boss."

Chapter 7

Barrett

Isn't this an interesting turn of events?

The beautiful woman standing in front of me is my new assistant. She's also the woman who sat down at my table at Atlas 22 the other night and inserted herself firmly into the middle of my date.

"You're my new boss?" Her eyes widen but her expression gives nothing away.

I live for moments like this.

Surprising an employee is always a test to their character. If they handle it well, they gain my respect. If they don't, that's a mark on their record.

I'm not a three strikes and you're out kind of man. Two strikes will land you in the unemployment line. If the infraction is serious enough, one strike is all it takes.

I value hard work, integrity, and honesty.

Self-control is a must.

Isabella Calvetti is about to prove if she has any.

"That's correct." I cross my arms over my chest.

Her eyes follow my movements. She takes in my tailored gray suit, black button-down shirt, and matching tie.

First impressions set the tone, so I chose carefully before I arrived at the offices of Garent Industries thirty minutes ago. Every person who works in this building will in some way be answering to me.

"You're mistaken." Her head tilts. "Where's Duke?"

That's complicated and messy. Tragic as well, but it's not my place to delve into the finer details of why Duke Garent isn't in this office, and I am.

"I need you to arrange the removal of this." I jerk a thumb over my shoulder at the monstrosity of a desk that Duke had hand carved. Personal taste is subjective, but Duke's is shit. "The chairs as well. All of the chairs."

She gazes past my shoulder. "Where's Duke?"

Persistence is admirable, but in this instance, it's a waste of time. "Ms. Calvetti, I want these items removed as soon as possible. I have new office furniture arriving at four."

She glances at the watch on her wrist. "I'm not doing anything until you tell me where my boss is."

"You're looking at him."

Her hands drop to her hips. "I need to make a call."

"Good." I exhale. "The sooner they take this out of here, the better."

"I'm not talking about Duke's furniture." She stomps a foot. "I'm going to call Ivan Garent. You've wandered into the wrong office, Mr. Adder. I'll find out where you're supposed to be."

"Adler," I correct her. "And I'm exactly where I need to be."

"We'll see." She points her index finger at me. "Don't touch anything until I come back."

I round the desk and take a seat in the chair, or throne.

Whatever the fuck it is, it's uncomfortable.

Watching her march out of my office stirs my cock.

Her ass is utter perfection in that tight red dress she's wearing. I shake away that thought because business mixed with pleasure is a recipe for career disaster.

I hear the distant sound of Isabella's voice as she places a call. I assume Ivan is on the receiving end of that.

I'll give her a moment to accept that this is her new reality. Once that happens, Ms. Calvetti is going to realize that for the next twelve months, she works for me.

Whether she likes it or not.

***

Isabella has more influence than I expected.

Her call to Ivan Garent brought him rushing up from the floor below us.

I was under the impression that he was in a meeting and couldn't be disturbed.

"Tell Mr. Adger that he doesn't belong in here." Isabella stands in the doorway of my office with Ivan by her side. "He wants me to have all of Duke's furniture removed. I can't do that."

"Adler," I correct her again.

She shakes her head as if she doesn't give a fuck about the correct pronunciation of my surname.

Ivan squints at her. "Barrett is taking over for Duke."

She recoils with a step back, bumping her curvy ass against the doorjamb.

Her gaze is pinned to Ivan's face. "Why?"

I learned about Duke on Saturday morning when Ivan called me and offered up the job of CEO of Garent Industries. I just happened to be in New York City for the weekend visiting my oldest friend, and making a new redheaded friend.

I've been spinning my wheels as the COO in Chicago for the past five years.

This isn't how I anticipated landing the job, but I wasn't about to turn it down. Ivan needs me to run the ship, so I'm moving to Manhattan to take on the task.

"Let's talk outside." Ivan gestures toward Isabella's desk. "Give us a minute, Barrett."

I nod.

There are no words. He held his composure through our discussion about his son. I feel for the man. I feel for Duke too, but I have a company to run and the sooner that Ms. Calvetti accepts that I'm her boss, the better.

Chapter 8

Bella

I don't say a word as Ivan explains what happened to Duke on Friday night after he left the office.

I take in everything he says, and the emotion that he can't contain. When he finally takes a breath, I step closer. I let him gather me into his arms because he needs it. I need it too.

"He'll need our support, Isabella," he whispers. "We can't visit him yet, but I'm hopeful that once we're given the green light that you'll want to see him."

I wasn't working for Duke the last time this happened. I was still an intern.

Rumors about Duke's addictions were the only thing anyone talked about when he didn't show up for work one day.

That absence turned into a three-month stint in rehab for alcohol and drug addiction.

Duke collared that beast.

He went to meetings, sometimes twice a day. His commitment to sobriety was inspiring.

Sometime between then and now he lost the battle. He was arrested for public drunkenness and disorderly conduct on Fire Island late Friday night.

This morning, he was on an airplane headed to an addiction treatment facility just outside of Boston. His mom is making the trip with him.

Ivan steps back, his arms crossing his chest. "He needs to focus on his recovery. I need to be available whenever he needs me. Barrett agreed to take over as CEO."

"In the interim?" I ask, hopefully. "Duke came back to work after a few months the last time…"

"No," Ivan interrupts me with a shake of his head. "I fear I put too much pressure on my son."

Guilt favors those who love deeply.

I can tell that he thinks Duke's fall from grace is his fault.

"If…no, when, he comes back to Garent, we will figure out where he feels most comfortable." His gaze drops. "That's not something to think about today. Duke's recovery is what matters. My son has a bright future ahead of him."

He's right.

Duke has a lot of life left to live. He's only thirty-six-years-old. The company will still be here when he's ready to come back.

"I should have explained all of this earlier." He glances at the open doorway of Duke's office. "I was trying to juggle too many things at once this morning. I assumed you'd take a longer lunch and I'd get to you before you got to Barrett."

I look over to where Barrett is standing next to Duke's desk. He's focused on the phone in his hands.

"I offered you the new contract to keep you here, Isabella. You're Duke's closest ally. You know every deal, every contact, everything. My hope is that with you by his side, Barrett's transition to CEO will be seamless."

All Mr. Garent needs from me is reassurance, so I give that to him. "I'll do my best, sir."

"You always do." He straightens his jacket. "I'm going take Barrett down to marketing to introduce him to the team. You'll hold down the fort until we're done with that?"

"Of course. You'll let me know how Duke is doing?" I lower my voice. "If you or Mrs. Garent need anything, I'm always here for you."

"I'll check in regularly." He lets out a deep breath. "I only need one thing from you. Do your job exactly the same way you have for the past six months. You're the best executive assistant my son ever had. I expect you to be the same to Barrett."

I wait until he walks into Duke's office before I unlock the top drawer of my desk and pull out my copy of the contract I signed earlier.

I scan it quickly, noting that nowhere does it mention Duke by name.

When I reach the bottom of page three, I stop and read the last line.

Isabella Calvetti will report directly to the CEO of Garent Industries, Mr. Barrett Adler.

Dammit. I just found the fine print.

***

An hour later, I let the ringing office phone go to voicemail. I know that I'll have to explain to whoever is on the other end, that Duke is no longer in charge. I've already had that conversation with three Garent employees. All of them had the same reaction; shock and disappointment.

I'm still reeling from what happened earlier.

Leaning back in my chair, I close my eyes. I'm exhausted, and it's not even three o'clock yet. There's no harm in a five minute nap to refuel and recharge before I return that call.

"What are you doing?"

My eyes pop open to find my new boss standing in front of my desk. I look past him to the closed elevator doors. How did he get here? I should have heard the elevator. He must have taken the stairs from the floor below us.

Straightening in my chair, I look him dead in the eye. "I'm working, Mr. Adver."

"It's Adler." He points at my left hand. "What the hell is that?"

Twirling the white stick in my fingers, I sigh. "It's a heart-shaped lollipop."

I follow that up with a quick lick of the cherry flavored candy.

"A lollipop?"

"A cherry lollipop." I pop it in my mouth and slide it out over my lips.

Watching every move I make, he repeats my words back. "A cherry lollipop."

"It's delicious." Without thinking, I push it toward him. "Do you want a bite?"

What the hell is wrong with me? Who asks their boss a question like that?

Before I have a chance to drop my hand, he reaches for the lollipop, spinning the stick between his fingers. In one fluid movement, he tosses it over my shoulder toward the wastebasket.

He misses.

I turn to see shards of red candy on the floor.

Jumping to my feet, I round my desk. "Why did you do that?"

"Satisfy yourself after hours."

He did not just say that. "Excuse me?"

Glaring at me, he shoves a hand through his hair. "Satisfy your sweet tooth after hours. You're my executive assistant. It's not professional for you to be sitting here sucking on that."

"Duke never cared if I sucked it at work. He liked it."

Did that come out the way I think it did?

I scrub a hand over my forehead. "What I meant to say is Blanche Heald brings them in for the staff whenever she makes up a bunch for her grandkids. Duke loved them too."

Crossing his arms over his chest, he narrows his gaze. "Blanche from accounting?"

I nod. "She's a good friend to the Garents. Duke always kissed her on the cheek to thank her for the candy."

Contemplating that, he looks around the office. "Blanche and I are not friends, and I hate candy. I never want to see another one of those in this office."

"Fine." I drop my hands to my hips. "I'll save them for when I'm done work."

Staring at the broken candy on the floor, he lets out a heavy exhale. "You're done now. Leave, Isabella."

Done? Is he firing me over this?

With a shaking breath, I glance at his face. "I'm done?"

"I don't need you for the remainder of the day." His gaze drops to his watch. "We'll start fresh tomorrow morning."

I heave a sigh of relief, grateful that I haven't screwed myself out of the best job I've ever had.

***

My grandmother, Martina Calvetti, rushes toward me. "It's the middle of the afternoon, Dolly. Are you sick? You're not pregnant, are you?"

Dolly. The name my grandma has called me since the day I was born. She's told me the story over and over, and I'd happily listen to it a million times more.

When my dad put me in my grandma's arms at the hospital, she told him it was like looking at a perfect little doll; her perfect little doll.

I glance down at the front of my dress. "Do I look pregnant to you?"

"No. You don't have the glow."

I shake off the comment with a smile. "I have the rest of the afternoon off. I came to bring you these."

I swing my hand from behind my back to reveal a small bouquet of peonies. They're my grandma's favorite flowers.

"You're too good to me, my sweetheart." She plants a kiss on my right cheek.

I know she's left a bright pink lipstick imprint. I won't wipe it off. I live for the reminders of how much my grandma loves me.

"Walk with me. Talk with me." She motions to the kitchen of her restaurant. "My girl looks troubled."

"It's frustration," I confess. "I have to report to someone new at work."

I leave out the part about crashing my new boss's date a few nights ago, and I skip right over the fantasies that have been playing on repeat in my mind since I met him.

She turns to face me just as we reach the entrance to the bustling kitchen. "You'll do the job they pay you to do. It doesn't matter who you report to if you do your best."

I glance at the friendly faces that cook the delicious Italian food that has been a staple of my life for as long as I can remember.

"I have time to help in the kitchen today," I offer because being in this restaurant has always brought me peace.

"We'll see." She dumps the dying daisies my sister brought her last week into the trash before she plops the peonies in the same vase. "First, you'll eat."

Chapter 9

Barrett

I've never had an assistant who looked like Isabella Calvetti.

At this moment, she's outside my office with her back to me.

That's affording me a clear view of her shapely ass. It's wrapped in a dark green skirt today.

The sheer black blouse she's wearing is nice, as are the black heels that have granted her a few inches in height. It's the skirt that I can't tear my eyes away from. Or maybe it's the ass underneath.

She glances back over her shoulder at me. Her eyes flit across my face. "Is there something you need, Mr. Admer?"

It's a simple question with such a ripe choice of possible answers.

"Adler," I correct her yet again.

She turns to face me. "Where did you put Duke's furniture?"

"Where it will never see the light of day again," I say with a straight face.

That draws her two steps closer. "What does that mean?"

"It's ugly as hell." I smooth a hand over the top of my steel desk. "I didn't want to subject another person to that misery."

She twirls a piece of her hair around her index finger. "Duke will want it back when he returns to the office."

"Your devotion to the man is misguided."

Her nostrils flare as her eyes widen. Her irises are popping with more gray than blue today. "Duke was the best boss I've ever had."

"Until now," I point out.

"The best boss I ever had," she repeats.

Shot fired. Target missed.

I lean back in my chair, my hand adjusting the dark blue tie around my neck. "I'm not here to win a popularity contest, Isabella."

"Good." Her hands drop to her hips. "You'd lose."

Her attitude makes me want to dig my teeth into her shoulder as I pump my dick in her...

I shake off the thought.

I've had female assistants in the past, but not one has ever gotten under my skin this way, and we're only on our second day.

"I'd like a cup of coffee." I change the subject before I say something in response to her insult that I'll regret.

"There's coffee in the break room down the hall."

I laugh.

Her hand moves to the center of her chest. "Why are you laughing?"

"Get me a coffee." I glance down when my phone chimes. "No sugar, no cream."

"I'm not that kind of assistant," she stresses the last word. "Duke always got his own coffee."

I look to the left, before gazing to the right. "Duke isn't here."

"Right now," she adds.

If she wants to hang tight to the hope that Ivan will reinstate his son at some point, that's her pipe dream. It's not reality.

I signed a three-year contract for this position with a yearly seven-figure salary and a list of perks that put hers to shame.

"My coffee." I rest my hands on my desk. "Or would you prefer to discuss what happened at Atlas 22 the other night?"

Her expression shifts from indignation to shock. "We don't have to talk about that. It was an unfortunate misunderstanding."

Her cheeks bloom pink. She's embarrassed.

I found her kryptonite.

"How's Dale?" I ask with a perk of my brow. "The actual Dale. How is he?"

She stomps a shoe on the floor. "I'll get your coffee, Mr. Adwer."

"Barrett," I say with a smile. "Call me Barrett."

***

I spoke of the devil earlier and… No. The man wandering near the reception desk in the lobby of the Garent Industries building doesn't resemble the devil. This guy is timid and nervous.

He's also lost.

"Hey," I call out to him. "You're Dale, aren't you?"

He glances over at me, his shoulders straightening. "Dale Samuelson."

He offers his full name along with a hand. I take it for a quick shake.

"Have we met?" he asks, his eyes searching my face.

I don't blame him for not being able to place me. His attention was on Isabella at Atlas 22 on Friday evening.

"Barrett Adler." I pinch my brows together. "What brings you to Garent today?"

I know the answer to that question.

Dale's gaze wanders past my shoulder to the bank of elevators behind me. His face lights up like a kid who is handed every toy he ever wanted. "I'm meeting someone. She works here."

I hear the click of her approaching heels. The sound slows as she nears us.

"Bella," he says her name with a smile. "You look beautiful."

I resist the urge to turn and look for myself. I spent most of the day watching her as she sat at her desk.

I left two hours ago to take a meeting uptown. I expected to have a few minutes alone with her before she clocked out for the day, but time wasn't on my side.

I smell the sweet scent of her perfume as she walks next to me.

"Dale." She moves to him, reaching out a hand. "It's nice to see you again."

Dale takes it as an invitation. He wraps his arms around her.

I watch her eyes close briefly. I shouldn't give a shit if his touch does something to her.

"We should go," Dale suggests, taking her hand in his. "I made a reservation for six at an Italian place in Brooklyn I think you'll like. Donini's. I hear they make great fettuccine."

Her grandmother owns the restaurant that serves the best Italian food in the state. Taking her for pasta anywhere else is an insult.

Dale should have blocked out five minutes out of his day to research Isabella. I did last night.

She lets out a soft sigh. "Let's go."

I level my gaze on her. "Goodnight, Isabella."

"Goodnight, Mr. Adjer." She pauses before she adds, "I hope you enjoy your evening."

I might if I called Minna, the redhead I had dinner with at Atlas 22 the other night. Our evening ended early when I ducked out after dessert with an excuse about a pressing business matter.

I slide my phone out of the inner pocket of my suit jacket. Scrolling through the unread text messages, I land on one sent by Minna an hour ago.

Minna: Let me show you around Manhattan. I'll start the tour in my bedroom.

She's attractive, willing, and just what I need to take the edge off.

I thumb out a reply.

Barrett: Dinner was enjoyable. I'll skip the tour. Take care.

I delete her number and drop my phone back in my pocket.

I may regret turning her down, but I know another way to take the edge off.

Work. It's never failed me. I walk to the elevators, press the call button, and make a mental list of everything I want Isabella to do for me tomorrow starting with coming to work an hour early.

Chapter 10

Bella

I glance down at my phone when it buzzes.

A text message pops up on the screen.

Unknown: Be at the office tomorrow at 8 a.m. sharp.

Seriously? Did Barrett just text me? He knows I'm on a date.

I smile across the table at Dale. "I don't mean to be rude, but it's a work matter. I can handle it with just a couple of text messages."

He nods. "I'm enjoying my dinner. Take all the time you need."

I type out a response.

Bella: You must have texted the wrong number. Have a nice night!

Unknown: I didn't text the wrong number. This is your boss.

I roll my eyes and bite back a laugh.

Bella: Duke? Thank God it's you. I miss you like crazy.

Unknown: Not Duke. Barrett. I need you at the office at 8.

Bella: My contract says I start work at 9. I'll see you then.

I place my phone on the table, but it buzzes almost instantly with a reply.

Unknown: Your new contract states that you work the hours I request.

All my common sense disappeared when I saw the six-figure salary and perks. I know better than to sign a contract I haven't read over carefully.

Barrett sends another text before I can respond to the last one.

Unknown: I'll see you at 8. How's Donini's?

I glance at the half-eaten cheeseburger and the handful of fries left on my plate.

I couldn't go to Donini's. If I ever set foot in that restaurant, I'd have to put myself up for adoption.

No member of Marti's family eats Italian food anywhere but at Calvetti's. That's an unspoken rule that I will never break. I convinced Dale that I was in the mood for a burger, so he brought me to this cowboy themed restaurant in the heart of Times Square.

I add my new boss's name and number to my contact list before I type out a response.

Bella: We never made it to Brooklyn.

I know it's rude to make small text talk with Barrett while I'm on a date with Dale, but it's not even seven p.m. and I've already had dinner. I'm ready to go home.

Alone.

Dale isn't going to get to first base tonight.

"What do you want to do after dinner?" Dale wiggles his brows at me.

I scratch my chin. "My boss needs me to go into the office extra early tomorrow, so I have to go home soon."

His gaze drops to his watch. "It's six fifty."

I resist the urge to look at my phone when it buzzes again.

"Are you free tomorrow night?" He asks before I can come up with a believable excuse about why our date is ending. "I'll buy you a drink after you're done work for the day. I don't know many people in New York."

The corners of his lips dip into a frown. I think he's trying to go for a lonely puppy dog look.

Max and I are supposed to go to a movie tomorrow night, but we can squeeze in a drink with Dale before that. "Text me where and when and I'll be there."

His entire face lights up with a smile.

I should be all over this, and him. He's single, good-looking, and he works in the mayor's office in Philadelphia. He seems like an all-around great guy, but he doesn't light a spark inside of me.

I move to stand, but Dale is on his feet before I'm out of my chair.

"I can see you home, Bella," he offers. "I don't mind."

I give my head a shake. "Thank you, but I can make it on my own."

Disappointment flits over his expression. "I'll text you in the morning about our drink tomorrow night."

I reach in to give him a chaste peck on the cheek. "Thanks for dinner, Dale."

He sighs. "Every minute was my pleasure."

My phone buzzes again as I step away. I look down at the screen to find two messages from my boss.

Barrett: Does a man fall into the clueless category of one and done if he doesn't realize that you're a direct descendant of Martina Calvetti, founder of Calvetti's?

I laugh out loud as I exit the restaurant.

Navigating through the pedestrian traffic, I read the other text.

Barrett: I'll take your silence as a yes. Be at your desk by 8 a.m. tomorrow.

Shaking my head, I drop my phone in my purse.

The extra five figures a year is worth getting out of bed an hour early. I can handle anything Barrett Adler throws my way.

Chapter 11

Bella

I arrive at my desk at one minute before eight. I planned that on purpose. I was hanging out in the lobby with my sister before I got on the elevator.

Gina has a meeting around the corner with a fashion designer.

My sister is living the dream of so many that post content online hoping to find an avid audience. She's a social media influencer. She has millions of followers across different platforms. Her corporate sponsorships keep her in the latest high-end fashions and pay for the mortgage on the apartment she owns.

I rent a bedroom from her and do most of the cooking.

We took the subway uptown together this morning. I read a book while she responded to some of the thousands of comments posted beneath a picture of the new mascara she used today.

I rest the cup of coffee I picked up at Palla on Fifth on my desk.

"Where's mine, Isabella?"

I shoot a glance in the direction of Barrett's office. "Palla's is a block over. You can make it there and back in under ten minutes if you catch the elevator at the right time."

"I know where it is." He pushes back from his desk to stand. "Use your expense account to pick me up a cup every morning on your way to work."

I don't pay for coffee at Palla on Fifth.

My cousin, Rocco, owns the business with our cousin, Arlo, and his wife, Palla. Whenever I stop in to pick up a medium cup of dark roast, Palla insists that I put my wallet away.

He goes on, "I want a cup on my desk when I arrive tomorrow."

"I usually start work at nine. You prefer to start earlier," I point out with a finger jab at the face of my watch. "Make a pit stop there on your way here."

I expect more push back from him, but all I get is a stern glance and a cross of his arms over his chest.

We both know that I'm not in a position to negotiate anything since my pay was doubled days ago, but it doesn't hurt to try.

"We'll discuss your hours another time." His shoulders tighten. "I take it you read over the email I sent you last night."

He looks gorgeous in the gray suit he's wearing today. His blue shirt is a shade lighter than his tie.

It's also the same color as the dress I picked out of my closet this morning. Gina told me to pair it with nude heels, so I did. I got two thumbs up from her before we left the apartment.

"I didn't get a chance," I confess.

I switched my phone to silent mode when I got home from having dinner with Dale. I'm halfway through a novel by my favorite author. I didn't want any distractions, and I knew that Max would have questions.

I'll answer those tonight before we meet Dale for a drink.

"You didn't get a chance?" he parrots back with a tilt of his head.

"I was reading a book." I take a sip of coffee.

His eyes follow my movements. His tongue darts over his bottom lip.

It's coffee envy. I get it.

"I expect you to read every email I send as soon as it arrives." His tone sharpens.

I take another drink from the cup in my hand. "Duke always told me that once I left this building, my work was done. He insisted that I spend my time outside of the office doing things that make me happy."

"Things that make you happy?" He takes a step closer to me. "Does that include going on blind dates?"

I doubt he'll stop reminding me of the night we met.

I take up the challenge that's woven into his question because he expects me to back down. I showed weakness when he first brought up our unintended meeting at Atlas 22. I won't make that mistake again.

"Bind dates have made me happy," I half-lie.

One blind date two years ago made me happy. I met a man I thought I paired well with.

That all changed on our third date. He left me to pay the check in a four-star French restaurant. The text message he sent me later that night to explain his sudden absence only added salt to my already wounded ego.

He took off with a woman he met in the corridor leading to the washrooms. It was love at first sight his message said.

That was confirmed when I ran into him three months ago. He had a ring on his left hand and a picture of his newborn son on his phone.

"So Duke was giving you time to pursue more of that?" Barrett smirks.

I set the coffee cup on the corner of my desk. "Duke cared about my happiness."

"Did you tell him about the string of one and done men that you've met?"

I widen my stance. "What I did or didn't tell Duke is privileged information."

The corner of his mouth twitches in an almost grin. "As interesting as this conversation is, we have work to do. Check your email, Isabella."

I shrug my shoulders in exasperation. "Fine. I'll do that now."

I expect him to stroll back into his office, but he stays glued in place.

I fall into my office chair, flip open the cover of my laptop, and wait for it to pop to life. Once it does, I open my email program and scroll through the dozens of messages waiting for me.

I can skim through them, and reply to all within ten minutes, but I take my time, typing out a response to one of Garent's marketing reps about a dinner party she's hosting at her home two weeks from now.

"I'm standing right here." Barrett taps the corner of my desk with his hand. "If you have a reply to my email, say what you need to say."

I glance up at him, pasting a fake smile on my lips. "I'll get to your email. I'm responding to them in the order in which they were received. That's the way Duke preferred I handle work emails."

"I prefer you to handle the work I assign you, so I'll paraphrase the email for you," he says in a pissy tone. "I need you to prepare termination documents for the list of employees I've included in the email."

Clicking open the email, I furrow my brow as I read through a list of at least twenty names of Garent Industries employees.

Most of them have held their positions for years. Some I met on my very first day as an intern.

"I need that done now, Isabella." He taps his hand on my desk again. "The first soon-to-be-former employee is due here in less than an hour."

Termination documents? Soon-to-be-former employee?

I look up to find his blue eyes locked on my face. "Are you firing all these people?"

"All of those people and more," he says without missing a beat. "This is the first round of cuts."

I know every person on the list. I've been to the wedding of one and the housewarming party of another.

"You can't do this," I point out. "These people have families. They have financial responsibilities."

His left brow rises. "I have a responsibility to this company. It's time to clean house. Prepare those termination documents now."

I raise my middle finger to his back when he turns to walk into his office.

"Tyrant," I whisper under my breath, dropping my hand.

He glances back over his shoulder. "What was that?"

The word edges over my tongue, aching for me to release it to his face, but I need this damn job.

"Nothing, Mr. Adper."

"Barrett," he corrects me with a grin. "Get to work."

Chapter 12

Barrett

I stand in my office and watch my assistant give one hell of a hug to a man who just lost his job because of me.

Fred Molfor, the former head of research for one of Garent's subsidiaries, is taking full advantage of Isabella's compassion.

Every person who has left my office without a job today has landed in my assistant's arms. Most take the hug offered for what it is and break free after a respectable ten to fifteen seconds of full-body contact.

Fred's hug is heading into minute two, and he's not letting go.

I clear my throat to break them up, but they ignore me. I step just outside my office doorway so I'm within five feet of the hug-fest.

This time I resort to a muffled cough, but the embrace continues with Fred's hand inching its way down Isabella's back. It's on a direct path to her ass.

"Isabella," I snap her name off my tongue.

That sends her a step back, breaking Fred's death grip on her.

"What?" Fred looks at me. "What now?"

All respect and pretense disappear when you steal a person's career out from under them. Fred was a gentleman when he shook my hand twenty minutes ago. He had no idea that I called him into my office to kick him out of the company.

"I was talking to my assistant," I point out. "You need to go, Fred."

"Bella and I were in the middle of a private conversation." He shoves a hand into the front pocket of his cheap suit pants.

My gaze drops to follow the movement. I catch an unfortunate glimpse of the obvious bulge under the dark brown fabric.

He's sporting a hard-on even though he just lost his job. Potential hardship isn't raining on his dick's parade.

His attention shifts back to Isabella. "I could really use a friend right now. Can you meet me for a drink tonight? Around eight, maybe?"

Isabella's gaze volleys between Fred's face and mine. "I have plans."

Fred shakes his head. That shifts the gray hair that's covering a bald spot. He flips it back in place with his left hand.

I've had enough of this ridiculous exchange. Fred is clearly none and done in Isabella's eyes. He's a few decades older than her and he's unemployed. I interrupt whatever the hell this is because I have work to do and I need my assistant's undivided attention. "Isabella, get Curtis Mayview on the phone."

"What about right after work?" Fred ignores the hell out of me and hones in on Isabella with a hand on her wrist. "You must have some time to fit me in."

She tugs her arm free. "I'm having drinks. I have a date tonight…with… with two men."

That mess of words tumbles out of her in a breathy stutter.

"With two men?" Fred repeats that back slowly. "You're into threesomes? I have a friend who I know would be willing."

What the fuck is going on?

Enough is enough, so I place a hand on Fred's shoulder. "Collect your things from your office and leave the building."

He glares at me. "I'm not ready to go yet. I haven't finished my conversation with Bella."

The man is delusional if he thinks he stands a chance with my assistant.

"I need to get to work." Isabella steps toward her desk. "Good luck with everything, Fred."

That brush-off comes with the same megawatt smile she gave me at Atlas 22 when she thought I was Dale.

"I'll call you." Fred cups his cell phone in his hand. "Thanks for everything, Bella."

"No problem," she mumbles back.

He turns to me, stopping mid-step to shove a finger into the center of my chest. "You're an asshole."

I've heard it before. I'll likely hear it again before the day is over.

I step back to cease contact between my body and his. "Go now, Fred."

"Duke didn't fire people for no good reason," he seethes. "He would never kick people out on the street like this."

He's right. Duke overlooked the bottom line to employ people who did virtually nothing all day. His last name gave him carte blanche to do whatever the fuck he wanted with his dad's company.

In the process he was wasting millions of dollars a year. It's my job to see that Garent Industries survives the whims of Ivan's prodigal son.

"Duke's not here." I cross my arms over my chest. "Your position doesn't exist anymore, Fred. If you saved wisely, you could retire on that and the severance I generously gave you."

"Generous?" He laughs in my face. "Duke was generous. You don't know the meaning of the word."

He's likely right.

I glance at Isabella. Her fingers are nervously picking at the nail polish on her right thumb. Her gaze is focused on that, but I know she's keenly listening to the exchange between Fred and me.

"It's been a pleasure." I toss Fred a grin because if nothing else, I'm sure as hell calm in the face of an insult. "See your way out of the building within the next fifteen minutes, or security will assist you."

"Fucking jerk," he shouts. "You can go straight to hell."

I take a step to the side to allow him a clear path to the elevator.

"He was mad," Isabella points out the obvious. "He needs that job."

"He needs a stiff drink." I button my suit jacket. "Your evening plans sound interesting."

Pink blooms high on her cheeks. Jesus, she's beautiful.

Whatever is on her agenda tonight, I'm certain it won't end with her in bed with two men. Maybe that's the bite of envy I feel making that assumption.

"It's just drinks with Dale and..." Her voice trails when her desk phone rings.

"Good afternoon," she chirps into the receiver. "Mr. Adler's office. How can I help you?"

I watch her lips move as she launches into a conversation about the projected purchase of a company Duke had his eye on.

I'll crush that deal later. I'm stuck back where she confessed that she's meeting Dale and someone else for drinks.

I want to know who the 'and' is in that equation.

A name will mean nothing to me, but I crave it for some goddamn reason.

My cell phone starts on a ring in my jacket pocket. I should ignore it and wait until Isabella is done so we can continue our conversation at the point it left off.

She wiggles a finger at me, alerting me to my incoming call as if I'm oblivious to the jarring sound.

I curse under my breath, drag the phone out of my pocket, and answer it in a steady tone. "Ivan, how are you?"

I would have ignored anyone else, but my boss is an instant answer. I turn and walk away, pushing my office door closed with my shoulder as I try and shake off the unwanted mental image of Isabella's nude body pressed between Dale and another man.

Chapter 13

Bella

I slipped out of the office at five o'clock on the dot. Usually, I'm at my desk until well past six clearing away the day's emails and following up with phone calls. Today, I tied everything up early.

Barrett was on a call with his office door closed, so I left without a word.

I don't owe him a goodbye or a have a swell night.

I had to reluctantly spend my day consoling people who don't have a job waiting for them tomorrow morning.

I thumb out a quick text to Max since I haven't heard from him all day.

Bella: We're meeting Dale for a drink before the movie. Before you respond to this text, remember that you owe me one.

I round the corner while I wait for him to reply.

The smell of Greek food wafting from one of the street carts is tempting, but I keep walking. I have leftovers waiting for me at home. I'll heat up my dinner and eat it while I'm getting ready.

I look down when my phone buzzes in my hand.

Max: I'll be your third wheel as long as I get to pick the movie.

I laugh out loud, drawing the glances of two women walking near me. I pop a brow at them and toss them a wave.

They both wave back with wide smiles on their faces.

This is one of the reasons why I love Manhattan as much as I do. A stranger's smile can brighten your day.

I need that. Today was hell. I've never been so emotional at work before. That's likely because Duke never fired anyone while I worked for him.

My pace slows as I near a pretzel cart. I could snack on one on my way home. It wouldn't ruin my dinner. It would be more of an appetizer before the main course of warmed up chicken and dumplings.

I fish in my purse for my wallet, but my phone buzzes, stealing my attention.

I expect to see Max's name on the screen, but it's my boss.

Barrett: Where are you?

I glance over at the stack of baked pretzels. I can almost taste the first bite. It wouldn't hurt to buy one for me and one to give Max later.

My fingers graze over my leather wallet just as my phone sounds when another message arrives.

"Dammit," I mutter under my breath.

Barrett: I needed to speak with you before you left the office. Call me ASAP.

I should ignore him since I'm off the clock, but I did walk out of the office without a word earlier and I am being paid an exorbitant amount of money to be his assistant.

I compromise. Instead of calling him, I send him a text message. I'm not that excited about meeting up with Dale for a drink, but I am looking forward to hanging out with Max. I'll handle my boss now, so that I can spend my evening in peace.

Bella: I'm officially done work for the day. Can this wait until tomorrow?

Barrett: No.

I expect another message, but there's nothing. No snippy reply. No three bouncing dots signaling he's writing something to send back to me.

Bella: What is it?

I turn my back on the pretzels and set off down the sidewalk again. I'll splurge on buttered popcorn at the movie tonight so the pretzel will have to wait for another time.

I glance down at my phone when another text buzzes its arrival.

Barrett: Meet me at Axel NY at 8.

For a split second, I wonder if he's sent me a message meant for the redhead he was having dinner with the other night.

His next text clears away all potential confusion.

Barrett: Ivan wants to see us both at 8. You do know where Axel NY is, don't you?

Jerk.

I know exactly where Axel NY is. I've been to the restaurant twice on blind dates in the past year and at a handful of times with Duke and his dad.

I can't exactly say no to Mr. Garent, so I type back a simple response knowing that I have to skip out on my movie plans with my best friend.

Bella: I'll be there.

***

"Wait a minute, Bella." Max's hand darts in the air. "You're telling me that the guy you thought was Dale is actually your new boss?"

Slipping on my shoes, I nod in silence.

"Why the hell didn't you tell me about this sooner?"

I point at the belt around my waist. "My belt is red, and my shoes are black. Is that a fashion faux pas?"

Max gives me a full once-over. "Your dress is tight enough that it doesn't matter."

I turn to the side to look at myself in the large mirror propped against my bedroom wall. "I should change. Should I change?"

"You're not changing. Dale is going to fucking love that dress." Max fans his face with his hand. "Wear the red lipstick you bought last week."

I walk to my dresser to find the tube of lipstick. "You forgive me for not going to the movie with you, right?"

"That's already forgotten." He crosses his legs. "I haven't forgiven you for keeping your boss's identity a secret."

I glance over my shoulder to where he's sitting in the big blue armchair in the corner of my bedroom.

Gina decorated before I moved in. Everything in this room is a product gifted to her by one of her sponsors. The chair and bed are courtesy of a new home furnishings company. They get high marks for aesthetics. They fail miserably in the comfort department.

"I'm sorry I didn't tell you until tonight," I say honestly. "I was embarrassed."

It's not a lie. I haven't told anyone that I dropped myself into the middle of my boss's date because I thought he was at Atlas 22 to meet me.

I would have told Max sooner, but I was stalling because he's going to remind me about it every chance he gets.

"He must have thought that you lost it." He throws his head back in laughter. "Some random sits down at his table and starts hitting on him."

I roll my eyes. "Do I look presentable? Does my outfit scream, 'I'm here for business.'"

Max stands, tucking the hem of the green T-shirt he's wearing into the waistband at the front of his dark jeans. "It's the perfect little black dress, Bella. Mr. Garent is going to be impressed."

That's all I really care about.

It doesn't matter if Dale likes what he sees. Barrett's opinion of how I look is a non-factor to me.

Or it should be.

I steal another glance in the mirror.

"You look like a million bucks," Max says with a wink. "Duke's replacement won't be able to keep his eyes to himself."

"Barrett," I say quietly.

"Barrett?" he repeats back. "That's his name?"

Scooping up my red clutch from the corner of my bed, I nod. "Barrett Adler."

"I'll have to stop by the office to meet, Mr. Adler." He grins. "If you mistook him for Dale based on my description, he must be screaming hot."

Hot doesn't even begin to describe Barrett.

"You've got that look on your face." Max circles his finger in front of me.

Laughing, I pinch my brows together. "What look?"

"The look you always have when there are butterflies in your stomach."

I glance down at the front of my dress. "There are no butterflies in there."

"Liar." he chuckles. "What I really want to know is are you feeling that way because of Dale or your new boss?"

I pat my stomach. "No butterflies. No feelings. End of discussion."

He lets out a puff of air from between his lips. "You're not fooling me, Calvetti. One of those men has you tied up in knots. Or maybe you want one of them to tie you up in knots."

Holding back a giggle, I shake my head. "I don't. Let's go."

He swoops a hand toward my bedroom door. "Lead the way."

Chapter 14

Barrett

Every head in the restaurant turns when Isabella Calvetti walks in.

At Atlas 22, all eyes were on her because she flipped the place upside down in an attempt to get away from me. Tonight, her beauty is putting her in the spotlight.

She's headed in my direction in a little black dress that looks like it was custom made for her body. The woman is breathtaking and oblivious to how much attention she's drawing.

Her hair is wind-whipped. It's messy and her effort to tame it with a hand brushing through it is futile.

With rosy cheeks and brisk breaths, she takes unsteady steps through the crowded dining room.

As I glide to my feet, I suddenly realize what's going on.

My assistant looks freshly fucked.

What the hell?

I thought this meeting with Ivan and I would cancel her plans, but it seems that she compensated by shifting her date to earlier in the evening.

As she nears our table, her gaze swings from my face to the back of Ivan's head as he stands in anticipation of her arrival.

A glance over his shoulder brings a broad smile to her face. I get nothing when she looks at me again.

"Mr. Garent," she says his name softly. "It's nice to see you again."

"Isabella." He scoops her into his arms with as much enthusiasm as Fred did, but Ivan is a happily married man, so the embrace is short and sweet.

"How are you?" Her forehead furrows. "How's Duke?"

"We're taking it day-by-day." He reaches for the back of the chair between us. "Have a seat."

She takes the invitation, carefully lowering herself into the wooden chair. Ivan and I do the same. I'm not offered anything but a view of the back of her head as she shifts so she's facing Ivan.

"Good evening, Isabella," I finally say.

"Hi." The word leaves her lips without a glance in my direction or even an acknowledgment that I exist.

"You look lovely." Ivan's gaze is glued to her. "Did you have plans tonight? We didn't step on anyone's toes when we asked you to meet us, did we?"

"No toes were stepped on." She settles back in her chair, giving me a perfect view of her profile. "I met a couple of people for a drink earlier."

"Was Max one of them?" Ivan asks casually with a small grin.

Isabella's face lights up. "Yes. You remember him?"

That sets Ivan's head back with a burst of laughter. "Max is unforgettable. He was the life of the holiday party last year."

I've never seen the senior Garent laugh like this. Whoever the hell this Max guy is, he's earned his way into Ivan's good graces.

"He had the very best time at the party." Isabella shoots me a tepid look. "He loves Duke. He asked about him earlier."

She knows how to score points with my boss.

Ivan cups Isabella's hand in his. "You tell Max that my boy is doing his best and thank him for his concern."

It was my duty to ask about Duke when I met Ivan here for dinner an hour ago. I dropped that ball because I was anxious to dive into our discussion about Duke's latest passion project. He was set to sign on the dotted line to buy a bookstore in Brooklyn.

It's a money pit and I'm here to convince Ivan of that with hard numbers. I've spent the past hour doing so. He was ready to pull the plug on the deal when my assistant walked in.

During our call this afternoon, Ivan mentioned that he'd be stopping by the office tomorrow morning to see Isabella before he heads to Boston. I suggested that he save the trip by having her meet us for dessert tonight.

I thought the bookstore deal would be in the grave by the time she sat down.

"I have a question for you, Isabella," Ivan says as if he can read my mind. "It's about an acquisition that Duke had his eye on."

"Hold that thought," I chime in when I notice the waitress approach. "Let's get Isabella a drink first."

"What would you like?" Ivan asks politely. "If my memory serves, your drink of choice at the holiday party was white wine."

I'd suggest a cosmopolitan, but that would raise Ivan's eyebrow. His stance on interoffice relationships is that they shouldn't exist. I got that lecture in Chicago during my first year with the company. I took a colleague to bed. Ivan took us both to task for it.

I may have tried to derail Isabella's plans tonight, but that was a momentary lapse of judgment. If she wants to hop in the sack with two men, who am I to throw a roadblock in her way? Obviously, she found her way around it tonight.

"A glass of cold water would be amazing." She glances up at the waitress, giving her a wide smile. "I ran three blocks just now, and I'm so thirsty."

"You ran three blocks?" Ivan questions, obviously surprised.

"Max and I met a friend for a drink at this bar that Max loves." She lets out a laugh. "Max started telling stories about when we were kids and boom, I looked at my watch and it was five minutes to eight, so I ran here."

The fact that she sprinted here explains her flushed cheeks and the tangle of hair around her face.

I hone in on Max because I've met Dale. "Max is an old friend?"

"They met when they were children," Ivan says before my assistant has a chance to reply. "Max told me all about it at the holiday party. He's like a brother to Isabella."

Isabella glances over at me. "Max is my best friend."

She took her best friend to meet Dale tonight. That seems like a step up the relationship ladder. Whatever's going on between them is full throttle.

I swallow what's left of my whiskey to tame the jealous knot in my gut.

"Back to business." Ivan eyes me before he shifts his attention to Isabella. "Barrett and I were discussing the proposed acquisition of Rusten's Reads. You're up to speed on the company, aren't you?"

"I'm at full speed." She laughs. "I was there the other day, and last week, and..."

Ivan can't contain a smile. "You were there?"

"At the store," she clarifies. "I buy all my books there. I've been going there since I was a kid." Judging from the sales figures I've seen, I wouldn't be shocked to discover that Isabella is their only customer. The business is bleeding money. It doesn't need Garent Industries to take it over. It needs to call it a day and shut the doors for good.

"Do you view it as a worthwhile acquisition, Isabella?"

I expected he'd ask her opinion, but I have no idea how much value he's going to put in that. Ivan is as frustrated with the current financial state of Garent as I am. I admit that I was mildly surprised that he upped her salary as much as he did, but I sense that he did that to keep her behind her desk.

Isabella's adjusting to the fact that Duke is gone and I'm taking his place permanently. The extra money Ivan offered her is a guarantee that she'll remain at her post.

"Honestly?" she asks, looking at me before she glances back to Ivan.

"Of course," he answers without hesitation. "Give it to us straight. If you were in charge of the acquisition of Rusten's Reads would it be a go or a no?"

She drops her gaze to the glass of water the waitress just placed in front of her. "It's a special little shop with the best selection of used books, but…"

"But?" I interrupt. "But what, Isabella?"

She grabs hold of the water glass and brings it to her ruby red lips. She swallows a mouthful, her lipstick leaving behind an imprint on the glass.

It's sexy as hell, but I shake away the thought of those crimson lips wrapped around my dick. I can't go there. I won't go there.

"If Garent Industries invested in it at this time, I think it might lose its charm." She looks at Ivan. "It needs a careful and committed hand to help it flourish. Duke had that. He saw the vision that Rusten and his wife, Misty, have for their store."

I read Duke's notes on his most recent acquisitions. He ran Garent with his heart. He'd pick up failing small businesses left and right just to keep their owners happy. It's virtuous but reckless.

"Do you think with your help, Barrett can breathe new life into it?" Ivan leans closer to her. "Duke saw something in that bookstore. I don't want to overlook any potential that's hidden behind the low revenue."

"Duke had some ideas for it including changing the name to something more whimsical that would fit the feel of the store." She circles a fingertip on the table in front of her. "He had plans for book signings but not with well-known authors. Duke wanted to showcase up and comers. He even considered having an author in residence program at the bookstore and a community corner where the people who live in the neighborhood could gather and talk books."

I watch the expression on Ivan's face morph from stoic concern to joy.

Well, shit.

Duke and his penchant for saving the underdog are about to win this battle, and there's not a damn thing I can do about it.

Chapter 15

Bella

I pass on dessert when it's offered. Ivan and Barrett do the same.

Both men are dressed in gray suits and blue ties. That's where their similarities end. Barrett is on his second glass of whiskey since I arrived at the restaurant. Mr. Garent is nursing what looks like a vodka and tonic. I'm assuming that's what it is since it's the only drink he ever ordered when he'd join Duke and me for working lunches or dinners.

I miss those meetings. I miss Duke.

Talking about Rusten's Reads brought a flood of memories to the surface. Duke was passionate about breathing life into the bookstore since he met the owners a few months ago.

Duke has given dozens of small businesses a second chance. If the owners could convince him that their dream was worth saving, he'd strike a deal to take them under Garent's umbrella as a subsidiary.

The owners would continue to focus on day-to-day operations, and Duke would find ways to breathe new life into those struggling businesses. I've watched him succeed a few times since I became his assistant, but not all of those rags-to-riches stories ended with a happy ending.

Garent Industries is funding several ventures that won't succeed. I have no doubt that Barrett will shut them down within the next few weeks.

Ivan touches the top of my hand with his finger. "Isabella, I'm leaving in the morning for Boston. I don't expect to be back in New York for at least a couple of months."

I manage a small smile. Being near his son is important to him, even if he can't see Duke at the moment. The Garent family is as close as the Calvetti clan. I understand his need to leave New York City.

"I'll be checking in with Barrett weekly," he goes on, "I'll call you as well. As soon as I'm able to see Duke, I'll let him know that you're thinking of him."

He steals the words right out of my mouth. That's the only message I want him to convey to my former boss. I've never dealt with addiction, so I don't know firsthand what the Garents are facing, but I'll do what I can to help.

"Thank you." I pat his hand.

"We'll hold down the fort," Barrett chimes in. "I don't want you to think about business while you're in Boston, Ivan. I can handle anything that pops up."

Ivan nods slowly. "That's why you're the CEO. I have faith in you, Barrett. I know that every decision you make will be for the good of Garent. I trust that you'll only reach out if the matter is pressing."

I glance at Barrett and the smug smile on his face. Ivan is handing him the keys to the Garent kingdom. Every decision going forward will be Barrett's alone.

He may not say it aloud, but the look on Barrett's face is easy to read. The Garent Industries that existed when Duke was the CEO is about to change forever.

***

I wave one final time as I watch Ivan round the corner and disappear out of view. He may live in Chicago, but he keeps an apartment a block from here in a pre-war building.

"I have a car." Barrett points at a dark sedan parked next to the curb in front of the restaurant. A gray-haired driver sits at the ready behind the wheel. "We can drop you at your place."

I firm my grasp on the clutch purse in my hand. "That's wasteful."

His lips curve into an almost grin. "What's wasteful?"

I glance down the sidewalk toward the nearest subway stop. "Manhattan isn't that big. You can get where you need to go by foot, or by subway."

"The car is a perk of the job, Isabella."

"It was a perk when Duke was CEO and he took the subway or walked to the office," I point out.

"I'm not Duke." He glares at me. "The sooner you accept that he's no longer your boss, the better."

I can't fault him for speaking the truth. He's not Duke. He's nothing like Duke.

"How are you getting home?" He questions with a glance at the driver.

"I'm taking the subway," I say proudly.

The sound of a chime lures his hand to the pocket of his suit jacket. He tugs out his phone. Without a word to me, his fingers fly over the screen.

"The subway is the easiest way to get around the city," I continue my pitch for public transportation. "Once you get accustomed to it, it's a breeze."

He moves toward the car, tapping a knuckle on the passenger side window. The driver lowers the glass and mumbles something in a tone so low that I can't make it out.

"I'll get home on my own," Barrett says. "I won't need you again tonight."

Home?

Curiosity peaks my interest. He only transferred here from the Chicago office days ago. How is it possible that he already has a home?

When he turns back to me, I blurt out the question that's sitting on the tip of my tongue. "Where do you live?"

My question sparks something in him. I see a flash of satisfaction pass over his expression before his left brow peaks. "Why do you want to know where I live?"

I instantly regret asking the question. I scramble for an explanation that makes sense. "I…well…I was wondering whether you live within walking distance of the office. If you do, you'll probably save a lot of time traveling on foot instead of in that car."

He turns to watch the car as it pulls into traffic. "Because that's what Duke did?"

There's a bite of frustration in his tone. I know it irritates him when I mention Duke. I can use that to my advantage. It doesn't hurt to know your boss's weaknesses.

Pasting a fake smile on my face, I give him a curt nod. "Duke set a great example."

"Until he didn't," he quips.

Anger swirls in my belly. Duke is a good person. He doesn't need this jerk making rude comments behind his back.

My phone buzzes in my hand. I glance down at the incoming text message.

Dale: Did I tell you how beautiful you were tonight?

I look up to find Barrett gazing down at my phone. I cradle it against my chest. "Excuse me. This is private."

"What do you call a man who has made it past the first few dates but he's boring as hell?"

This riddle is hitting too close to home. I've seen Dale three times, counting when I met him at Atlas 22, but I still feel nothing. I won't give Barrett the satisfaction of knowing that.

"I call him a great guy."

He smirks. "So Dale is your first..."

"My first?" I bark out a nervous laugh. "Um, no. I'm not a virgin."

"No." Barrett chuckles. "I wasn't asking that, Isabella. I sure as hell don't want to know that."

My cheeks heat with the flush of embarrassment. I look around at the people passing us by. I envy all of them. They aren't standing in the middle of the sidewalk fumbling their way through an awkward conversation with their boss.

"Dale is obviously not a one and done," he says, glancing down at his phone when it chimes. "I take it he's the first man who hasn't fallen into that category in some time?"

What the hell?

Am I supposed to respond to that? I won't. My personal life is not his business.

The buzz of my phone saves me from my internal debate over whether his question was rhetorical or not.

Dale: I'm still at the bar. If you're up to it, we can end the night with one last drink.

"Interesting," Barrett drawls.

I don't need to look up to know that he's caught a glimpse of Dale's latest message. I have to start turning my back to him before I read my incoming texts.

"I'm leaving," I announce, wondering if I should take Dale up on his offer or not.

"It seems we both have plans for one last drink before we call it a night." He glances over my shoulder. "I'll see you at the office in the morning."

"I'll set up a meeting for you with the owners of Rusten's Reads for ten o'clock sharp."

He studies my face. "What for? I'm still considering the acquisition."

"It's not your decision." I point out with a tilt of my head. "Mr. Garent was clear about what he wants. It doesn't matter if he's in New York, Boston or London. His word is the last word."

I don't catch the curse that falls from his lips, but I do see the clench of his jaw. "I expect you to be at your desk at eight, Isabella. Goodnight."

He brushes past me. Against my better judgment, I turn to watch him walk away. I get more than a clear view of his back. A blonde-haired woman wearing faded boyfriend jeans and a black blouse rushes toward him before he takes her in his arms.

Chapter 16

Barrett

Isabella has perfect timing down to a science. It's ten seconds before eight when I look up and finally see her settling behind her desk.

I know that she put in a fair amount of overtime when she worked for Duke. She stayed past five most nights and even showed up in the office on the occasional Saturday or Sunday.

I can't question her dedication to the company. Duke sent a string of memos to Human Resources commending his executive assistant. She doesn't have one unfavorable mark on her record.

She'll keep on track with that winning streak as long as she understands that certain things have changed since I took over as CEO.

"Isabella," I call out to her.

Her head pops up, her dark hair floating around her shoulders. She straightened it since I saw her last night at the restaurant. I was tempted to ask her to stay when Ivan announced he was leaving, but I followed them both out the door of Axel NY.

She's my assistant, and on top of that, she's a decade younger than I am. I've always been drawn to women my age or older. I've never contemplated dating or fucking someone more than a year or two younger than me.

"What is it?" she questions with a perk of her dark brows.

Her makeup isn't as dramatic this morning as it was last night. Today she looks fresh and young. She's wearing a lavender wrap dress. Ivan would silently disapprove since his idea of business attire is a suit or skirt in black or dark blue paired with a shirt in a neutral color.

I much prefer Isabella's idea of what's office appropriate. My cock has no complaints either.

I adjust myself in my chair, hoping my dick will lose its enthusiasm before she walks into my office. I'm a gentleman. I was taught to rise to my feet when I greet a woman. I can't do that now, or my executive assistant will see that what I want from her is more than a brief chat.

She strolls toward me, stopping at my office door. She leans a hip against the wooden doorjamb. If there were a master class in effortless seduction, Isabella Calvetti would be the professor.

Her hand falls to the front of her dress. Adjusting the neckline, she keeps her eyes trained on mine.

"I want to be clear about your hours," I say, breaking her gaze. "You report to work at eight each day. You stay until I tell you that you can leave."

A nod is the only response I get from her.

"If I need you here at seven or even six a.m., I'll let you know the night before."

I doubt like hell I'll ever need that since I'll never have my ass in this chair before seven-thirty, but I'm going for the reaction.

I don't get anything, but a blink of her eyes.

I'd push on the coffee issue, but I need to put the brakes on the amount of caffeine I consume. I didn't fall asleep until three this morning. I can't blame a woman for that. I was home alone an hour after I said goodnight to Isabella.

I spent the next few hours pacing the floor while I picked my life apart.

"Is there anything else?" she asks with a sigh. "I have a busy day."

Working for me, I should point out, but I let it slide because my calendar is crammed with meetings outside of the office that she booked for me.

I would take that as a hint that she hates me if her nipples weren't furled into tight peaks under the flimsy fabric of her dress.

I wonder what her tits look like. What does she taste like?

Her fingers dance over the screen of her phone. When I don't respond to her question, she finally looks up. "Since you're skipping out on the ten o'clock meeting with Rusten and Misty from the bookstore, I've arranged for you to spend that hour with Curtis Mayview."

Fuck that.

I reached my Curtis Mayview quota on the phone yesterday. He heads up our social media division. He wants an in-person meeting with me to go over his vision for the online future of a handful of our subsidiaries. I told him to put those ideas in an email and send them to Isabella.

"That's not going to work," I say firmly. "Curtis is sending you an email later today. I want you to sift through it and condense his thoughts into a half-page, bullet-pointed list."

A shake of her head accompanies her soft laugh. "I received that email this morning. I'll read it to you."

I hold up a hand to stop her. "There's no need. Go to your desk, summarize it and send it to me."

She ignores everything I just said. "It's right here. It's short and sweet."

"It is?" I'm skeptical, but there's a chance that I misjudged Curtis.

She clears her throat. "Dear Bella, I need to see him in person today. Curtis."

"Isabella." I lean back in my chair. "Cancel that meeting. He needs to follow my direction."

Her gaze drops to her phone. "You'll meet him at Palla on Fifth at ten o'clock."

"Cancel that meeting," I repeat.

"His contract clearly states that he has an in-person meeting with the CEO twice per month," she says matter-of-factly. "I can get Human Resources to forward you a copy of that if you'd like."

"Dammit Duke," I curse my predecessor under my breath.

"Curtis likes his coffee with one sugar and two splashes of cream." She glances over her shoulder when her desk phone starts to ring.

"Why the hell would I care what he takes in his coffee?" Irritation taints my tone.

"Garent's CEO supplies the coffee. That's in his contract too." A smug smile plays on her lips. "Make it a large. That will put him in a great mood. I need to answer that call."

She sets off toward the ringing phone on her desk.

Why the hell does it feel like she just won the latest round in our silent battle of wills?

Chapter 17

Bella

"Look at you. You're all nipples today." Max points at the front of my dress. "What's got you so excited?"

I glance down, wishing I had chosen a different bra this morning. "It's cold in here."

"It's not," he quips. "What exactly are you looking at?"

My gaze darts to the screen of my laptop. "Nothing."

I panic and try to close the internet browser by punching a few keys, but Max is too quick. He scoops the laptop in his hands and turns it until it's facing him.

His eyes skim the screen. "Holy hard abs, Bella. Who the fuck is this?"

I jab a finger in the air at him. "You can't talk like that here. Someone might hear you."

He looks around. "There is literally no one on this floor but the two of us. Your co-workers must have gotten the memo that they can leave the building during their lunch break. Why didn't you text me back?"

I should have read all the text messages Max sent me this morning, but I was busy answering a string of calls from nervous employees wondering if their jobs are in jeopardy. I couldn't reassure any of them because I have no idea what my boss's next move is.

"You didn't even hear me when I called your name after I got off the elevator," he goes on. "I see why. You were in a hot guy trance."

I heard the ping of the elevator as the doors opened, but I assumed it was Karley. She shows up every Thursday in the early afternoon to water the plants in the building.

I reach for my laptop, but Max tugs it closer to him. "Who is this, Bella?"

Lying won't work. Max can read me like a book. He'll know if I tell him a fib, so I lay it all on the line and brace for the inevitable assault of questions coming my way. "That's my boss."

"Like hell it is." He looks at the screen before he levels his eyes on my face. "This stunner in the board shorts is your new boss?"

I nod. "I thought I'd do a quick search online for him just for research, of course, and I stumbled on all of that."

"You fell down the rabbit hole." He winks at me. "See what I did there? You and your rabbit vibrator."

"Shut up." I jump to my feet. "I don't have that anymore."

"You broke another vibrator?" He huffs out a laugh. "They come with instructions, don't they? Maybe you need to give those a read before you get down to business."

I cover my mouth with my hand to shield the uncontainable smile on my lips. "Stop talking, Max."

"Why are there so many pictures of your hot boss online?" He scrolls a finger over the screen. "He looks just as good in a tux as he does out of one."

I can't argue with that.

Tugging the laptop from his hands, I snap the lid shut. "An ex-girlfriend of his took most of those pictures. I stumbled on her social media accounts and there he was."

Skepticism knits his brow. "You must have been digging pretty deep to find that treasure trove. Did the ex tag him in all those pictures?"

"Something like that," I say with a shrug.

It's nothing like that. I found those pictures because I typed 'who is Barrett Adler dating' into Google.

I expected nothing to pop up, but instead of zero results there were thousands. Most of them were articles about his relationship with a former reality TV star.

Alyssa Wells went on national TV to find a husband. She struck out but met Barrett at a grocery store in Chicago a week after the final episode of her season aired. Every online gossip site was all over their relationship.

Max takes a step forward so he can peek into Barrett's empty office. "I take it that Mr. Hunk of Burning Lust isn't here right now?"

Barrett doesn't need a nickname, so I stop that train on its tracks. "Mr. Adler is out at meetings all day."

Max tosses his head back in laughter. "Listen to you being all professional."

I set my laptop on my desk. "Exactly why are you here?"

Doing one full turn with his arms outstretched at his sides, he cocks a brow. "What do you think?"

"I think you're the best friend in the world," I say with a smile.

His bottom lip pouts out. "Bella, pay attention. Something is different about me."

I study his face. It's just as gorgeous as it was the last time I saw it. His hair hasn't been trimmed in the past two weeks. No beard. No new face piercings. I didn't expect any of those since he took out his eyebrow and nose ring years ago.

He's wearing a black polo and dark gray dress pants. I've seen those before.

I could prolong this in the hope of not hurting his feelings, but Max and I aren't skating on that thin of ice. We tell it like it is, so that's what I do. "Nothing is different about you."

He sighs through a wide smile. "Look down."

I inch around my desk and take in the new shoes on his feet. Wingtip and expensive leather are both on Max's must-haves in footwear.

"Those just came in today?" I point at his feet.

"Bright and early this morning." He taps a toe on the polished concrete floor. "I'm giving them a test drive as we speak."

"Those are keepers." I tug on his hand. "They're perfect for you."

Lifting my hand to his lips he gives it a sweet kiss on the palm. "And that is perfect for you."

"What's perfect for me?"

"Your new internet obsession slash boss." He squeezes my hand. "Get yourself some of that, Bella, and your vibrator problems will be a thing of the past."

I tug my hand free, using it to slap him on his chest. "That's not going to happen."

"Why not? I know you haven't had that kind of fun in a while, so why not mix business with pleasure?"

"I have over a hundred thousand reasons why I can't mix business with pleasure," I point out. "I want to make my dreams come true. Working here is the quickest way to fund those dreams."

"True, true," he says with resignation. "Get back on your laptop and order a new rabbit because you're going to need it if you keep stalking your hot-as-hell boss."

Giving my head a shake, I smile. "I don't need any help in that department. Barrett Adler will not be making any appearances in my fantasies."

I wait for him to call me out on that lie. Instead, he leans forward, kisses my forehead, and drops his gaze to the floor. "Let's walk over to Palla's to get a coffee and a sandwich. It's time to make the men of Manhattan wish they had a pair of these shoes."

Chapter 18

Barrett

"Two plus two is six."

I stop in place as the elevator's doors slide shut behind me. There's no way in hell that I just heard a child's voice, is there?

"You're wrongo bongo. Two plus two is seven."

Another child's voice and another wrong answer to one of the most basic math equations in existence.

"It's four," I say as I approach Isabella's desk and the two small brunette-haired people sitting in her office chair.

"I'm four," one of them says with a lift of her hand in the air. "I turned four one hundred and twenty-two days ago."

The brown-eyed little girl has some grasp on numbers.

The boy sitting next to her is shaking his head so hard I wonder if he's going to fall off the side of the chair.

"I was three one million, twelve twenty-two hours ago," he blurts out. "So there."

I have no idea if he's talking to me or not since his gaze is stuck on the ceiling.

I glance into my office, but my assistant is nowhere in sight. I look back at the two pint-sized math geniuses to find them staring at me.

"Who are you?" The little boy spits out. "Are you a stranger?"

I volley his first question right back at him because I need an explanation and these two are my best bet for getting one. "Who are you?"

"I'm his sister." The girl jerks a thumb into the side of the little guy's head.

"I'm her brother." He pokes a finger at her, just missing her left eye.

I'm lost.

"I'm back," Isabella's voice comes at me from the right.

I turn to see her on the approach with a juice box in each hand. Her pace slows the second she lifts her gaze and spots me.

"Why are you here? You're supposed to be in meetings all afternoon."

That's not the greeting a CEO expects from his executive assistant, but I'm learning that Isabella has a certain attitude when it comes to me. I, on the other hand, have a certain question that I want an immediate answer to.

"What's going on here?" I point in the general direction of her desk.

"It's snack time." The little boy runs a hand under his nose. "Mommy forgot to pack us a snack, so Bella went to get some juice."

"In the break room," she answers, brushing past me. "I ran there. I didn't leave them out of my sight for long."

I need zero explanation about her abilities as a childcare provider because she's my fucking executive assistant and nowhere in her job description does it mention babysitting mop-haired toddlers in the middle of a Thursday afternoon.

She hands a juice box to each of the kids. "I have some animal crackers in the bottom drawer of my desk. Do you want those?"

I wait for her to turn her attention back to me, but she carries on like I'm not staring a hole in her back.

I'm fighting every urge inside of me to glance at her ass, but there are children in the room and I consider myself somewhat of a decent man.

Clearing my throat, I watch as she rounds her desk, bends over and slides open the bottom drawer.

I get a brief flash of the top of her breasts before she stands up again.

Jesus.

Animal crackers spill onto the top of her desk when she tugs on the package to open it.

The kids burst out in laughter. Isabella does the same, so I stalk into my office, shutting the door behind me. I have no idea what the hell is going on, but as soon as my assistant is alone, I want answers.

***

"Come in, Isabella," I call out an hour later when she finally knocks on my office door.

I heard the screech of excitement from both kids when someone exited the elevator five minutes ago. I had no interest in getting up to see who came to claim them. They shouldn't have been here in the first place. It's an unwritten rule that anyone who can't do basic math shouldn't be in the building.

Garent Industries has yet to host a 'bring your kid to work' day.

It would cut into productivity and cost the company too much in potential revenue.

Ivan brought Duke to work every day and that was a fucking disaster.

My office door inches open slowly. She clears her throat before she speaks. "I come bearing a gift."

"A gift?" I repeat in a neutral tone.

Her hand darts into view. She's waving something in the air. I inch ahead on my chair and narrow my eyes to get a better look.

What the fuck?

Before I can order her inside my office, she pushes open the door and marches in with a smile on her face.

A bright, I-have-no-care-in-the-world, smile.

"Sit down," I order, pointing at the two chairs facing my desk. "Take a seat now."

The smile doesn't fade as she plops herself in one of the chairs. Crossing her legs, her hand moves to close the slit at the front of her dress.

She's not quick enough to steal my chance to get an unobstructed view of her thigh.

I lean back in my chair. "Explain to me what was going on out there."

Her gaze darts over her shoulder briefly. "I was watching Ansel and Elara."

Putting names to their cherub faces makes no difference to me. They're kids. They belong in places where children play, not in the office of the executive assistant of the CEO of a Fortune 500 company.

"You were babysitting?" I ask the question, even though it's rhetorical.

"I was watching over them," she clarifies as though I don't understand the definition of babysitting. "I do that every second Thursday afternoon. Duke loved having the kids in the office."

Why the hell doesn't that surprise me?

My jaw clenches. "Who are they? I want to know who they belong to."

She cradles the gift she brought me in her palm. "Marcy Clover."

More information would be helpful, but Isabella isn't offering it, so I roll a hand in the air. "Who is that? Your friend? A relative?"

Her mouth thins. "Marcy Clover runs Empire Soaks."

And Garent Industries owns Empire Soaks. It was another acquisition from Duke's era that is bleeding money. Unless something changes dramatically, their doors will close permanently before year's end.

"Marcy Clover needs to make new childcare arrangements for every second Thursday." I scrub a hand over the back of my neck.

Her head shakes defiantly. "No."

"No?" I question back. "We're not running a daycare here. Tell their mother to find someone else to take care of them."

She slides back on her chair. "I can't do that."

"You will do that." I keep my gaze focused on her face. "You work for me, not her. Simple."

"It's not simple." That draws her to her feet in a huff. "If you'd just give me a chance to explain."

"The topic isn't open for discussion." Glancing at my watch, I get up from my chair. "I have a meeting in ten minutes."

She drops her gift on my desk. "Marcy thought you might appreciate this. It's Empire Soak's body wash for men."

I pick up the plastic bottle that's shaped like a baseball. I crack open the lid to the smell of a muddy swamp.

"What the fuck?" I recoil, clamping the lid shut before I shove the bottle back in her hand. "Get rid of that."

An audile gasp escapes my assistant. "Marcy worked hard on developing this. Duke loved it. He bought it by the case."

Duke's lack of taste in furniture can only be matched by his absent sense of smell. I swear to fuck I'm lightheaded after getting a whiff of whatever the hell was in that bottle.

Empire Soaks just shot to the top of my list of Garent subsidiaries that need to be shutdown.

"Keep children out of the office, Isabella." I wait for a beat before I go on, "You're free to leave at six."

She glances at the bottle in her hand before she offers a snappy reply. "Fine."

Chapter 19

Bella

Ignoring Barrett on Friday was easy because he left New York City. The only warning I got that he wouldn't be in his office was a text message from him late Thursday night. It was brief and to the point telling me that he was called away to Illinois.

He sent me an email right after he landed in Chicago. I opened it to find a list of twenty-six tasks that he wanted completed before I could step into my weekend.

I finished everything on the list by noon, so I forwarded the office number to my cell and took Max out to lunch at Calvetti's.

Marti made baked tortellini for us. To repay her, I took her to a movie on Saturday afternoon. My grandma loves romantic comedies and she can pack popcorn away like no one I've ever known.

We ended the day back at the restaurant enjoying a big bowl of minestrone while she told me stories about my dad when he was my age.

Santo Calvetti is my hero. He's also Marti's youngest son.

Daydreaming about my weekend stops as soon as I hear the elevator ding its arrival on this floor. I sat down at eight a.m. sharp. It's almost eleven, and Barrett still hasn't made an appearance.

I suppose I could have texted him to make sure he's still alive, but the crossword puzzle I've been working on won't finish itself.

I slide it under a file folder on my desk as I hear heavy footsteps approach.

Glancing up, I see my boss staring at me.

Woah. Just woah.

Unshaven, disheveled Barrett Adler is enough to make any woman forget her name. He's wearing a pair of jeans, a wrinkled light blue T-shirt, and shiny black shoes. A weathered dark duffel bag is slung over his shoulder.

"I'm on my way home," he says before I can ask what's going on. "I need you to arrange a meeting for me with Darien Penrew at noon."

Darien Penrew, the man who heads accounting at Garent Industries, is on medical leave. He had open heart surgery two months ago.

"Mr. Penrew isn't…"

"Shit," Barrett hisses, interrupting me. "He's got that heart thing going on."

At least he has a heart.

Those words linger on my tongue, but I don't say them, even though I want to.

I had to explain to Marcy Clover that I couldn't watch over Ansel and Elara every second Thursday anymore. I didn't bring up the fact that my new boss is a jerk who insulted her best selling product while he flat out refused to listen to me.

A mass email I sent to the employees of Garent Industries on Saturday morning asking for help taking over my spot with Marcy's kids resulted in a huge outpouring of support. Ansel and Elara will spend a few hours every second Thursday with the wife of one of the doormen who work in the lobby of this building.

"Clara Boyman is running the accounting department at the moment." I sigh. "I'll arrange for you to meet her at Crispy Biscuit at noon."

"My office at noon," he snaps.

"Clara likes to eat and work." I pull up her contact information on my laptop. "The fried green tomato sandwich at Crispy Biscuit is her favorite."

He pushes a hand through his already messy hair. "What is that? A restaurant? A food truck? I have no idea where the hell it is."

"I'll draw you a map." I try not to stare at his bulging bicep when he moves his arm. "I'll jot down where to catch the subway and where to get off."

"No need. I'll call my driver." His jaw flexes. "I'm heading up for a shower and change of clothes. I'll be back down here in fifteen minutes. I expect the most recent sales numbers for Rusten's Reads on my desk when I return."

Wait? What?

"What do you mean you're heading up for a shower and change of clothes?" I ask, knowing I shouldn't. "I thought you said you were going home."

A sly smile slides over his sinfully sexy mouth. I see satisfaction dancing in his eyes. "I knew you were curious about where I live."

Nervous laughter bubbles out of me. "No, I'm not."

"You are." He stares into my eyes. "I live in one of the penthouses on the top floor of this building, Isabella."

I scratch my chin, trying not to let on that I had no idea that there is an actual penthouse or penthouses above us. I assumed that floor was undeveloped since that's what Duke told me when I asked him about it after I pointed out the button labeled PH on the control panel in the elevator.

"I need a shower." Barrett's gaze slides over my black blouse. "I'll be back in ten."

"I'll be here," I say quietly.

I watch him walk to the elevator looking like he slept in his clothes. I know there's a story there, but it's not my place to ask. It's not my place to daydream about my boss in the shower either, so I shake off the thought of what he looks like naked and I get to work printing out the sales numbers for Rusten's Reads so that bookstore deal can finally be signed and sealed just the way Duke wanted.

Chapter 20

Barrett

I swing open the door of my penthouse to find a familiar face standing in front of me with a case of beer in one hand and a wilting potted plant in the other.

"Happy fucking housewarming." Dylan Colt brushes past me. "Thanks for skipping town with no warning this weekend."

My Monday has been the stuff of nightmares. My lunch meeting with Clara Boyman ran over two hours and then I had to put out three fires that Duke set before he left. He made reckless promises to a handful of Garent staff members that I have no intention of keeping.

I was banking on a quiet night at home staring at the television screen in nothing but boxer briefs, but Dylan called fifteen minutes ago to tell me he was on his way over.

I put on a pair of black sweatpants and a matching T-shirt, called the doorman and told him to send the smug bastard up once he arrived.

Dylan takes in the massive open space that I now call home. "Nice digs. I take it you were in Chicago playing hide-and-seek with Mommy Dearest?"

Dylan knows my story. We've been friends since we were kids. He's had a front-row seat to the circus that is my family for years.

"You know it." I reach for the beer. "Took me a couple of days and a bunch of calls but I tracked her down."

Dylan drops the plant on the round marble coffee table. "How's Monica?"

Monica Adler is a retired struggling actress. She never made it professionally so all that wasted talent has fueled her role as my mother.

I'm her only child and the oldest of my father's four kids.

One of my half-siblings was born while he was still wearing the gold ring my mom slipped on his finger at their wedding.

"She's fine." I take the simple route because my weekend wore me out. "How's Eden?"

"Beautiful." His hand leaps to his chest. "She's working late so she told me to give you this."

He leans in and plants a kiss on my right cheek.

I shove him back with a playful punch to his shoulder. "Tell your fiancée I'd prefer if the kisses come from her."

"Duly noted," he responds, straightening his tie.

Dylan's a divorce attorney. Eden works for the prosecutor's office. I don't know how the hell they balance all that with their relationship, but they make it work.

I've never seen two people more devoted to each other than they are.

Dylan yanks two bottles of beer from the case, handing me one. "So you're actually going to live here?"

I unscrew the cap and take a swig from the bottle. "Yep."

He gives the room another full glance. "You like this?"

I get where the question is coming from. I lived in a one-bedroom, eight hundred square foot walk-up in Chicago. It wasn't in the best neighborhood. It could have used a few coats of paint on the walls, and the oven didn't work, but it was home.

I saved for the down payment. I negotiated the mortgage. I owned the place.

I still do. I'll hand the keys to a friend in real estate the next time I'm back in the Windy City so he can list it. Manhattan is home now.

"It's rent free," I point out with a lift of my bottle in the air. "And it's close to the office."

Dylan huffs out a laugh. "You're two minutes away from your office. You can't beat that in this city."

My gaze wanders to the plant on the table. "You can take that with you when you leave."

"I found it in the lobby." He shakes his head. "You need to fire whoever is in charge of keeping plants alive in this building."

"My assistant will handle it."

"Your assistant," he repeats my words with a cock of his dark brows. "You always called Julia by name, so I take it she didn't want to drop everything in Chicago to move here with you?"

I tried. Jesus did I try to convince my executive assistant to pick up her life and follow me to Manhattan. She wasn't buying what I was selling. That included a substantial raise, a moving allowance, and tickets to every goddamn Broadway musical that's playing.

I thought the show tunes she hummed every day were a clue to her weakness. It turns out I don't know shit about music because it's the opera that owns her heart.

She took early retirement and jetted off to London with her husband of thirty years for a performance at the Royal Opera House. I doubt like hell she'll be back anytime soon.

"I have a new assistant." I take a seat on one of the uncomfortable white leather armchairs that flank the hard-as-hell black leather sofa in the room. "Isabella Calvetti."

Dylan drops onto the sofa. "For fuck's sake, I think I broke my ass."

Comfort takes a back seat to stylish design when you're Ivan Garent. He picked out, personally approved, and paid for everything in this place right down to the gold utensils in the kitchen drawer.

When he offered me the keys I snatched them up without a second thought.

"Calvetti?" Dylan mumbles Isabella's surname. "Like the Italian restaurant?"

I nod. "She's the owner's granddaughter."

"Wait." He cocks his head to the side. "Are you talking about Bella Calvetti?"

"She's my executive assistant. You know her?"

The concept is foreign to me, but it shouldn't be. Dylan has lived in Manhattan for years. Isabella must know hundreds, if not thousands, of people on this island.

"She took me for five hundred bucks." He holds up two fingers. "Twice."

That's a story that I want to hear. "Details, Colt. I want details."

He tugs his phone from his pocket when it chimes. "Give me two minutes. I ordered a pizza. It's here."

I'm in. It's nearing nine p.m. and the last time I ate was shortly after noon at Crispy Biscuit.

Dylan slides to his feet. "The security guard in the lobby is sending the delivery guy up. Crack open another couple of beers, and I'll tell you everything I know about your new assistant."

Chapter 21

Bella

Another day. Another round of brutal cuts by Barrett Adler.

My boss is heartless.

That's putting it mildly.

There are a lot of other words I could use to describe him, but it boils down to the simple fact that he doesn't have an ounce of compassion in his body.

He does have a lean frame and muscular arms.

I saw that yesterday when he was wearing a T-shirt and jeans. Today, he's back to a dark blue suit paired with a white dress shirt and a deep purple tie.

"What can I do for you, Isabella?" He calls from behind his desk.

Dammit. I was staring again.

I pluck a piece of lint from the front of my red skirt. "Nothing."

I hear the creak of his chair as he gets up. I know he's headed in my direction. The rhythmic beat of his shoes on the concrete floor is a dead giveaway.

I finally look up when I sense him standing next to me. "What can I do for you, Mr. Adler?"

His lips curve up in a satisfied smile. "It's Barrett, but I'm glad to see you finally mastered the pronunciation of my surname."

I twist my lips in a scowl. "No problem."

I knew when I arrived at the office this morning at ten seconds to eight that he would be firing more people today.

He sent me an email last night with a list of the names of twenty-five employees of Garent Industries and three simple words: Prepare Termination Documents.

I didn't respond because I couldn't say what I really wanted to.

I'd lose my job if I called him an arrogant asshole to his face or in an email.

I bite my lip to ward off the temptation to share my true feelings. This job is the ticket to my future, so I need to hold onto it.

"I found out last night that we share a mutual friend."

My stomach knots at that announcement. He's going to tell me that he's dating someone I went to high school with or one of my cousins. Please don't let that be it. I loathe him, but I don't want anyone I know to sleep with him.

Guilt would consume me since I've been thinking about Barrett's body at night when I'm in bed alone.

I look up into his blue eyes. "Who?"

He traces a path over my lips with his gaze. "Dylan Colt."

I straighten my shoulders. I may have had a crush on Dylan for a hot minute the first time we met two years ago. It was at my cousin's apartment. Rocco Jones is the eldest of Marti's grandchildren. He's also a retired professional poker player.

Rocco taught me how to play cards using peppermints for chips.

Once he felt I was ready, he invited me to one of his monthly poker nights. A handful of his friends were there.

I emptied every wallet in the place, including Dylan's. I did the same three months later.

"You know Dylan?" I ask. "How?"

"We went to high school together in Chicago." He leans forward. "We've been friends for a long time."

"That's surprising," I blurt out without thinking.

His eyes widen. "Surprising? How so?"

From what I remember, Dylan is charming and funny. He hugged Rocco when he arrived and ordered pizza for everyone at the table. It's hard to imagine that he has anything in common with my boss.

I shrug a shoulder. "You two seem different."

He looks to the elevator when it dings. "We are different. I'm nothing like him."

"You can say that again," I whisper under my breath.

"What was that, Isabella?" He tilts his head, cupping his hand over his ear. "I didn't catch that."

I turn my attention to the approaching footsteps. It's Linus Adamsen, the Assistant Director of Quality Control for Garent and the first name on the list that Barrett sent me last night.

I look down when Linus raises his hand in a friendly greeting. He's on top of the world right now, but when he steps back on that elevator, his life will be forever different because of my boss.

***

I'm waiting around until Barrett's office door opens because I know he has something he wants to say to me.

I'm not a mind reader. I am very diligent about reading every last word of the emails my boss sends to me. The last one sent ten minutes ago at six-fifteen p.m., told me to stay in place until he was done with the call he's on.

He has to be talking on his cell because the office line is free and clear. I know that because I tried to connect him with a woman who heads development for one of the country's biggest beverage companies, but he didn't pick up.

I even emailed him to tell him that he needed to take the call. He responded almost immediately with three simple words: Take a message.

I slide the half-finished crossword puzzle from under the file folder on my desk. Giving it a glance, I hone in on the clue I've been stuck on for days. "Five letters for busy."

I tap my pen against the side of my lip. "Not me."

I laugh to myself. When I worked for Duke, I always had something to do. Barrett doesn't delegate nearly as much as my previous boss. It has to be a control issue. That, or he doesn't trust me as much as Duke did.

The sound of heavy footsteps sets me in motion. I drop the pen, slide the crossword puzzle back into it's hiding place, and open an already completed document on my laptop.

My fingers jump to the keyboard. I might as well appear to be busy when Barrett comes out of his office.

"Listen to me." His voice carries through the wooden door. "It's not your damn decision."

The door flies open, revealing a man on a mission. His gaze doesn't land on me as he charges right past my desk. "Say what you need to say, but it changes nothing. Do you hear me? Nothing will change."

I stare at his back as he heads toward the elevator. When he jabs his finger into the call button over and over again, I rise from my chair.

I should stop him, shouldn't I? He said he needed to talk to me.

Before I can round my desk to chase after him, the elevator doors pop open, and he steps inside. The doors glide shut, and I watch as the car climbs to the penthouse floor, leaving me with questions I don't think I'll get the answers to tonight.

Chapter 22

Bella

I wait a full thirty minutes before I turn off my laptop and lock my desk drawers for the night. Shouldering my purse, I skim my hands over the front of my short sleeve black sweater, tucking the hem into the waistband of my skirt.

I make my way to the elevator and push the call button. I should go straight home and cook a quick stir-fry with all the fresh vegetables that are sitting in the fridge. I bought those days ago to make a tofu dish for Gina. She stumbled on the recipe online and sent it to me via text message. She didn't have to ask if I'd cook it for her. I always do.

My sister has been good to me. I couldn't find another room to rent for five hundred dollars a month that offers a fully equipped chef's kitchen, laundry in the apartment, and a stellar view of Manhattan.

We've gotten closer since our older brother, Dominick, moved to Italy six months ago. Gina and I miss him, so our bond has grown stronger in his absence.

Just as I'm about to send Gina a text asking if she's at home so I can cook for her, the elevator doors spring open. My eye catches on something on the floor of the car.

I step forward and scoop it into my palm.

It looks like a black credit card.

No. It's a keycard. The Garent logo is on the front. Underneath are the words Penthouse Two etched in raised gold lettering.

The elevator was on the penthouse floor until I pushed the call button. I know that for a fact because I kept watch from my desk to see if my boss would take a ride back down to his office. This keycard has to belong to Barrett.

I study the silver panel hanging on the wall in the lift. I can press any button other than PH and I'll be taken directly to the corresponding floor. I know that because I've tried pressing the PH button and it's never lit up.

I tap the card in my hand against the control panel and the PH button shines yellow.

That draws me back a step. I need to think this through. I can hold onto the card until tomorrow and return it to my boss when I see him in the morning, but what if he goes out tonight? He won't have a keycard for the elevator.

Returning the card is the right thing to do, so I press the PH button and suck in a deep breath.

I'm a good employee. That's all this is. I repeat that to myself over and over again as the elevator rises toward the penthouse where Barrett lives.

***

As soon as I step off the elevator, I'm greeted with a choice. To the left is a door marked Penthouse One. To the right is Penthouse Two.

Both are at opposite ends of a long corridor.

I've worked in this building for years and had no idea that this existed. I imagined undeveloped space with dust everywhere, but this is beautiful. The floor is dark stained wood. The walls are painted light gray and dotted with framed works of art. The design has Ivan Garent written all over it. He appreciates art more than anyone I've ever met.

My knowledge of the creative world is reserved to the colorful drawings my cousin's kids give me when I see them at Calvetti's or family gatherings.

I set off toward the door marked Penthouse Two. My mission is simple. I need to get this keycard back in the hand of my boss. As soon as I do that, I can head home to prepare a feast for my sister.

I stop just short of the door to Barrett's apartment. I run a hand over my hair. Why do I care if I look nice and why the hell are there so many butterflies in my stomach?

I'm just here to drop off a keycard. This is not a date.

Sucking in a deep breath, I knock softly on the door. I wait in silence hoping that I'm not interrupting anything. I assume he's done with his call by now, but what if he isn't?

A flash of regret passes over me just as the door opens.

Holy hell.

Barrett leans his bare left shoulder against the doorjamb and flashes me a brilliant smile. "Isn't this a surprise?"

I stare at his body, covered only in a pair of black sweatpants. It's gorgeous unmarked skin and muscles.

Pushing the keycard at him, I mumble. "For you. It's yours."

His gaze falls to my hand before he locks eyes with me. "I must have dropped that."

I nod my head up and down like a fool.

"You didn't have to come up here to return it." He takes a step back affording me a clear view into his apartment. "I'm glad you did. Come in, Isabella."

I step forward once and then again until I hear the click of the door behind me.

Chapter 23

Barrett

I walk back into the main living area after sliding on a black T-shirt. Isabella's face lit up when she saw me shirtless. I gave her the time she needed to take it all in. I work out. I'm in great shape. Appreciative looks like the one Isabella shot my way are all the motivation I need to hit the gym three times a week.

"Can I get you anything?" I offer because she looks like she could use a drink. "I have some red wine, a beer, whiskey if you're up for it. I don't have the makings of a cosmopolitan, but this is New York so I'm sure I can order one up from the restaurant across the street."

Her gaze bolts to the wall of windows that border the main living area. "Water. I'll take water."

Smart choice. I'm not as grounded, so I grab a beer from the fridge and pop it open before I take a swallow. I empty a small bottle of sparkling water into a glass, dropping two ice cubes in it.

When I hand it to her, the tremor in her fingers is noticeable.

My assistant is a bundle of nerves.

The expression on her face was a clear indicator that she didn't expect an invite into my apartment, but I wasn't about to turn her away after she took the brazen step of using my keycard to gain access to this floor.

"I thought you might need that tonight." She points to where she dropped the keycard on a table in the foyer next to a tall vase holding some type of fake flowers. "I was worried that if you had plans, you wouldn't be able to get back up to this floor."

"The doorman knows me. He would have let me take the ride up here. Besides, I have an extra keycard."

"Of course," she says, shaking her head. "I should have thought of that."

I'm glad she didn't. I was facing a night alone going over a few of the acquisitions that Duke has made in the past five years. He created one hell of a mess when he was in charge. Spending time with my assistant is a welcome buffer between the call I was on earlier and dealing with Duke's fuck-ups.

"Do you have plans tonight?"

My question lures her brows up. "I'm cooking dinner for my sister."

I know about the sister. Gina Calvetti is a rising social media star. She's three years older than Isabella and a recognizable face in the Instagram ready world.

"What are you cooking?" I draw this out because I'm enjoying watching her squirm. Her hand hasn't stopped shaking. All the deep breaths she's been taking aren't helping.

"A tofu stir fry thing." She scrunches her nose.

I point the bottle in my hand at her. "I've learned that if the chef makes that face when they're talking about their food, you need to find a new place to eat."

Eat. Jesus. Why the fuck did I have a flash of my head between Isabella's thighs?

"It's not my first choice," she acquiesces with a shrug of her shoulder.

I step right through that open door. "What would be your first choice?"

Her blue eyes meet mine, and I feel the spark of something between us. I don't know what the fuck it is, but it's undeniable. It's dangerous, but it feels so damn good.

She's my assistant. She's my much younger assistant.

I drill that into my brain as her lips tug up into a smile. "My first choice?"

I give her a nod. "If you could eat anything for dinner tonight, what would it be?"

A bite to the corner of her bottom lip sets my dick over the edge. I harden inside my sweatpants. Another drink from the beer does nothing to quell the growing need I feel inside me.

"Greek food," she announces with a sigh. "I should say Italian because I'm a Calvetti, but sometimes I crave Greek food."

Guilt lures her gaze to the floor. I should punish her.

I need to get a fucking grip.

I also need air. Cool New York City night air.

I empty the bottle in my hand in one last swallow. "Where do you go when you want great Greek food?"

"There's a food truck not far from here," she answers hesitantly. "Why?"

"Tell your sister she needs to cook her own dinner." I drop the bottle on the dining room table on the way back to my bedroom. "Give me two minutes to change."

"Change clothes?" She steps toward me.

I turn back, tempted to curl my finger at her in an invitation to follow me, but Garent's goddamn rules and regulations keep my hand by my side. "I haven't had dinner yet. Neither have you. We'll walk down to the truck together."

"Together?" she parrots back. "You and me?"

I clarify because I can't tell what's going through that beautiful head of hers. "I want details about the party supply store Duke bought into. I'm killing that deal, and I need to know everything you do about Duke's plans for that venture. We'll walk and talk about that."

Her lips part. "It's a working dinner."

If there's disappointment in her tone I sure as hell don't hear it. I sense she's relieved that I'm not trying to sweep her off her feet. "That's what it is."

"I'm ready when you are." A smile blooms on her mouth.

I take off down the hallway toward my bedroom. This evening took a hell of a sharp turn in a direction I wasn't planning on heading, but I'll go along for the ride.

Greek food with Ms. Calvetti should prove to be interesting.

Chapter 24

Bella

What do they say about a well-dressed man?

It should be that every woman turns to get a glimpse of him. That's what's happening now as Barrett and I walk down Fifth Avenue side-by-side.

He changed into charcoal gray pants and a black button-down shirt before we left his apartment. He rolled the sleeves on that and left the top two buttons open. He looks gorgeous and seriously delicious.

Scrap that last thought.

I have to stop thinking that way about him, even though I did see his bare chest less than an hour ago. That image is imprinted on my brain for eternity because of his abs and biceps and that gorgeous happy trail of dark hair that disappeared under the waistband of his sweatpants.

"Isabella?" His deep voice shatters my thoughts about his sexy-as-sin body.

It was so much easier working for Duke because he wasn't my type.

"Yes?" I glance over at him.

"I asked you twice what your thoughts were about the acquisition of the party supply store."

It was a reckless move on Duke's part. I saw the sales numbers for the mom and pop run store. I warned my then boss that he needed to rethink how he could help the elderly couple, but he dove into the deal with both feet.

That's how Duke is. He jumps first and asks questions after everyone has signed the contracts.

I slow as we near the Greek food cart. The man in the suit standing at the window placing his order is all too familiar to me.

Without a word from me, he turns in our direction. Recognition lights up his handsome face. "Bella?"

His voice is just as I remember. Soft and soothing. It offered me comfort after a long day or a hard-fought battle with an exam. He was a vital part of my life when I was in college. I thought he might be important to me forever.

"Emil," I whisper his name to keep my tone even.

I've seen him from time-to-time when our paths cross on the sidewalk or in a restaurant, but a part of me always feels a stab of sadness when I run into him.

He looks just as he did the last time I saw him. That was at least five months ago, maybe more. His black hair is the same length, his green eyes as sharp as always.

The seriousness that surrounds him fades when he smiles because the man could light the darkest sky when joy grabs hold of him.

"Who is he?" Emil keeps his eyes pinned to me. "You're seeing someone?"

"Barrett Adler." My boss steps beside me, snaking a hand past my shoulder toward Emil. "I work with Isabella."

"You go by Isabella now?" Emil questions with a draw of his brows together. "It's so formal. It's so not you."

He doesn't know me. I thought he did, but how can a man know a woman if he doesn't understand her soul? Emil's sights were set much higher than mine when he graduated from NYU two years before I did.

"I'm Emil Burdeon." He shakes Barrett's hand. "Is Bella still working as an assistant at Garent?"

There it is; the innocent question with the unmistakable undertone of my value hidden within the words.

"Always be better than someone else's best. Aim higher, Bella. There's no triumph in being second to anyone."

Emil thought he was helpful when he said those things to me over and over, but they cut into my self-esteem until I had to cut myself free of him.

My grandma taught me that my value couldn't be measured in the size of my paycheck or my job title, but in what I do for others that won't earn me a dollar.

"You're one of those Burdeon kids, aren't you?" Barrett sizes Emil up from head-to-toe. "Your dad owns the Burdeon vineyards. Is that right?"

It's Emil's claim to fame. He runs the family business. It was his calling from the start. His degree in business only cemented his place in the legacy founded by his great-grandfather.

He convinced himself that he beat out his brothers and older sister to take the reins when his father was looking for a CEO to lighten his load. Emil always felt he earned it by hard work and determination, but no one else wanted the responsibility. They all had their own dreams to chase.

Emil's face beams almost as brightly as his diamond cufflinks. "That's right."

"My father owns Adler Estates." Barrett scratches his chin. "He's running circles around you at the moment."

Adler Estates? Barrett's father owns the company that produces some of the best wine in the country?

"I wouldn't say that." Emil glances down the crowded sidewalk. "We're focused on development at the moment. Expect our spring offering to trump yours."

"Not mine." Barrett laughs off the comment with a shake of his head. "I don't work for my old man. I carved my own path. You should try it sometime."

"Sir?" A woman sticks her head out of the window of the food truck. "Your order is up."

Emil grabs the offering, not bothering to thank the woman. "I need to take off. I'm heading to California later tonight."

"Safe travels," I quip as I approach the window.

"Cheers, Emil," Barrett says from behind me. "It's been a slice getting to know you."

***

"I need you to arrange a meeting for me with the owners of the party supply store tomorrow. Damn, if I can remember the name of that place."

I look up into the face of my boss. "Party Hearty."

"Hate it," he quips. "What the fuck was Duke thinking when he dropped a load of cash into that?"

I toss the wrapper from my gyro into the trash. "He was thinking that he was helping the owners keep their dream alive."

Barrett taps a finger on the side of his mouth. "You have a little something there."

Of course, I do. This night has been nothing but one disaster after another. I saw my college boyfriend. I dripped yogurt sauce on my sweater and now I'm proving to my boss that I can't eat without leaving a trail of food on my face.

I swipe a finger over both sides of my lips to be extra certain that I got whatever was left behind.

Barrett leans forward on the bench we're sitting on. "Emil Burdeon. Let's talk about him."

I thought we'd skip over the subject of my ex when we got our food and sat down. Barrett launched into a long-winded speech about everything that is wrong with Party Hearty. I didn't say a word because every point he made was valid.

My silence wasn't just because I agreed with him. I was in shock. Seeing Emil was jarring. I'm over him, but there's still a bite of something when I see him. Maybe it's regret that I stuck it out as long as I did.

"What's the story with you two?" Barrett presses for more. "Does he fall into the one and done category?"

I close my eyes briefly before I turn and look at him. "No. I thought Emil was the one until it was done."

Chapter 25

Barrett

The one.

That's a concept I've never been able to wrap my head around. How in the hell does a person decide to devote himself or herself to one human being for eternity?

The deer-in-the-headlights look on Isabella's face when she saw Burdeon told me enough of their story that I knew he was someone special to her.

To hear that he was almost "the one" is still surprising.

When I was in my early twenties, I couldn't nail down a decision about what to eat for breakfast. Isabella was light years ahead of me if she was contemplating whether a guy was the forever to her happy-ever-after.

I don't talk rainbows, butterflies, or anything related to hearts, but I dive in because this is a story I want to hear. "You were in love with him?"

She looks just as surprised that I asked the question as I am. She nods. "For a time, I was, yes."

Not giving a shit that the question is completely out-of-line, I ask it. "What happened?"

She shifts on the bench. "Life happened."

It's none of my fucking business. That's what her body language is telling me. She's as uncomfortable now as she was when she saw me without a shirt. The problem is that this time, I'm pushing her to a place she doesn't want to go.

Just as I'm about to suggest we hit up a bar a block over for a drink to talk business, she darts to her feet. "I need to go home."

Like hell she does.

Tossing the paper cup in my hand in the trash, I stand. "What's the rush?"

"I start work early."

"You start at eight," I point out.

Her gaze darts over her shoulder. I follow her lead and spot Burdeon rounding the corner headed in our direction.

She knew. She fucking knew he would come back looking for her. This has to be his pattern because she sure as hell doesn't seem surprised to see him.

Resignation pulls her shoulders forward. She's weary. This asshole has worn her out emotionally. I saw the same expression on my mother's face each time my father circled back around, proclaiming his undying devotion to her.

"It looks like you have company," I say in an even tone.

Her eyes find mine. "He thinks…"

"That you'll want him back at some point," I finish the thought for her.

Burdeon approaches at an even pace. I keep my gaze locked on him.

"Yes," she answers quietly. "Our break up was messy."

I round her so I'm the one he has to face. I don't know why the fuck I'm putting myself in the middle of this, but I have an overpowering need to protect Isabella.

"What?" I bark at him as he nears.

"Bella," he calls out to her even though her back is still to him. "Give me thirty minutes. I'm asking for one cosmo for old time's sake. Amore Mio, please."

I feel her move behind me. Those words pierced something inside of her because she's next to me and face-to-face with him before I realize what the fuck is going on.

I sense her gaze floating over the side of my face, but I keep my eyes trained on Burdeon. I want to tell him to go to hell, even though I know that Isabella can fight her own battles.

"Don't call me that," she says quietly. "You can't call me that anymore."

Amore Mio. It's Italian for my love.

I used the same phrase the summer after I graduated from high school when Dylan and I took to Europe for a backpacking trip. I tried to pick up an Italian woman at least ten years my senior by calling her my love. With a pat on my head and a string of Italian words I'll never understand, she left me standing in the middle of a coffee shop with a bruised ego.

"I have something to say." He gestures toward me without making eye contact. "I need to do that when we're alone. I'm not asking for more than a few minutes, Bella."

"I can't." A shake of her head punctuates the words.

"It's about Venla." He reaches out a hand. "You'll want to hear this."

The bait works. She drops her hand in his and steps forward. "What about her? She's alright, isn't she?"

This is a conversation I have no right overhearing even though I know he's pulling on Isabella's heartstrings because she's a good person. She's too kind. She's too much of an angel for this twisted, hardened world.

She glances at me. "I'll see you in the morning?"

I've been brushed off with a beautiful smile. "Sure thing."

"Good to meet you, Baron." Burdeon drops Isabella's hand to extend his to me.

I ignore it and him.

"Barrett," Isabella corrects him. "His name is Barrett Adler."

I catch her gaze briefly before I turn and walk away, leaving her in the clutches of a man who will never fully appreciate the beautiful woman standing right in front of him.

Chapter 26

Bella

"How's Venla?"

I turn to the sound of Barrett's voice. He's standing in his office near the window staring out at the skyline of Manhattan.

It's ten minutes to eight. I'm a touch early because Gina had a meeting three blocks from here with a producer for one of the national morning shows. If I can ride the subway with my sister, I'll do it. That's for her, not me. The train makes her anxious. I always give her hand a squeeze when we board so she knows I'm right beside her.

"Venla is fine," I say.

I'm not getting into the details about Emil's teenage sister. The big reveal was that she was accepted to Columbia University. I haven't spoken to her in years, but I'm still happy that she's going to the college of her dreams.

Before Emil could start in on how we still belong together, I told him I needed to go home. I'll never be with him again. I owe myself more than a man who thinks my best is not enough.

"Who is Venla?" Barrett turns to look at me.

He's dressed down today in a pair of jeans, a black sweater, and a dark gray suit jacket. I like the look. It's classic, but has an edge that his tailored suits don't offer.

"Emil's sister." I shrug. "We were close a long time ago."

He studies me from a distance with the morning sun shooting a ray over his broad shoulders. He's a tall man. I'd guess around six foot three since he towered over Emil. With the sunlight haloing him, he almost looks approachable, even kind.

"I fired Daphne this morning."

The halo shatters into a million pieces just like that. The devil seeps back out in the sly grin on his face.

Daphne Clegg was a Garent lifer. She was with Ivan from the start. She's held so many positions in the company that I've lost count. Most recently, she was in charge of economic development for a new division that was focused on educational endeavors.

Some Garent employees thought she made the position up herself so she could take a pay raise. I try to block out office gossip because I've been the focus of it more than once when people thought Duke and I were pairing up behind closed doors.

That never happened.

If Daphne was fired that puts her pension in jeopardy. Her plan was to retire next year. She was thinking about buying a condo in Florida a few months ago so she'd be all set when she walked out of the office for the last time.

Holding out hope that a caring heart beats in his chest, I ask a question I'm not sure I want to know the answer to. "You mean you offered her early retirement, right? You did this to save the company money by shutting down her new division."

"I. Fired. Her." He pauses between each word, so his message is loud and clear.

I step into his office. "Why would you do that?"

He rakes me from head-to-toe taking in the navy blue and white striped dress I'm wearing. "Because it was necessary."

As Duke's assistant, I had access to all the employee's records and I know, for a fact, that Daphne gave her all. She never had a warning or a write-up. She rarely missed a day of work. Ivan once called her the cream of the Garent crop.

"Mr. Garent won't like this."

Barrett rubs the back of his neck. "Ivan has a lot to worry about, Isabella. I doubt that he will give a shit about Daphne losing her job."

He's wrong. He is so wrong. He doesn't know Ivan the way I do.

I fist my hands together at my sides. "I suggest you talk to Mr. Garent about this before Daphne does."

That sets him a full step toward me. "I suggest you call Human Resources and tell them that Daphne Clegg was terminated with just cause. Make it clear that there is no severance option here. She'll be paid for time earned, nothing more."

Indignation rolls through me. "What about her pension?"

"That's not your concern." He turns to the side. "Go make that call, Isabella. I want Daphne out of the building within the hour."

***

I slip the crossword puzzle out from under the file folder that keeps it hidden from the prying eyes of my boss.

I glance at it, stopping when my gaze catches on something written in bold black ink. I look at the blue pen in my hand.

The clue is five letters for busy.

DOING.

Who filled that in?

Wait. Barrett always has a silver pen in his hand. In fact, he sent me an email yesterday telling me to order a box of pens for him. He underlined the requirement that I order the black ink model, not the blue ink one. He included a link to the website he wants me to order them from. It just so happens to be the biggest retail site on the planet. I buy virtually everything there. Duke did too, which is why I set up a corporate account for Garent Industries on the site.

I slide the crossword back under the file folder. If I ignore the fact that he was snooping around my desk, maybe he will forget that I've been doing crosswords on company time.

I wake my laptop with a tap on the screen. Navigating to the shopping site, I send a text to Max on my phone.

Bella: Missing you.

I key in the brand of pen and black ink into the search bar on the site. Two different options pop up.

My gaze drifts to my phone when a new message arrives.

Max: If it isn't my rich best friend. I thought you forgot all about me.

Laughing, I type out a response with one finger.

Bella: Not possible. Dinner tonight?

I click on the black ink pens that Barrett can't live without. I choose the two hundred count box because it's the most economical. Clicking on the 'add to cart' button, I catch sight of a new text message out of the corner of my eye.

Max: Calvetti's? At seven? I miss your grandma almost as much as I miss you.

Bella: She misses you too.

The sound of the elevator pinging its arrival sets my back straight in my chair. I type out another text.

Bella: I think my boss is back from lunch. I need to go.

The elevator doors spring open and Barrett strolls out. His eyes don't leave mine as he stalks toward my desk.

A chime from my cell goes ignored because I won't lose this staring contest with my boss. As he nears, his gaze drops to my computer.

"What are you working on, Isabella?" he asks smugly. "I told you earlier that I want the quarterly sales reports for Stems & Scents on my desk by five. Are you still on track for that?"

"I'm ordering those pens you like." I tap a finger over the place order button. "That's done, and the sales reports are done. You'll find them on your desk organized by date."

His expression gives nothing away. Why would it? He fired a long-time employee, and he hasn't batted an eyelash. In fact, I think he went out to celebrate. A woman named Felicity called the office this morning wanting to speak to him about their lunch plans. I patched her through to his phone only to hear him laughing before he ended the call and waltzed out of here like he didn't have a care in the world.

Smug jerk.

He starts toward his office door before he turns back to me. "One last thing."

Shutting my laptop, I glance over at him. "What's that?"

"This was dropped off for you at reception." He yanks a white envelope out of the inner pocket of his suit jacket. "Carol or Cheryl or whatever her name is that works the desk handed it to me on my way up. It's for you."

"For me?" I hold out my hand.

"There's no return address." He taps the corner of the envelope against his palm. "It's marked personal and confidential."

I wiggle my fingers, curiosity nipping at me. "Give it to me, please."

He slides it into my hand, his fingers grazing mine briefly. "Here you go."

My gaze drops to the envelope. I don't recognize the handwriting. "Thank you."

When I look up, his eyes search mine for something, but I can't place it. Clearing his throat, he says, "I'll look over those sales reports now."

I wait until he's in his office with the door closed before I slide a fingernail under the seal and open the envelope.

I unfold the simple sheet of white paper and read the printed words. I reread it, before I slip the paper back into the envelope and drop it in the bottom drawer of my desk.

Chapter 27

Bella

"Are you working hard to earn all that extra money Mr. Garent is throwing at you?" Max glances over to where Marti is standing next to a table occupied by six people. All of them have heaping bowls of spaghetti and meatballs in front of them. "Your grandma is beautiful. You see it, right?"

She's breathtaking.

Her face is heart-shaped with blue eyes that mirror my own. Each fine line on her face is a testament to a life lived with tender love and caring concern.

I sigh. "I hope when I'm her age I look that good."

"Don't count on it," Max quips with a wink. "You're looking good today though. That dress is cute."

"Stripes suit me." I laugh. "We're twins."

He tugs on the front of the blue and white striped button-down he's wearing. "This is one of my favorite shirts because my favorite girl bought it for me."

It wasn't me, so I stick out my tongue.

"My mom, Bella." He laughs. "She still likes buying me clothes. What am I supposed to do about that?"

"Enjoy it." I smile. "Your mom knows what you like. If my mom bought me clothes, I'd look like a grandma."

"And that would be a bad thing?" Marti asks as she nears our table. "You're talking about me again, Dolly, aren't you?"

"Dolly always talks about you," Max says with a straight face. "I was just asking her about her work."

My grandma skims her palm over my cheek. "Work is work. You leave it at the office, and then you live life. You're living life, aren't you?"

I glance up at her with a smile. "Every day."

A tear wells in the corner of her eye. "You're my treasure. You know that sweetheart, don't you?"

"I know. I always know," I whisper.

She shakes off the moment with a brush of her hand over her forehead. "Your dad was here today. He fixed the loose tile on the floor in the kitchen."

My dad loves helping his mom whenever he gets the chance. He'll help anyone who needs it.

"You should meet him here for lunch one day," she suggests with a pop of her eyebrows. "I'll make linguine with clam sauce. You can invite the people you work with."

"And me," Max adds. "I'm all for having lunch with Bella's new boss."

"The new boss too," Marti says as she turns to walk toward the door of the restaurant to greet a group of people who just arrived. "You tell me when. I'll cook and tidy the place."

Never.

Barrett doesn't strike me as the type of man who wants to sit down for a meal with someone else's family. I've never heard him mention his own family other than his dad.

"I'm ready to go if you are," Max announces with a push back of his chair. "I'm going to hide some money under the napkin to cover our meals."

"Marti will never talk to you again." I laugh. "Bring her some peonies tomorrow. She'll love you forever if you do that."

"Done." He reaches a hand to help me up from my chair. "I do want to meet the new boss. If we're not going to do lunch with him here, at least invite me to the office when he's around."

"You don't want to meet him." I laugh.

"Why not?" He inches my hair back over my shoulder. "Duke and I got along. Ivan loves me."

"He's nothing like either of them." I roll my eyes. "He's heartless. He fired Daphne this morning."

Max and Daphne took a few spins on the dance floor at the holiday party. He had a blast listening to her talk about her kids and grandkids.

Skepticism clouds his expression. "You're joking."

"I'm dead serious." I shrug. "He fired her on the spot. She's officially a former employee of Garent Industries."

"Maybe I don't want to meet this guy." He offers his arm to me. "I'll take you home now."

Passing my grandma on our way out, I tap her on the shoulder so I can hug her. "I'll see you soon."

She holds me tight and whispers the words she always does when we say goodbye. "Look both ways before you cross the street, my sweet Dolly."

***

"I'll come in for a glass of water, and then I'm heading out." Max exits the elevator first, leading the way down the corridor toward my apartment. "I'm stuck doing inventory this week, so I'm going back to the store."

I walk quickly to keep up with him. "Why didn't you tell me? I'll change and go with you."

He spins on his heel to face me. "You don't have to do that. I can handle it on my own."

"I'm going with you." I march past him. "Let me throw on a pair of yoga pants, and a T-shirt and we'll head back uptown."

I hear his footsteps behind me as I reach the door to my apartment. It's slightly ajar. Voices seep out from inside.

I recognize my sister's husky tone, but there's something about that other voice. Why does it sound so familiar to me?

Pushing open the door, I face the man having a random conversation with Gina about the weather.

"Hot boss is here," Max drawls from behind me.

The sound of his voice lures Barrett's gaze to us. Gina's follows. With a wink, she tosses me a knowing smile. "Bella, look who dropped in to see you."

Chapter 28

Bella

"Why are you here?"

It's not the best way to greet your boss, but the words tumble out of my mouth because I'm in shock. My apartment is my safe place. I come here after work to unwind and hide from the stress of my day.

Duke hasn't been here. I would never have invited him because I cherish my personal space, but apparently, Barrett Adler doesn't understand boundaries and the fact that I'm not tied to him twenty-four seven. Wait. Maybe I am considering the size of my paycheck.

Gina taps me on my shoulder. "Manners, young lady."

It's one of our mom's favorite sayings. We throw it at each other every chance we get. This time I don't find it funny.

"Your boss is here to see you," Gina announces from beside me. "Why don't you invite him to sit down?"

I turn to make a face at her. It's my shut-the-hell-up-Gina look, but she's gone in for a hug from my best friend.

I hear Max whispering to her about the black jumpsuit and boots she's wearing.

"Isabella?" Barrett's hand lands on my forearm. "The pens you ordered this afternoon arrived at the office."

What? He came to my apartment to tell me that the shopping site lived up to their promise of same-day delivery?

He's still wearing the jeans, black sweater, and suit jacket he was earlier. It looks like he rushed over to give me the good news.

"That's great," I reply because what am I supposed to say.

"I brought the other item you ordered over."

My brow knits in confusion as I drop my gaze to his hand and the brown paper shopping bag in it. I recognize the logo on the bag. It's from the deli a block from the office. I order lunch from there at least once a week. I noticed an empty bag on the foyer table in Barrett's penthouse, so I assumed he took my lead and tried the pastrami on rye for himself.

I lean forward to try and peer in the bag, but he's gripping the twine handles so tightly in his fist that I can't see what's inside.

A pat on my shoulder lures my attention away from the bag.

I turn to see Max staring at me. "You haven't introduced me to this handsome man yet."

The emphasis on the word handsome doesn't get lost on me, or Barrett. When I glance at him, his lips are twitching in a suppressed smile.

With anxiety twisting my stomach in a tight knot, I give Max my best not-now-Max look, but it has as much impact as the look I shot my sister earlier.

"I'm Max Polley. I'm Bella's best friend." Max pushes me aside to approach Barrett.

Barrett extends a hand to Max. "Barrett Adler. It's good to meet you."

"Bella has told me a lot about you," Max says, giving Barrett's hand a shake that lasts two seconds too long.

I sigh. "I haven't."

Barrett's gaze drops to my face. "What exactly has Isabella told you about me?"

"Isabella," Max repeats in his best swoony voice. "I tried to call her that when we were kids but she kicked me in the knee. How times have changed."

Needing this to be over, I grab Barrett's attention again. "I told Max I had a new boss. That's the extent of our conversation about you."

"No, it's not," Max jumps in. "She said that you…"

"What's in the bag?" I interrupt because I want Barrett out of here.

The walls feel like they're closing in on me, even though the apartment is spacious. We're all gathered in the foyer. Barrett keeps stealing glances at the living room. It's decorated in an array of oversized navy and gray furniture pieces that were given to Gina by a company in New Jersey in exchange for an online shout-out to her millions of followers.

I'm not inviting him to take a seat so he can get comfortable. I want him to go, but first I need to know what the hell is in that bag since I didn't order anything but the black ink pens.

Barrett's gaze slides over my sister and Max before it lands back on me. "I need to speak with you privately."

"We're leaving." Gina turns her attention to Max. "'I'm on my way to a boutique in Tribeca for a clothing line launch party. If you're headed home we can ride the subway together."

"I'm going to that party with you." He scoops her hand in his. "Consider me your plus one."

This time I turn to both of them and say what I want, instead of tossing them warning looks that fly right over their heads. "Don't go yet."

Max leans forward to plant a kiss on my cheek. "I know we had a date to count sneakers, but I can't turn down a launch party with this beauty."

Gina flicks her long brown hair over her shoulder. "I'll be back before midnight, but I can crash at Max's place if you want the apartment to yourself tonight."

They giggle in unison.

"It was good to meet you, Barrett," Gina says, reaching for the doorknob.

"I'll second that," Max chimes in.

Just as they're walking out the door, Barrett calls after them. "Enjoy your evening."

I shut the door behind them before I turn to face him. I'll clear this up quickly so he can leave and I can breathe again. "I only ordered pens today. If something else was shipped with them, it's the store's mistake. I'll return it tomorrow and have the amount credited back to Garent's account."

He runs his fingers along his jawline. "I called the customer service number listed on the packing slip after I opened the box. They assured me that there were two items in the cart when you placed the order. The box of pens and this."

Before I can ask what the second item is, he reaches into the brown bag and yanks out a rectangular box.

Oh my God.

There is a vibrator in my boss's hand.

Chapter 29

Barrett

I could have handled this tomorrow in the office. I probably should have, but I'm not a man who puts off an important conversation. Besides, curiosity brought me to Isabella's apartment. I wanted to see where my executive assistant spends her nights.

Meeting her sister and her best friend was a bonus. Max Polley seems like a good guy. Gina is just as I imagined she'd be. She's attractive but in a much different way than Isabella is.

Gina is pretty. Isabella is the type of beautiful that graces this earth once in a lifetime.

At the moment, her skin is flushed pink, and her blue eyes are wide. I shocked the hell out of her when I pulled the vibrator out of the bag.

The box was delivered no more than five minutes after she left the office for the day. I set it on her desk but decided to pry it open to see how many pens she'd ordered. I laughed out loud when I saw it was two hundred. I expected ten, maybe twenty, but Isabella saw fit to go for the best deal.

The laughter went up a notch when I noticed the other item in the box.

I ordered take-out from a deli near the office and sat down to debate what the fuck to do. By the time I swallowed the last bite of food, I had formulated the ingenious plan to swing by here to deliver the vibrator to my executive assistant.

Not a squeak has left her pouty lips since I showed her what's in my hand, so I clear my throat. "You did order this, didn't you?"

I've cornered her. We both know she ordered the damn thing. My question is why charge it to the company? She knows better. I don't give a shit about the money. I'll bury the small amount under entertainment expenses, but I'd like to understand how this made sense to her.

Her bottom lip trembles and for a split second I think she might start crying. I don't know her well, but that seems out of character. Isabella has proven that she can go toe-to-toe with me. I can't imagine her crumbling under the weight of embarrassment.

She sucks in a deep breath and manages a small smile. "It's a funny story."

I hold back a chuckle. Still holding the vibrator, I lean my shoulder against the foyer wall. "I can't wait to hear it."

Her gaze darts to the living area before it lands back on my face. "Do you want to sit down?"

That's an invitation I didn't expect. Pushing the box at her, I nod. "You take this, and I'll take a seat."

***

After handing me a glass of cold water, Isabella settles into an armchair that faces the gray couch I'm sitting on. The apartment's décor looks like it jumped off the pages of a magazine. It's got a much more welcoming feel than the penthouse I'm learning to call home.

Emptying the tall glass in one large swallow, I place it on the distressed wood coffee table and wait for her to start talking.

Anxiously picking at the nail polish on her thumb, she keeps her gaze pinned to her lap. I watch as her lips move silently as if she's rehearsing what she's about to say.

"It was a mistake," she blurts out. "I put that in my shopping cart a couple of weeks ago because mine is wearing out."

She wore out a vibrator?

A fleeting image of her in my lap riding my cock with abandon flashes in front of me. I choke it back with a cough. "What did you just say?"

"Nothing." She taps the middle of her forehead with her index finger. "I thought I put that item in the shopping cart in my personal account, but obviously, I was mistaken. I must have been logged into the Garent Industries account when I did that."

It's an innocent mistake, but I let her go on because she's still drilling away at that nail polish.

"Right before Duke left, he told me to work at home for a day, so I brought my office laptop here." She sighs. "That was the day I was looking for a new… anyways, I added it to my cart so I could think about it. When I went to order the pens today, I didn't check the cart. That was my mistake. I'll return the fun and done tomorrow."

I huff out a laugh. "Fun and done?"

Her eyes widen with the realization that she let those words slip out. "That's not what I meant."

"You call that," I pause to jerk a thumb over my shoulder at the box sitting on her foyer table. "You call it a fun and done?"

I have to admit I've heard a host of names batted around for vibrators, but this is the first time I've heard anyone call one that.

She crosses her legs and then uncrosses them. "That's what it is. I have fun with it, and then it's done, and I put it away."

I give her credit for not buckling during this conversation. She's held her own, even looking me straight in the eye when she delivered the answer to my last question.

We're stepping dangerously close to a line that I can't cross. I want to tell her to trash the thing and show me the way to her bedroom. She's doesn't need anything between her legs but me.

"I'll return it first thing in the morning." Rising to her feet, she looks toward the foyer. "If that's all, I'll show you to the door."

I can see the fucking door from where I'm sitting, but I take the hint and stand. Buttoning my suit jacket, I look her over.

This woman shouldn't be so pent up with sexual energy that she has to resort to a toy so often that she wears the damn thing out. She can go at me all night and into next week if she wants.

My cock hardens against the inside of my jeans. That's my cue to take off. "I'll see you in the morning, Isabella."

She leads the way to the door, her ass swaying with each step she takes. The need inside of me only grows. I'm going to have to go home and stroke one out to the thought of her. I've done that too many times to count since she started working for me.

Looking up at me, the gray flecks dance inside her blue irises. "I'm sorry, Mr. Adler. Can we forget this ever happened?"

"Barrett," I correct her as I lean down. "I want you to call me Barrett."

"Barrett," she repeats in a hushed whisper. "I'll send it back tomorrow, and we'll never speak of it again? You won't mention it to anyone?"

She wants my reassurance that I won't tell Ivan, so I give her that and more. "Consider this our secret."

Her lips curve into a smile. "Maybe you're not so bad after all."

"Maybe I'm not." My gaze roams her face, following the curve of her neck until I reach the valley between her full breasts. When I look back into her eyes, there's a question there waiting to be asked. "Is there anything else we should talk about, Isabella?"

With the softest touch of her hand to the center of her chest, she shakes her head. "There's nothing else. Goodnight."

Caught in her spell, I somehow make me way out of her apartment and into the elevator. When the doors slide shut, I let out a deep exhale. "You're fucked, Adler. You are so fucked."

Chapter 30

Bella

I should be proud of myself for the way I handled things last night, but I'm too tired to feel anything but numb. I finally gave up trying to sleep shortly after five this morning. I could hear Gina softly snoring behind her bedroom door, so I quietly showered, dried my hair, and applied my makeup.

I put on a pair of black pants and a light pink sleeveless blouse. It's not my best look, but with the cute white fitted blazer I slid on over the blouse, it's presentable enough for a day in the office.

After Barrett left my apartment last night, I paced the floor for over an hour thinking about what we talked about.

I was tempted to run out the door to another state to start a new life when he showed me the vibrator, but I made a promise to myself when I was nineteen that I'd never be ashamed of my sexuality.

I'm a woman. I like sex. I prefer it if it involves a man. That's not always possible, so I take care of myself if I need to.

I refused to let the situation overwhelm me. I owned my mistake. It's an error I plan on fixing as soon as I get to the office. That's why I tucked the vibrator box in my oversized red purse last night. It's going right back where it came from. I'll reorder it when I'm logged into my personal account.

My biggest hope for today is that there's no added tension between my boss and me because of last night. He promised that it would be our little secret, and I trust his word. Time will tell if that's a smart move on my part or not.

I breeze through the lobby of the Garent Industries building, heading straight for the elevator. My purse is slung over my shoulder, and I have a large coffee from Palla on Fifth in my hand.

I stopped in there at seven-fifteen. When Palla offered me the larger cup, I took it without question. I'll need the extra boost of caffeine to get through my longer-than-usual day.

I could have hung out at home, but I have work I can do. I'll answer my early morning emails until Barrett shows up to give me the day's itinerary.

As soon as I arrive on my floor, I know that Barrett has beaten me to the office. His deep voice carries through the space, booming against the walls.

I take a step off the elevator and freeze. The doors slide shut behind me before it races to another floor.

"You don't get it, do you?" Barrett's voice snaps through the silence. "I'm going to see her whether you like it or not. You can't dictate who she has a relationship with."

I can't string anything together with those bare-bones pieces of information, so I move closer to his office door, being careful to stay out of his view.

"I know you're her father." He laughs, but it's not joyful, it's filled with spite. "She's an adult. Any control you had over her ended years ago."

Whoever she is, she's damn lucky to have him fighting so hard to be with her.

"This discussion is over."

I inch back toward the corridor that leads to the washroom. I'll duck in there if need be. I don't want him to know that I was listening to a private call.

"Let her live her damn life." His voice cracks. "Isn't it time you let her choose?"

I hear a muted curse followed by footsteps.

Before he's out of his office, I'm in the ladies' room with the door slightly ajar, listening to the tap of his shoe against the concrete floor as he waits for the elevator.

***

Twenty minutes later Barrett strolls off of the elevator with a large cup from Palla on Fifth in his hand and a smirk on his face.

He's dressed impeccably today in a light gray suit, a white shirt, and a dark blue tie. The man has excellent taste in clothing and coffee.

"You're here early," he remarks as he nears my desk. "You must have snuck in when I went to get a coffee."

Sure. That's it.

I avoid telling a lie by using the tried and true tactic of deflection. "Marcy Clover called a few minutes ago. She'd like to see you this morning."

I know he's set on shutting down Empire Soaks as soon as he can. That's why I made a few phone calls over the weekend to try and stop that in its tracks. I have strings to pull and favors to cash in. The Calvettis know a lot of people in New York.

He glances at the watch on his wrist. "Schedule that for ten. I can give her fifteen minutes."

"She can't leave the store, so I told her you'd be there from ten until eleven since you have nothing else booked."

"You what?"

There's a bite of irritation in his tone. I don't need to look up into his face to know that he's frustrated, but I do anyway.

Yep. His handsome face is twisted into a scowl.

"It will give you a chance to see the store," I say calmly. "The subway runs two blocks from Empire Soaks. I can send you directions if you want."

His eyes widen. "You can send a message to my driver telling him to get down here before ten to pick me up."

"It's going to take longer to get there in a car. Traffic is hell in Manhattan." Smiling sweetly, I tilt my head to the side. "Hop on the subway, and you'll be there in no time flat."

"What is it with you and the subway?"

Laughing, I shake my head. "I've taken it all my life. It's the best way to travel this city. You have to give it a chance."

"Fine, but you're going with me." He raises a brow. "I need a subway guide, and you seem to be the expert."

I wouldn't say that, but I can show him the ropes. The bonus is I get to see the look on his face when he walks into Empire Soaks and sees their new spokesperson.

Today is already ten times better than yesterday.

He starts toward his office door but stops to turn back to me. "Don't forget to return the fun and done, Isabella. Unless you'd prefer I take the cost out of your paycheck so you can keep it."

"I'm on it."

His brows perk as a sexy grin lifts the corners of his mouth. His gaze drifts to my chair. "You're on it?"

Shit. Today is worse than yesterday.

"I'll have it sent back before we leave for Empire Soaks." I reach for the invoice that he left on my desk. "I should get back to responding to emails."

He nods before he walks into his office, shutting the door behind him.

Chapter 31

Bella

"You lived." I look up into Barrett's face as we reach the top of the stairs leading up from the subway platform. "That wasn't so bad, was it?"

Taking in our surroundings, he brushes a hand over his brow. "You don't want me to answer that question honestly, do you?"

Laughing, I toss my hair over my shoulder, looking for some relief from the mid-morning heat that's engulfing Manhattan. "You didn't tell me that you had a MetroCard."

"I'm not the subway virgin you think I am."

It's hard to imagine him as a virgin in any capacity. I glance down the street to chase the moment away, hoping that he'll think the sudden pink flush on my cheeks is from the warm air circling us.

"I did take the subway on occasion in Chicago," he goes on, loosening the knot on his tie. "I picked up the MetroCard after you gave me hell that night outside Axel. I thought I better learn to ride the rails like a real New Yorker before you give me shit again."

Smiling, I wave a finger at him. "It takes time to become a real New Yorker. This is just the first step."

"What's the second step?"

I glance down the busy sidewalk. "Learning where the best cupcakes are. There's a bakery three blocks from here. We have enough time that we can stop in there and pick up a few for Marcy and her kids."

He steps back to make room for a woman walking five dogs. He gives her a curt nod when she smiles at him. "It's a business meeting, Isabella, not a tea party."

"Who says you can't have cupcakes at business meetings?" Curling a finger so he'll follow me, I set off. "I'll give you a mini-tour of the Upper West Side. The bakery is on Amsterdam Avenue. We'll take 78th Street to get there."

"No." His voice comes out in a strangled whisper. "Stop."

I turn and face him, noting the heavy exhale that escapes him. He's digging a finger inside the collar of his shirt. Sweat is peppering his forehead. I can't tell if the steady rush of people passing us on the sidewalk is making him uncomfortable or if it's the heat in the air.

"I'll get you some water," I offer looking around for a bodega or a drugstore. I could take him to my parents' apartment. That's only a few blocks from here, and my mom is a retired nurse, but she might not be home. I do have a key since I lived there for the first eighteen years of my life, but it's in the purse I usually carry with me. That's back at my place.

"I'm fine," he insists with a hand on my forearm.

He's not fine. He looks like he's on the verge of passing out. Getting him to Marcy's air-conditioned store is my best move. The cupcakes will have to wait for another day when my boss isn't melting from the heat.

I tap my hand over his. "Let's go."

His fingers wrap around mine in a death grip. "No detours. We're going straight to Empire Soaks." I look up and catch him staring at me. He's flushed, but there's more to it. I see something in his eyes I haven't noticed before. It's panic.

His gaze falls to the sidewalk. "Let's get this over with. The sooner I get back to the office, the better."

I fall in step beside him as he maneuvers through the heavy pedestrian traffic, headed for Marcy's store with my hand still in his.

***

Ansel and Elara run at me full-force when I walk into Empire Soaks. They bypass Barrett with ease, sidestepping him to land right in my arms.

I giggle when they scream, "we missed you so much," in unison.

Kneeling, I take them both in for a big hug. "I missed you too."

Elara cradles my face in her small palms. "You'll come over to play soon, right? Mommy said you'd come."

When Marcy asked me via text if I'd stop by her apartment for playtime with the kids, I responded immediately that I'd love to. I'm going to take everything I need to make tacos for dinner once we figure out which night works best.

Letting them go, I gaze up to find Barrett staring at me. He took off his suit jacket before we walked in the door. His hair is a mess from where he repeatedly ran his hand through it. He doesn't look anything like he did when we left the office.

I can tell he's overwrought about something, but I have no idea what that is. He didn't say a word to me on the walk here from the subway stop.

"Bella!" A man's voice turns Barrett's head toward the checkout counter.

Empire Soaks is busy. It's filled with people carrying wire baskets containing many of the products that Marcy developed. Everything is organic-based, and I'm confident that once we spread the word, she won't be able to keep up with the demand.

"Trey," I call back. "You made it."

"Is that Trey Hale?" Barrett mutters under his breath as I head across the store to the handsome man wearing a green Empire Soaks T-shirt.

I let him take me in his arms for a big bear hug. "How's my favorite Calvetti?"

Taking a step back, I look into his brown eyes. "Marti is your favorite."

Trey dropped into Calvetti's for the first time two years ago when I was helping in the kitchen. It was just days after he pitched the winning game in the World Series. My grandma had no idea who he was. She still doesn't understand that he's one of the best major league baseball players. To her, he's just a "sweet boy who loves spaghetti."

"I love her," he admits on a sigh. "She's the best. You're lucky to have her."

I give him a knowing nod. "You should stop by to see her soon."

"Today," he promises with a smile. "I'm going to put in a few hours here, and then I'll head over there."

The sound of a throat clearing behind us lures Trey's gaze over my shoulder. "Who's the suit?"

"My boss."

"Barrett Adler." Barrett's hand shoots out in Trey's direction. "You're Trey Hale."

Trey smiles politely. "Guilty as charged. It's good to meet you."

When Marcy turns to look in my direction, I raise a hand to wave to her. I'm gifted with a silent, "thank you," from her lips. Even from this distance, I can see tears welling in her eyes.

"What are you doing here?" My boss asks Trey the obvious question.

Trey tugs on the front his T-shirt. "You're looking at Empire Soaks new spokesman."

"New spokesman?" Barrett shifts his focus from Trey to me. "You knew about this? Who authorized it? I didn't see a contract."

"I'm doing it as a favor to Bella." Trey rests a hand on my shoulder. "After she told me about what Marcy has been through since her husband died, I jumped right in to help. I'll do what I can. I'm donating my time, and I've got a photographer friend headed down here as we speak to get some shots of me with the products. Empire Soaks will be trending online before the day is over."

Chapter 32

Barrett

It's been four days since I shook Trey Hale's hand. His social media posts touting the products that Marcy is selling put Empire Soaks on the map. Not only did the store shut its doors early that day because they ran out of inventory, but their website crashed.

Last week I was contemplating when I'd close the business for good. Today, I've been on the phone for hours working out a manufacturing deal with a supplier in the Midwest. They can replicate Marcy's products on a large scale right down to the last drop of essential oil.

One call from my executive assistant to Trey Hale altered the course of the lives of Marcy and her kids. They've all struggled since the unexpected death of her husband five months ago.

Grief therapy has kept Marcy's feet moving forward. Every second Thursday afternoon she's there with her mother-in-law. The woman is Elara and Ansel's nanny. That's why Isabella was watching over the kids that day. Their mother and grandmother have been trying to navigate their way through an unthinkable loss.

I left Empire Soaks alone the other day with a full picture of Marcy's life and business. Isabella hung back to work on promotional details with Trey.

Since then, I've been working my ass off. I've kept my assistant just as busy. She clocked out on Friday night with a wiggle of her fingers in a wave to me while I talked on the phone.

I wanted to ask her to join me for a drink to celebrate the stellar week we had, but she was out of the building before I could wrap my call up. I took it as a sign and headed up to my penthouse to pour over the details for a merger that Duke was keen on. It won't see the light of day. Some deals can't be saved.

I look up when I see Isabella dart into my view through the open door of my office. She met Max for lunch an hour ago. She checked in before she left to see if I wanted her to bring me back anything. I declined. I need to take off to a meeting of my own.

Standing, I clear my throat, hoping to grab her attention.

It works. She drops her purse on her desk then whips around to face me.

Soft gray is definitely a color that works on her. It plays off the flecks in her eyes. The dress she's wearing is clinging to her. It's simple, but on her, it looks fucking spectacular.

Tapping one of her black stilettos on the floor, she drops her hands to her hips. "Is there something I can help you with?"

The raging hard-on I seem to have every time I'm near you.

Seeing as though I'm not a seventeen-year-old kid with zero self-control, I swallow those words and go for a more business like approach. "I have a meeting to get to. I need you to stay on top of all the moving parts for Empire Soaks. I've been in touch with a new website developer, and I'm waiting to hear back from the supplier."

Her brow crunches together. "You have a meeting? I don't recall seeing that on your calendar."

Pushing back from my desk, I stand. "It's personal."

Narrowing her eyes, she steps into my office. "Should I interrupt you if something comes up?"

"No." Buttoning my jacket, I round my desk. "I'll be back by four to address any issues. Keep things at bay until then."

I can see the wheels turning behind those stormy blue eyes of hers. She's trying to piece together what the hell I'm doing. I want her to ask questions because I'm aching to see a flare of jealousy cross that beautiful face of hers, but she's stoic. She contemplates me for a few more seconds before she shrugs a shoulder and turns to leave.

I head straight to the elevator. I jab a finger into the call button twice even though I know the second time is useless.

"Barrett?"

Hearing Isabella's voice behind me, I turn. She's standing next to her desk with a pen in her hand. Tapping it against her palm, she takes a heavy breath. "Is the meeting in your penthouse or somewhere else?"

"A hotel," I answer succinctly.

The pen slaps her palm harder and then again, even harder. "Well, I hope you have fun."

There's no mistaking the sarcastic bite to the last word. Maybe my assistant is as attracted to me as I am to her.

I board the elevator once the doors slide open. Turning back to face her, I shoot her one of my dimpled smiles. "Have a great afternoon, Isabella."

"You too," she drawls with a forced grin. "I hope you have the time of your life."

***

Why the fuck do I do this to myself? I know better.

"Barrett, are you listening to me?"

I look over the rim of the glass in my hand. It's perched at my mouth. I'm not a day drinker, but today is a special occasion. I've spent the last two hours in a hotel suite with my mother. If that doesn't call for getting inebriated mid-afternoon, I don't know what the hell does.

"I'm listening," I say calmly. "You were talking about Stella Jerkins and her hair extensions."

"Her wig," she corrects me with a manicured fingernail wagging in my direction across the table. "The color is dreadful."

It's probably a step up from the ruby red mess of curls sitting atop my mother's head. She wants the world to believe that she's never donned a wig, yet I know that she has a collection that numbers in the hundreds.

She tips her stylist extra well to keep the secret hidden from her friends back in Chicago.

I empty the last of the alcohol in my glass. I've ordered room service multiple times since I arrived since my mother couldn't decide what to eat for lunch. Each order was punctuated with a glass of whiskey for me. I lost count, but I'd guess it's up to three or four.

I can still walk a straight line, so I stand readying to raid the mini bar. "I need another drink. Do you want anything, Mother?"

"You should call me Monica."

I give her a look that can only rival the ones she must get when she walks down the street with that wig on her head. "Why the hell would I do that?"

"I look too young to be your mother." That's followed by a nervous laugh from her.

"You were thirty-two when I was born." I point out waving the empty glass in the air. "That makes you sixty plus."

"Shush your mouth." She tosses a linen napkin in my direction. "You may be thirty-four, but you still need to show me respect."

I respect her. I respect that she held it together when my father couldn't keep his hands off other women. Monica stuck it out through those affairs because she wanted me to have a stable home life.

It was an innocent mistake on her part. I knew what my dad was up to. I overheard the phone conversations he had with his mistresses. I smelled the overly sweet perfume on his clothes when he'd come back to Chicago after his business trips to New York.

"Why are you here?" I ask the question I've wanted to ask since she surprised me early this morning with a call that started with the words I wasn't in the mood to hear. "I'm in Manhattan, son."

She pops out of the chair she's been settled in. "Your father called me after all these years. He said you've been asking questions. I thought it would always be us against them."

Them. My half-siblings. They are the three people on this earth that she's fought to keep me from.

She used guilt as her ammunition. I fell in line for the most part because my efforts to contact my oldest sister were always met with silence. After years of trying, I gave up until now.

"Times have changed." I glare at her. "A mother shouldn't expect a sacrifice like that from her only child to satisfy her selfish need to punish his father."

"You know that he didn't want you around after that day. It was too hard after what you did."

A slap in the face wouldn't sting as much. My dad cut me from his life almost twenty years ago. Monica hopped on that bandwagon and steered it in the direction she wanted it to go.

She alienated me from my family so she could call me her own.

"You should have stood up for me." I clench the glass in my hand. "I was a fifteen-year-old kid."

"I'm standing up for you now." She rushes toward me with her arms outstretched. "I'm telling you what you need to hear. Don't reach out to them. They'll never accept you after all this time."

Selfishness knows no bounds in her world.

"You're too late," I say, loudly. "I've already reached out and there's not a damn thing you or Irving can do about it."

The mention of my father's name sets her back a step. "We promised we'd never say his name. You know how much that hurts me."

"It's been years, Monica," I hiss out her name. "Let it go. Let me go."

Chapter 33

Bella

I stand in the lobby of the Garent Industries building and stare at the man sitting on one of the black leather benches that border the windows overlooking Fifth Avenue.

I've spent more than two hours waiting for Barrett to return to the office. He said he'd be back by four. When he didn't show, I called him twice and texted him three times. There were decisions to be made regarding Empire Soaks. I took the liberty of handling a few matters myself. I left everything else for him to deal with.

He doesn't look like he's in any shape to do that now.

With his eyes closed, his head is leaning back against the glass. From this distance, he looks like he's fast asleep.

Maybe he is.

The end of his tie is hanging out of one of the side pockets of his jacket. His shirt is unbuttoned enough that I can see the smooth skin of his chest as I near him. A late-day shadow of whiskers peppers his strong jawline.

I look around, wondering how long he's been here.

Other Garent employees are heading out the double glass doors for the day, seemingly unaware that the man who signs their paychecks is parked on a bench just a few feet from where they are.

I could follow them out and forget I ever saw him, but I don't. Instead, I take a seat next to him. Anxiety washes over me. What am I supposed to do now? Do I wake him up? Should I sit here until he rouses on his own?

I opt for the first choice. Tapping a hand on his knee, I lean in to whisper his name, but my hand is caught in his before I can get anything out of my mouth.

"Sweet Bella," he growls with his eyes still closed. "I'd recognize that perfume anywhere."

Bella. He's never called me that.

I lean in closer to him because I don't want any nosy Garent employees to catch our exchange. "Are you okay?"

He pries open one eye to glance at me. "What time is it?"

I drop my gaze to my watch. "Six thirty."

"Shit," he snaps. "I have work to do."

He's in no shape to work. It's obvious that he had a liquid lunch today that must have lasted for hours. I won't ask about that. It's none of my business.

"You should go home," I suggest. "Why don't you head up to your penthouse and call it a day?"

That lures his eyes to mine. "Will you come with me?"

A flash of vulnerability crosses his expression. He looks tired and weary. The least I can do is help him to his apartment. I nod. "I'll come."

His lips inch up into a sexy smile. "You will."

His words are simple, but there's a promise woven into them. Maybe that's wishful thinking on my part. I've imagined too many times what it would feel like to come with him inside me.

He drops my hand to push himself to his feet. He wobbles slightly to the left before he corrects his stance. "We're wasting time. Let's go."

***

By the time he unlocks the door to his apartment, his phone has started ringing again. There were two incoming calls when we were in the elevator, but he silenced both of those immediately.

"Should you get that?" I ask, crossing the threshold into the foyer.

"Hell no." He laughs, shutting the door behind me. "It's my mother. I spent the afternoon with her. That's my limit for today."

Relief washes over me. He was with his mom.

I have no claim to him, but still, I'm glad that he wasn't rolling around in a hotel bed with a woman. The mental image of that plagued me all afternoon.

"Do you want a drink?"

As tempted as I am, I shake my head. "I should go home."

Scratching his chin, he looks around the penthouse. "I'm hungry. Are you?"

I'm famished. I ate a granola bar for lunch. I dug it out of the bottom drawer of my desk. The expiry date was four months ago, but once I took the first bite and lived, I gobbled it up.

"Yes," I admit on a sigh. "I was going to heat up leftovers at home."

"Sounds like you have a wild night ahead of you."

I can tell that he's sobering up. His voice has leveled, and he's standing in place, not leaning to the left anymore. Not to mention, that he was quick to dish out that sarcastic remark about my evening plans.

Shedding his suit jacket, he looks over his shoulder at me. "I'll order some food. What do you want?"

I don't want food. I want to kiss him. I want to touch him. I have a wild desire to unbutton his shirt and slide it from his shoulders so I can run my hands over his chest and abs.

Rolling the sleeves of his shirt to his elbows, he studies me. "You're giving this a lot of thought. What will it be? Pizza? Greek? Do you want me to call Atlas 22? I can get them to send over a sampling of everything since you didn't get to enjoy the food the night you crashed my date."

The reminder stings, but I don't let it show. "Leave dinner to me. I know just what to get."

Chapter 34

Bella

The door to his penthouse is ajar when I get back with our dinner. I called Calvetti's when Barrett excused himself to take a shower. I spoke with Marti. She was ready to get in a taxi and bring the food down here, but I convinced her to send it with one of the kitchen staff.

I love my grandma, but if she set foot in this building with her food in her hands, she'd want to join Barrett and me at his dining room table. I wouldn't escape the night without my boss learning a few of the most embarrassing stories from when I was a kid.

"Is dinner here yet?" Barrett rounds the corner from the hallway that leads to his bedroom.

Holy hell.

Dressed in charcoal gray pants and a lightweight black sweater, he could double as a male model. His broad chest leads down to a trim waist.

I tear my eyes away from him to hold up the two red insulated bags that contain the food that my grandma sent.

I asked for the baked ravioli, but she told me she was sending the lobster linguine because she'd just finished making it. When I met Alfie, one of the kitchen staff, in the lobby just now, he told me that she'd packed an extra special treat just for me.

I kissed him on his cheek and tried to slip a twenty-dollar bill into his palm. He pushed it back at me, warning me that he'd get fired if Marti ever found out that he took money from one of her grandchildren.

"What did you settle on?" Barrett moves next to me as I place the bags on his large dining room table.

It's made of steel with black accents around the edges. The six black leather chairs that surround it are high-backed. It fits in with the décor of the space to a tee.

Smiling proudly, I zip open the larger of the two bags. "My grandma made dinner for us."

His head bows as he takes in the aroma of the linguine and the unmistakable smell of freshly baked rosemary focaccia. "Damn. I don't know if I've ever smelled anything this good before."

I glance to my left, meeting his gaze. "She's the best cook I know."

He stalls with his eyes glued to mine. We stay that way for what feels like endless moments, although it's only a few seconds.

"I'll get plates and utensils." He starts toward his kitchen. "Is sparkling water good for you?"

"It's good for me and you," I bounce back with a grin. "You're sobering up nicely."

His laughter follows the sound of a cupboard door closing. "I should have had lunch, but nothing on the room service menu sounded appetizing, so I went with what I know. Whiskey."

I open the tray of lobster linguine and the brown paper bag containing the already cut, still-warm focaccia. Peering into the other insulated bag, I let out a squeal.

"What was that for?" Barrett stalks toward me carrying a wooden tray. It holds plates, utensils, gray linen napkins, a large bottle of sparkling water, and two glasses. "I know excitement when I hear it."

I can't contain a smile. "She packed my favorite dessert. Honey ricotta cheesecake."

Setting the tray down, Barrett turns to face me. "I can't wait to taste everything."

My eyes linger on his lips. They're just the right shape and fullness. It must be incredible to kiss them.

He touches his hand to mine. "Did I lose you for a second? You drifted away."

The brush of his fingers on my skin is electric. The need inside of me is coiled so tightly that I may burst if I don't pull back. So I do. I take a step to the side, dropping my gaze to the food. "Let's dig in."

Pulling out a chair, he motions for me to sit. "You have to thank your grandmother for me, Bella."

Bella. Again.

Settling onto the leather, I whisper. "I like that."

He takes the seat at the head of the table, next to me. "You like what?"

Looking up, I pull in a breath to quiet my nerves. "I like it when you call me Bella."

"It suits you." He reaches for a plate, a napkin, and some utensils. "Isabella does too, but the more I get to know you, the more I see that you're my Bella or a Bella. I meant you're more a Bella than an Isabella."

His Bella.

It may have been just a slip of his tongue, but I liked the way it sounded and how it made me feel even if it was only for a split second in time.

***

Dale: Hey beautiful.

My eyes drop to my phone's screen and the incoming message. The chime lures Barrett's gaze to it too.

Dammit. I meant to change the settings on the messaging app so that my incoming texts don't pop up on my lock screen.

Dropping my fork on my plate, I slide the phone closer to me, just as another text arrives.

Dale: I'm still waiting for an answer to my big question.

Barrett clears his throat. "If you're going to Philadelphia to visit him, you need to run the dates by me first."

What the hell?

I take a second to process what he said and what it means. Drawing in a deep breath, I look him straight in the eye. "You read the letter, didn't you?"

Our pleasant dinner just ran into a roadblock in the form of my boss snooping through my desk. Dale dropped off an envelope at Garent's reception on his way to the airport. Barrett handed it to me sealed which means that he read it after I'd opened it.

Setting his fork down next to his half-eaten slice of cheesecake, he nods. "I did."

That sets me on my feet. "You had no right to do that."

He's up too, chasing me down as I head away from the table. His hand on my elbow stops me just as I reach the living room.

I turn and face him. "Why would you do that? I told you it was personal."

"Why did you listen to my phone conversation the day you came to the office early?"

Busted.

His hand slides down my arm to circle my wrist. "Curiosity, Bella. I was curious. It was the same for you when you heard me chew out my father."

I step back in shock. He knew I was there? He was talking to his father?

Reading my expression, his tone softens. "I smelled coffee. When you took off, I heard your heels on the floor. I know you hid in the washroom."

"You didn't say anything," I whisper, bowing my head in embarrassment. "I didn't mean to eavesdrop."

His finger finds my chin. Tilting it up until my eyes meet his, he smiles. "You did mean to eavesdrop. Just as I meant to read the letter."

Chapter 35

Bella

He's right. I can't argue his point. My eavesdropping was intentional. I had no idea that I was listening to his side of a conversation with his dad. His sister was the woman he was talking about. I wasn't aware he had a sibling. I didn't bother researching his family the night I was drooling over pictures of him online.

His hand leaves my chin, and I instantly feel bereft. I've never craved the touch of a man as much as I crave his. I shouldn't, but I can't control the need I feel every time I'm near him.

I cover my mouth with my hand to hide the heavy sigh that escapes me. My lungs ache. My body is both numb and on fire. Everything's changed, yet it all still feels the same.

He doesn't say anything, so I take the reins. "You have a sister?"

It's an obvious question after his confession that the man he was talking to was his dad. It's hard for me to imagine a confrontation like that with my dad.

"Three." His arms cross his chest. "Technically, they're all half-sisters. We share the same father. There are three mothers in the equation, including mine."

"Where do you fall in that? Are you the oldest, the youngest or in the middle?" I ask trying to piece his family tree together.

"Oldest." He half-smiles. "One is three years younger than me. Another is seven years my junior and then, last but not least is Henrietta. She's four."

Thirty years separate him and his youngest sibling. The span between Gina and me is barely three years, and I sometimes wonder if we have anything in common.

"My father likes being a father." He laughs. "To my sisters more than to me."

His confession is marred by a pained look behind the laugh. From the outside looking in, I can tell it's a complicated situation.

"I've lost touch with my sisters." He pushes a hand through his hair. "I'm trying to bridge the gap since two of them live here."

"In New York?"

Circling his thumb over my wrist, he nods. "My dad found love and a vineyard in California a few years ago, so Henrietta is a west coast kid. Before that, he settled here after my folks split up."

The sound of my phone chiming lures his gaze over his shoulder toward the table. When he turns his attention back to me, his jaw is clenched. "Dale is still waiting for an answer to his big question. Are you going to visit him in Philly?"

The invitation was in the letter Dale handwrote me. He thanked me for spending time with him and offered to pay for my flight to his hometown so we could "explore the attraction."

I responded the day after I opened the letter, telling him that I wasn't sure if I could get away from New York. It was meant to be a soft letdown. Dale's persistence is admirable. He's texted me almost on the daily asking if I could steal away for a weekend.

"You haven't said no to him yet," Barrett goes on, his gaze searching my face. "That means you're still considering it."

I study him trying to grasp what he's thinking, but it's impossible, so I ask a question that I have no right to ask my boss. "Why does it matter to you if I go?"

His hand slides up my arm. Slow grazes of his fingertips over my skin send a shiver through me. I almost let out an audible moan when his hand reaches the back of my neck.

"It matters, Bella."

I rest a hand on his chest. The unmistakable beat of his heart falls in rhythm with mine. "How?"

He leans forward, his breath grazing over my cheek. "You know how. You feel this."

"This?" I question on a sigh.

"This," he repeats before he takes my mouth in a kiss that leaves me breathless in a way I've never felt before.

* * *

My fingers are tangled in his hair when I part my lips to deepen the kiss. He moans a second before I do. Our smiles touch in the heated moment. It's a brief break from the intensity before his hand slides down to cup my ass.

He whispers something against my lips, and then again. The second time I make out the words. "You're fired."

Recoiling, I slap a hand over his hard chest. Stumbling back, I bark out the only word I can manage. "What?"

His hands are on me again, cupping the back of my neck, pressing against the small of my back. "I can't fuck you if you work for me."

That word, the rawness of his need, makes my knees weak. I stumble into him. "Barrett."

"I'll rehire you in the morning." His lips feather kisses over the skin on the side of my neck. "Tonight, I need you. Jesus, I want you so bad."

I feel the same. Running a finger over his chin, I look up into his eyes. "I want you too. I won't tell anyone. Ivan won't know."

He catches my hand in his. Nipping on my index finger, he growls. "He can't know."

The burst of pain clenches my core. I'm wound so tightly. I'll come as soon as he touches me there, anywhere. "It's our secret."

He kisses me again. This time it's softer. Tenderness lingers between us when he cups my face in his hands. "My bed, Bella. Now."

I won't argue with him. I can't. I want this man more than I've wanted anything in my life.

Wrapping an arm around my waist, he takes a step forward. I do too. A faint knock at the door halts my second step.

No. Please, no. Don't let anything interrupt this perfect moment.

Glancing at me, his brows rise. "Who the fuck is that?"

I let out a soft laugh. "You tell me. You're the one who lives here."

Another knock lures his gaze to the door. "Goddammit. The security guard at the front desk is about to lose his job."

I don't know if he's joking or not. Sighing, I state the obvious. "You should answer it. Maybe it's important."

Wrapping his arms around me, he kisses my neck. "Unless the building is on fire, it's not important."

A loud thud stops his lips just under my ear.

"Give me ten seconds to tell whoever that is to go to hell."

I nod as I watch him stalk to the door. Nerves dance in my stomach. What if it's a woman who has already been here? I didn't bother to ask if he's involved with anyone. Why the hell didn't I do that?

I face the door as he swings it open.

"Barrett." A petite woman with red curls wags a finger in the air at him. "You can't ignore me forever. Let me in."

Chapter 36

Barrett

"What are you doing here?" I snap. "You're supposed to be on your way to the airport, Mother."

"Monica," she corrects me with a pat to my forearm. "Aren't you going to invite me in?"

Her gaze is locked on something behind me…someone behind me. This is not a scenario I imagined in my worst nightmare. I don't need her getting in Bella's face.

I take a step to the side to block her entrance and repeat the question she failed to answer the first time I asked it. "What are you doing here?"

"Introductions are in order, son."

Goddammit.

I don't try and stop her when she maneuvers around me, suitcase in tow. That's not a good sign. If she thinks she's camping here for the night, she's mistaken. I want her out of my penthouse and out of the city as soon as possible.

"And you are?" Monica blurts out once she's got a clear view of Bella.

Before she has a chance to reply, I step in. "This is my executive assistant."

Bella's gaze volleys from my face to my mother's. "It's nice to meet you, Mrs. Adler."
My mother approaches her, not offering her a hand or a smile. "It's a pleasure, dear. I need time with my son, so if you'll excuse us."

Bella looks to me for guidance. The last thing I want is for her to leave. I want her in my arms tonight. I'm about to fight to make that my reality.

"We're busy." I direct my attention to Monica. "You'll miss your flight if you don't get to the airport within the hour."

I have no fucking clue if I'm speaking honestly. I lost track of time right around the moment when Bella and I sat down to eat dinner.

"I switched to a morning flight." Her gaze wanders the perimeter of the room. "I checked out of the hotel. I'll be staying with you tonight so we can continue our discussion."

Like hell she will.

"That won't work for me." I tug my phone out of my pants pocket. "I'll call the hotel and book another room for you."

Her hand trails over her forehead in an overly dramatic gesture of exasperation. "I can't bear another night there. You know the food is not up to my standards."

"Is anything ever up to your standards?"

The question flies over her head because she's too busy sighing heavily to notice anything but the performance she's giving.

"I should go," Bella says, starting toward the dining room table. "I'll grab my things and leave you two be."

"No." The word snaps off my tongue. "You'll stay."

Oblivious to what's going on, Monica gives Bella a nod and regal wave of her hand in the air. "Very well, dear. It was lovely to meet you. Do take care."

If this were an audition, my mother would be nailing the role of an eighteenth-century monarch, but this is my fucking penthouse, and the only two people bearing witness to her theatrics is the woman I want to take to bed and me.

I glance at Bella. She offers me a shrug and a soft smile. "I'll see you in the office in the morning." The urge to kiss her is strong, but I resist. This isn't the time to get into details with my mother about my relationship with my assistant. Hell, I don't even know how to define what's happening between us.

Scooping up her purse and the empty insulated bags, Bella moves across the room. With a quick look back, she opens the door and walks out, leaving me alone with the woman I thought had left Manhattan in her rearview mirror.

***

I spent last night listening to my mother run through every potential film and television role she could have had. Her screen time was limited to a one-liner in a western movie shot sometime before she got married and the nosy neighbor in two episodes of a sitcom a year after I was born.

That didn't stop her from being a raging force in the Chicago local theater scene. She went from center stage to director, pouring all she had into every production of the classics.

That's wound itself down the last two years. She's taken up painting scenery. The shift from one creative discipline to another hasn't been without issues. Just as my seeking out my sisters here in New York hasn't been easy for Monica.

I said goodbye to her an hour ago. Setting her off to the airport with the driver Ivan secured for me was a good move. He'll earn his salary since he has to entertain my mother until he drops her at La Guardia.

That's all she needs. A friendly ear to listen goes a long way in her world.

"Hi."

My head darts up at the sound of Bella's voice. I've been waiting impatiently for her since I sat behind my desk. I couldn't sleep. My mind kept circling back to kissing her.

She's dressed in red today. The dress is simple but contoured to her body. Her hair is pulled back into a tight ponytail. In her hands are two large cups of coffee.

I push back to stand. "Good morning, Bella."

Extending her right hand, she lets out a small sigh. "I picked up a coffee for you at Palla's. It's the way you like it. No cream and no sugar."

I take it from her, appreciating that she put in the effort to bring me a cup. "Thank you."

Blowing out a breath of air, she shuffles her red heels in place. "I'll get to work now."

I glance at her hand. The polish on her thumbnail is almost completely gone. She's been picking at it since she bolted out of my place last night.

I edge around her, closing the door softly. "What's wrong?"

She turns on her heel so she's facing me. "Nothing. I have a lot to do today."

"I haven't assigned you anything yet," I point out.

Chewing on her bottom lip, she glances at the ceiling. "There are things on my desk that I should finish up."

"Like that crossword puzzle?"

Her eyes widen, but she doesn't say a word.

"You were stuck on four letters for an unpleasant emotion."

"I thought it was love, but it doesn't fit," she whispers.

I take a step closer to her, studying her face. "Is love an unpleasant emotion for you?"

She cradles the cup in both hands. "Yes. With Emil it was."

He's a fucked up asshole who tore her heart apart.

"What about you?" she questions with a tilt of her head. "Is love an unpleasant emotion for you?"

I have no fucking idea. I'm feeling something for her, but I don't know if this tightening in my chest is the beginning sparks of love or pure lust or a combination of both. I answer honestly, "I haven't been in love."

The corners of her lips tug up. "Oh."

"Oh?" I repeat back, holding back a smile of my own. "You're surprised that I've never been in love?"

Taking a sip from the coffee, she eyes me. "I am, and I'm not. You're old enough to have been in love, but you seem like you prefer short term arrangements."

I don't take offense, even though I've never been the type to fuck and flee. Sex is always better with an emotional connection. I've had a handful of one-night stands. The only benefit I got from them was the knowledge that I need more than a casual roll in the hay.

"You didn't love Alyssa Wells?"

I haven't heard that name in forever. It's a part of my past I'd like to forget. Getting pulled into Alyssa's orbit was exciting at first. It was fun and easy until it wasn't. She wanted a wedding. I was satisfied with dating. That spelled the end of that.

I reach past her to place my coffee cup on my desk before I do the same with hers. "No, Isabella. I didn't love her."

Her bottom lip trembles. "You were a little tipsy last night. Do you remember the kiss? We kissed."

Reaching for her hands, I steady them in mine. She's shaking. "I remember everything about it. I want to kiss you again now."

Her eyes find mine. They're more gray than blue today, storming with emotion that's just below the surface. It's there in her face. I feel it in her hands.

"A four-letter word for an unpleasant emotion is fear," she says, her voice quiet.

It is fear. That's what I see in front of me. The most beautiful woman I've ever laid eyes on is scared to death of what's happening between us.

Chapter 37

Bella

I didn't intend on coming to the office to pour my heart out, but that's what happened. After I left Barrett's apartment last night, I went straight home. Gina wasn't around. I was grateful for that. I needed time and space to think.

I spent most of the night weighing the pros and cons of sleeping with my boss.

The pro list was four times as long as the con, but that didn't matter.

At the top of the list of potential negatives was a big one – a broken heart.

My broken heart.

It took me time to get over Emil. Gina told me it was puppy love. She said that when I found real love, it would consume me.

I laughed it off because my sister has never been in a serious relationship, but I'm beginning to wonder if she's wise beyond her experience.

I can't define what I feel for my boss. The physical attraction is undeniable, but there's more. I feel an unexplained connection to him that I never felt with Emil.

I know that when Barrett looks at me, he sees who I am, not who he wants me to be.

"Tell me what you're afraid of." Barrett grazes his thumb over my hand in a lazy, slow circle.

I don't know how to answer that without pouring my heart out. I don't want to be that woman who scares a man away because she's feeling too much too soon. We haven't even slept together yet.

"It's the job, isn't it?" he asks before I can say anything. "You're worried that we'll both get fired if Ivan finds out. I admit I'm concerned about that too."

It hadn't crossed my mind until right now.

"Ivan is in Boston." He smiles. "We can be discreet. No one has to know about this."

"If Ivan finds out..."

"He won't," he interrupts with a heavy exhale. "You're my executive assistant. It's your job to spend most of your time with me. No one will question if we work late or spend a few hours together on the weekends. You did those things with Duke and no one wondered, did they?"

I laugh. "They wondered."

His eyes narrow beneath a scowl. "Someone thought you were sleeping with Duke?"

"A few people did." I shrug. "Ivan brushed it off as office gossip. He knew better. He trusted us."

His hand slides up my arm. "He trusts us too."

I nod.

Cupping my cheek, he gazes into my eyes. "Whatever happens between us on a personal level has no bearing on the work we're doing. We're a solid team in the office, Bella. I promise we'll be better together in my bed."

A rush of desire washes over me. I've never taken such a brazen chance before. I always weigh the pros and cons, especially when it comes to my career or my heart.

I ask the question that's been racing through my mind since last night. "Are there others in your bed?"

He stills. "In my bed? Other women?"

"Are you sleeping with anyone else right now?" I keep talking because my anxiety is shooting through the roof. "You were on a date at Atlas 22. She was pretty and there was that woman in front of Axel NY. She looked really happy to see you."

I take a breath and continue before he can get a word in. "I like to know what I'm getting into before I have sex with a man so I can choose if it's right for me."

He quiets me with a soft kiss to my lips. "Bella, beautiful Bella."

I melt into the touch of his lips and his words.

Pulling back, he cradles my face in his hands. "That date at Atlas 22 was one and done. We had one dinner, and it was done. I left before dessert."

Hope blooms in my chest. "It was one and done?"

"How the fuck was I supposed to focus on anyone after spending time with you?" He growls through a smile.

"You didn't take her home?"

"To do what?" He brushes the pad of his thumb over my bottom lip. "So I could talk about you all night?"

I bow my head to hide the wide grin on my face. I had no idea that he left Atlas 22 with me on his mind.

"I haven't seen her since that night." He lets out a heavy exhale. "I haven't been with anyone since I moved to Manhattan."

Tugging me into his arms, he presses a kiss to my forehead. "You have no idea how much I want you."

I want him too, but I still have questions about the woman outside Axel NY. She ran into his arms. The expression on her face was pure happiness, but he's not sleeping with her. He told me that no one has been in his bed. I believe him.

"The wheels are turning inside there again." He runs a finger over my brow. "Is it fear? You're still scared of this? Of us?"

I'd be lying if I didn't admit that I have reservations about jumping into bed with my boss, but I'll handle those for a chance to be with him.

"I'm thinking about kissing you," I whisper.

Without a word, he crashes his mouth into mine. I moan into the kiss. The need to be with him is so strong. It's almost too much.

Breaking the kiss, he stares at me. His gaze is heated and filled with the same want that I feel inside of me. "We're working upstairs today. My penthouse. Now."

Taking my hands in his, he moves toward the door of his office. A soft knock greets us just as he's ready to swing it open.

"You've got to be fucking kidding me." He groans. "You didn't schedule anything for me this morning, did you? Do I have a meeting I'm not aware of?"

Shaking my head, I answer simply, "Nope."

"I'll fire whoever is on the other side of that door."

Tugging on his hand, I half-laugh. "You won't."

"My dick is hard as stone." He leans back to brush a soft kiss over my lips. "I need you naked now."

Desire pools between my legs. "Fire them."

"Done." He winks at me.

Dropping my hand, he swings open the door. Standing in front of us is the woman who launched herself into his arms outside Axel NY. Without a word to him, or me, she does the very same thing now.

Chapter 38

Bella

What am I supposed to do now?

Do I take my coffee and calmly sit at my desk? Do I tap Barrett on the shoulder and ask who the hell the woman in his arms is or do I stand here waiting patiently for the two of them to pry themselves apart?

I don't have to make a decision because the blonde-haired woman clears her throat. "I can't tell you how much I've missed your hugs. I'm going to want one every time I see you now. You know that, don't you?"

Over my dead body.

"If memory serves, we didn't hug when we were kids," he says with a laugh. "I think we did fist bumps, right? That or high fives."

They go in for a fist bump, their hands in perfect unison with each other.

I catch the shimmer bouncing off the large diamond on her left hand. It's settled next to a plain gold band.

"You were too cool to hug me when you were a teenager." She playfully punches him in the arm. "I'm glad you grew out of that."

I take a step back. That catches her eye. Her gaze moves past Barrett's shoulder to settle on my face.

"I'm Felicity." Smoothing her palms over the skirt of her pink dress, she moves toward me. "You must work with my brother."

Brother?

The pieces all fall into place; the big hug, the playful banter, and the color of her eyes. They match Barrett's. So does her smile.

"This is Isabella." Barrett turns to face me. "Bella. She's my assistant."

She studies me. "You don't look like you're ready to strangle him. Is he a good boss?"

Biting back a smile, I shrug. "It's early. He hasn't had his coffee yet."

Peering past me to the two cups of coffee on the desk, she cocks a brow. "Palla on Fifth? Fancy schmancy, Adler. We should stop there on our way."

Barrett looks to me before he settles his attention on his sister. "On our way where?"

Lowering her voice, she leans closer to him. "She wants to see you. I explained what happened with daddy keeping you away from us. She's eager to see you. Can you come to her place with me now?"

Staring at his profile, I watch his bottom lip tremble. "Jesus, yes. Hell yes."

Felicity reaches up to adjust the light blue tie around his neck before she tugs on the lapels of his navy suit jacket. "She's not going to believe it's you. You're all grown-up."

Turning to me, he lets out a heavy exhale. "I need to go. It's my other sister."

There's no mention of what today held for us. The only thing I see on his face is hope.

"I'll take care of things here," I say softly.

I follow them out, standing in the doorway of his office as they walk hand-in-hand to the bank of elevators.

I may have lost my chance to make love with him today, but I have a feeling that he's getting a chance he's waited years for.

***

"Did your boss like the food, Dolly?"

My grandma stands next to the table I'm seated at in her restaurant. The smile on her face says it all. She knows he loved the food because everyone does.

"What do you think?" I tease.

"I think he loved it." She winks. "Did you like the dessert? I made it myself."

Taking her hand, I hold it against my cheek. "You know it's my favorite. It's always been my favorite."

"That's why I'll always make it for you." She pinches my cheek. "What are you doing tonight? You should be out having dinner with a handsome boy, not eating baked ravioli with your grandma."

I skirt around the core question by pointing at the vacant chair across the table from me. "You should sit with me."

On an exaggerated sigh, she plops into the chair, wiping both hands on the sauce-stained apron she's wearing. "I'll sit. You'll talk about your boyfriends."

"Boyfriends?" I pick at the corner of a slice of garlic bread in a basket in the center of the table. "I don't have any boyfriends, Marti."

She frowns. "Not one? Why not?"

Shrugging, I let out an exaggerated sigh. "It's not for lack of trying."

I can't tell her that I've kissed my boss twice. She'll show up at my office with a laundry list of questions for Barrett about his intentions. That's a complication that I don't need.

I know she means well, but I have to chart my own course. Barrett may only be looking for a one and done as in one fuck, and we're done with that fun.

"I'll ask around here if there are any single nice boys." Her finger curves in an arc as she surveys the room. "Leave it to me to find you a date."

"No." I reach across the table to tap her hand. "I'll find him one day, Marti."

"When you do, I'll tell him what a treasure you are." She squeezes my fingers. "I'll let him know that you're the most special girl in the world."

I hear the emotion in her voice before I see it in her eyes.

"Grandma," I whisper, darting from my chair to round the table so I can drape my arms around her neck. Pressing my cheek to hers, I relish in the comforting fragrance of her perfume. She's worn the same scent for as long as I remember.

"I know how lucky I am to be your grandma." She pats my arm. "I know how lucky I am that you're here with me."

Pulling back, I smile down at her. "I'm lucky. Marti Calvetti is my grandma. Not many people can say that."

That lures a grin to her mouth. "Your sister, your brother, and all of your cousins can say that."

Kissing her cheek, I laugh. "Good point."

Her gaze darts to something next to me. "I should get back to the kitchen, Dolly."

I'd join her, but I'm ready to call it a night. I was hoping that Barrett would reach out at some point, but I haven't heard anything from him since he left the office with his sister this morning.

I put in a full day, finally leaving work at six to come here for dinner.

I wait until she's on her feet before I take my grandma in my arms. "I'll talk to you soon. I love you."

Holding tight to me, she kisses my cheek. "I love you, my sweetheart. Be safe on your way home. Promise me you'll look both ways before you cross the street."

"I promise," I say, pulling back to lock eyes with her. "I always do."

Chapter 39

Barrett

She's going to give me hell for this, but I don't give a shit.

Lowering the back passenger window of the town car I'm in, I take a moment to appreciate how goddamn beautiful Bella is.

She's walking on the sidewalk, swinging a brown paper bag in her hand. Calvetti's is stamped across it in red ink.

I was headed in that direction after I stopped by the office to find it empty. A visit to her apartment resulted in a quick conversation with her sister. Gina was the one who suggested I check out the family restaurant.

I could have texted Bella or called her, but I wanted to surprise her.

As the car rolls to a stop at a red light, I reach forward to tap the driver on the shoulder. "I'm getting out here. Enjoy the rest of your night."

"Sure thing, sir."

I exit the car, keeping my gaze trained on my executive assistant as she strolls down the sidewalk, smiling at virtually every person she passes.

Her soul is gold. Happiness radiates from her.

I know she's too good for me, but I don't care. I want her. I've never wanted a woman more.

"Bella," I call out as I step onto the sidewalk from the street.

Her head bobs to the left, then the right. A glance over her shoulder lures a bright smile to her lips.

I put that there. I have to be the luckiest man in the world.

Pivoting on her heel, she tilts her head to the side. "Did you just get out of a car?"

Laughing, I narrow the space between us with hurried steps. "My subway guide was busy."

Her gaze drops to the pink box in my hand. It's tied with white string that is doubling as a handle. "What's that?"

"Bait to get you to come home with me."

She takes me in. I've been wearing the same suit and shirt since this morning. I left my tie at my sister's place after shedding it halfway through lunch. I know I look haggard, but it's in a good way.

I had my first family reunion today. It feels like I've been wrung inside out emotionally. Nineteen years of pent up feelings worked their way out, and by the time I said goodbye to my two sisters, I was spent.

A night alone and a glass of whiskey was what I thought I needed until I spotted a bakery in Brooklyn on my way back to Manhattan. I made my driver pull over. I hopped out, ran in, and came out with a half dozen cupcakes.

I don't buy cupcakes. I've never thought about feeding one to a woman until now.

Resting a hand on the lapel of my jacket, Bella leans closer. "A kiss is all the bait you need."

Wrapping my free hand around the back of her neck, I take her mouth in a deep, sensual kiss.

I hear a "yes, man," next to us, followed by a string of whistles.

When we break apart, her eyes are glazed. I swear to fuck that's exactly how I feel.

Running the pad of her thumb over my bottom lip, she smiles. "Lipstick."

"Come home with me, Isabella."

A soft kiss to my lips is followed by the only word I want to hear her say. "Yes."

***

With her back against the door to my penthouse, I give Bella another kiss before we enter. This one drops the bag from her hand as her fingers tangle in my hair.

I've been hard since I kissed her on the sidewalk. I could barely contain myself when we rode the subway here. It was packed, so we stood. Bella's ass was pressed against me the entire time. I dropped a hand to her hip to control our movement. Grinding against her in public may have been out of the question, but the friction of her ass brushing against my erection was enough to pull a soft moan from her when I pressed a kiss to the side of her neck.

"Inside," I groan against the corner of her mouth. "Inside now."

She leans back to look in my eyes. "I can't until you unlock the door."

All the blood in my body has rushed to my cock. I can't think straight. Pushing the box from the bakery at her, I fumble in my pocket for my keys. Tugging them out, I unlock the door quickly.

I wait for her to enter first. She bends down to pick up the bag she dropped. That gifts me with a perfect view of the top of her tits.

Her gaze meets mine when she straightens. "Were you checking me out?"

"I've been doing that since I met you at Atlas 22."

Shrugging a shoulder, she laughs. "Same."

Watching her walk, I follow behind a step. "You've been checking me out since that night?" She drops everything in her hands on the foyer table. "Every chance I could. I even found some pictures of you online."

I know what she's talking about. Alyssa kept a running diary of our relationship on her social media pages. After I broke things off, I asked her repeatedly to wipe my face clean from her online presence, but she insisted our relationship was "a chapter of her story."

"The only pictures of you online are on your Facebook page, and those are two years old," I point out.

That spins her around to face me. "You looked at my Facebook?"
I drop my keys and wallet on the table. "Don't pretend that you're surprised, Bella. You know I've been fantasizing about you for weeks."

She steps out of one of her heels before she does the same with the other. The loss of height puts her almost a full foot shorter than me.

"What did you think about when you fantasized about me?"

I fucking love that she's not too shy to ask. I love that her cheeks haven't bloomed pink out of embarrassment. She took my confession for what it is. I'm telling her that I've thought about her when I stroked myself.

Sliding out of my suit jacket, I drop it on the floor. "Your tits."

Her gaze falls to the front of her dress. "They're nice, aren't they?"

"From what I've seen, they're fucking magnificent." I edge a finger over the neckline of the red dress she's wearing. "I want to see more."

She turns slowly, lifting her hair with her hand. "Unzip me and I'll show you."

With a steady hand, I grab the pull and yank the zipper down in one fluid movement. The back of the dress falls open, revealing a black lace bra and the top of a black thong.

My knees shake, but I suck in a breath. She's going to fucking kill me with need.

The dress is on the floor before she spins back around, her hands at her sides.

I take it all in. The swell of her breasts pressing against the delicate lace and the darkened circles visible beneath are what draw my eyes down. Her nipples are perked and aching to be bitten.

I slide my gaze lower to her stomach and the small triangle of lace that covers her mound. She's smooth. I can see it under the sheer fabric.

"Is this what you saw in your fantasies?"

I have her up and in my arms, before I can form an answer. I tangle a hand in her hair, kissing her with abandon, not caring that our teeth crash into each other and I'm stumbling forward.

She wraps her legs around me, and I feel it. I fucking feel the need from inside of her. Pure heat is radiating from her skin.

I toss her onto her back on the couch.

A wince mars her perfect face. "That hurt."

"I'll kiss it all better," I growl, dropping to my knees.

I slide the panties down, every inch stealing another breath from my lungs until she's bare. Pink, wet, and perfect.

I lash my tongue against her tender flesh. "I need to taste you."

With a push of her ass off the leather, she curls her hands in my hair and breathes out in a moan. "I need to come."

Chapter 40

Bella

"Stop please," I beg as I tug on his hair.

Pull. I've been yanking on Barrett's head since my second orgasm. I'm barreling toward the third, and he won't let me breathe.

My lungs feel like they're collapsing within my chest. The room is spinning.

One of his fingers is inside me, hitting that spot that I knew existed in some faraway fantasy world. But I'm there now.

I'm close. So close.

I scream when it hits me. Tears well in my eyes not from anything but sheer pleasure. It's that good. It's been that good since he settled between my legs.

I thought it was a myth that men could be this good at oral sex.

His lips move from my core to my inner thigh. A trail of light kisses ends with a bite of the flesh on my hip. "Damn, Isabella."

Damn is right.

How am I going to go back to mediocre men now?

"You enjoyed that," he says as he straightens over me.

I answer with a nod of my chin even though he wasn't asking.

"Again?" The question is punctuated with a brush of his finger against my already super sensitive clit. "I can eat you until morning."

I shiver under his touch. "No. Please. It's so much."

Running the finger that just touched me over his bottom lip, he laughs. "That means you're in no shape to be fucked?"

I stay silent when he stands, watching in awe as he strips right in front of me.

He drops the shirt and then his shoes and socks before the pushes his pants and belt to the ground.

The large bulge under his boxer briefs is all I can look at.

"Come to my bed, Bella." He stretches out a hand. "If you're too weak, I'll carry you."
I fumble to my feet, grabbing for his hand for balance.

His fingers play over the strap of my bra. "Let's lose this."

I reach to unclasp it, but he beats me. His fingers glide behind me, and in one swift movement, the bra is undone and sliding off my arms.

"Every inch of you I uncover is more beautiful than the last."

I drop my gaze to his boxer briefs. "Can I see more of you?"

He reaches down, pushing his underwear down his legs until they're on the floor.

I stare at his naked body. It's powerful muscle and smooth skin. His cock is beautiful. Thick and long, it curves up toward his stomach.

"Your bed?" I question with a raised brow.

Taking my hand in his, he brings it to his mouth to press a kiss to my palm. "I'm not letting you leave tonight, my Bella."

The ache in my heart steals my breath. "I won't go."

I never want to go. I'd stay with this man, in this apartment, forever if he asked.

***

His body hovers me. The only light in the room is from outside. It's the glow of the city. It's enough for me to make out every detail of his handsome face.

He sheathed his cock while I settled on the bed, taking in the expansive bedroom.

It's barren except for the large king-size bed, and a pair of leather chairs tucked into a corner.

We don't say anything. Our eyes are locked, our bodies speaking their need with their movements.

I edge my legs apart, making room for his hips.

He grunts out a sound of need as the broad head of his cock presses against my core. I move my hips, relishing in the sensation when it grazes over my clit.

A smile takes over his face before it morphs into something else. It's something raw and primal when he notches his cock against my opening and pushes in slowly. Every inch is filling me more and more until I feel him deep inside me.

"Ah, fuck. So good," he growls out between heaving breaths.

I reach for his hips, holding him tight while we ride the wave together.

Deep, powerful thrusts that shake the bed are followed by slow, measured strokes that take me to the edge.

His eyes stay on mine the entire time.

I come with a cry that I don't recognize as my own. My voice bursts out in a strangled moan that sets him off.

He pumps harder and faster, chasing his own release and when he finds it, he calls my name over and over until he collapses on top of me with a kiss to my mouth and words whispered so softly that I can't make them out.

Chapter 41

Barrett

I sense her behind me before I hear her.

She clears her throat in warning as if I'm doing something I need to stop before she catches me.

"You're eating my leftovers." She laughs.

I'm on the couch with a tray of baked ravioli in my lap and a chilled water bottle next to me.

She fell asleep after we fucked. I cleaned her pussy with a warm facecloth, kissed her stomach, and before I could wrap her in a blanket, her eyes closed and she was drifting off.

That was over an hour ago.

I spent most of that time watching her sleep. I've never had that urge before, but I couldn't tear myself away from her. Her hair was a tousled mess around her shoulders. Her lips were swollen and pink. She looked at peace. I wanted to imprint that moment on my mind for eternity.

Waving my fork in the air, I motion for her to sit with me. "Do you want a bite?"

Tugging on the bottom hem of the white dress shirt she's wearing, she shakes her head. "No. I'm good."

Her hand shifts from my shirt to her other hand. She starts rubbing on her thumbnail. I don't want her to regret a second of what we did.

I pat the spot next to me. "Come sit with me."

She shuffles over on her bare feet. Tucking her legs beneath her, she settles in beside me. "It's good ravioli, isn't it?"

Forking a piece, I feed it to her. She parts her lips to take it, closing her eyes as she chews. When she swallows, she lets out a little moan.

Christ. I could watch that forever.

She's the sexiest woman I've ever known. The kindest. The most beautiful.

"I love my grandma's cooking," she says, sliding a finger over her bottom lip.

I take another piece of food in my mouth. Swallowing, I place the container on the coffee table. "It's fantastic. I understand why it's the best place for Italian food in the state."

Her gaze darts to me. "In the world."

Family pride is something I've never felt before. I felt it in spades today. My sisters are both teachers. They followed their dreams and made them come true. They're shaping the youth of this country.

I'm a lucky bastard to be their brother.

"Gina texted me." She drops her gaze to her lap. "That's what woke me."

I inch her chin up with my index finger. "What's on Gina's mind at this hour?"

It's after midnight. I suspect that her sister reached out to find out where she was or how she was. Gina knew I was on the hunt for her younger sister. She must know that I tracked her down.

When I went to grab the Calvetti's bag, I heard Bella's phone buzzing in her purse. I picked it up by the strap and dropped it on the floor next to my bed so it would be within reach once she woke up.

"She worries too much." She half-laughs with a roll of her eyes. "She wanted to make sure I was alright."

Turning to face her head-on, I cup her hand in mine. "Are you alright?"

"I'm good." A smile tugs on the corner of her full lips. "I'm way past good."

"Good." Leaning forward, I take her mouth for a soft kiss.

"I told her I was spending the night with you." Her chest moves on a sigh. "She won't tell anyone. Our secret is safe with her."

I don't want this to be a secret. I hate that it has to be, but I need the job and she does too.

"Is it time for dessert now?" Her eyes shine blue against the dim light from the lamp in the corner.

"I'm ready for dessert anytime." I pat my lap, tugging on the waistband of the black silk pajama bottoms I put on before I left my bedroom. "Let me kiss you and then I'll eat you."

The lures a laugh from her. "I meant whatever is in that pink box you brought home with you."

Ah, yes. The surprise for her taste buds.

There's no way in hell anything can taste better than her, but I'm still all for feeding her cake.

I push to my feet and cross the room. Scooping up the box, I turn to face her. The sight before me pulls all the air from my lungs.

Her hair is a mess, her make up is smudged, and my dress shirt dwarfs her, but she looks radiant. I want time to stop at this moment. I want her to stay in place forever.

Bouncing up to her knees, she points at me. "I think I'm going to love whatever is inside that box."

I think I'm in love with you.

The words I've never spoken to a woman play on my tongue, but I chase them away with a grin. "Get ready to have the best cupcakes in Brooklyn, beautiful."

Clapping her hands, she laughs. "They may be the best in Brooklyn, but they can't compete with the cupcakes from Sweet Bluebells on the Upper West Side. Remind me to take you there one day."

I'll never remind her. I'll never set foot in that part of the city again. My sister may have forgiven me for what happened there nineteen years ago, but I'll never forgive myself.

***

After finishing off a red velvet cupcake, Bella eyes me. "I admit they're good, but they're not the best I've ever had."

Am I? I don't need the reassurance, but I want to know that what we shared tonight was special. Sex is just sex to me. It's always been until now. What I experienced with Isabella was beyond the chase for an orgasm. Watching her come and being inside her consumed me.

I took one bite of a chocolate cupcake and reached my limit. I much prefer the ricotta cheesecake her grandmother made. A slice of that was my breakfast this morning.

"Your sister seems nice." She edges her bare leg over mine.

I grab hold of it, squeezing the flesh of her thigh. "Felicity is the best."

Her finger starts work on that thumbnail again. It's bare. Any trace of polish has long since disappeared. "Is your other sister like her?"

Her curiosity is feeding this. I don't want to shut her out, so I keep the conversation moving forward. "Felicity and Beatrice are the same in some ways, but very different in others."

"Felicity and Beatrice," she says their names as if she's testing how it will sound on her tongue. "And Henrietta."

"My sisters," I affirm with a nod.

"Not to pry," she starts before she shifts her ass so she's closer to me. "But it seemed like you were relived when Felicity told you that you could see Beatrice."

Grabbing her hand, I take her thumb between my teeth and nip on it.

"Ouch." She tries to tug her hand from mine, but I hold tight. "What was that for?"

"You are prying." I lean forward to kiss her mouth. "Don't preface anything with words you don't mean, Bella. If you have a question, ask me outright. I'll do the same with you."

Understanding washes over her expression. "What happened between you and your sisters?"

"I fucked up," I answer honestly, tugging her closer to me so I can wrap my arm around her. "I was in New York visiting my dad when I was a teenager. I was watching over Beatrice one day. There was an accident. I was exiled back to Chicago. I didn't see my sisters again until I moved here."

"An accident? She was hurt?" I hear the concern in her tone. "If you saw her today she must be fine, right?"

"Better than fine." I smile. "She's thriving. Happier than I could have imagined she'd be."

"Good." Her eyes shine bright. "Your dad should have taken a minute to calm down. There's nothing a kid can do that deserves a punishment like that."

She's wrong. I deserved what was handed to me. I let too many people down that day.

Fortunately, for me, I've been given a second chance to prove I'm a better man now than I was when I was fifteen-year-old kid.

"What should we do now?" Her eyebrows dance. "Do you have any ideas?"

I yank her onto my lap, pulling a scream from her. Another follows when I rip open the front of my dress shirt, sending buttons scattering around us.

"You just ruined your shirt," she points out looking down at her naked body.

"It was worth it." I cup her tits in my hands. "I haven't had a taste of these yet."

Lowering my mouth to her right breast, I swirl my tongue over her hard nipple. "Give me an hour or two to savor every inch of your body and then we'll decide what's next on the agenda."

Chapter 42

Bella

I open my apartment door to find two faces staring right at me.

"It's not even eight a.m.," I point out with a tap of my finger over the face of my watch. "What are you doing up, and why are you even here?"

"I have an early call time for a photo shoot," Gina answers first.

"I'm her stylist for the day," Max adds. "That and I had the most amazing date last night. I had to tell someone, and you were missing in action."

I look at my sister. I'm surprised that she didn't call Max to give him all the details of my overnighter at Barrett's apartment.

"I told him you were doing your boss." Gina throws her hands up in mock frustration. "He only wanted to talk about himself and the hottie that he met at the launch party we went to."

"You met someone there?" I drop my purse on the couch. "What's he like?"

"Prince Charming," Max swoons. "Seriously, Bella, he looks like every picture of Prince Charming I've ever seen."

"Every cartoon drawing you mean." Gina taps him on the shoulder.

"Whatever." Gus swats her hand away. "He's a doctor. He's smart and funny. He's a good guy."

I smile. "I'm happy for you."

Taking me in his arms, he gives me a full bear hug. "I'm happier for you. You broke your dry spell."

"You didn't just say that." I push back to stab a finger into the middle of his chest.

Adjusting the collar of the green polo he's wearing, he laughs. "Don't deny it. You look like you were fucked into next week."

Gina's head pops up. She gives me the once-over. "You do, Bella. You look good."

Wiping a hand over my forehead, I sigh. "I have to shower and get ready for work."

"Mr. Hot Stuff couldn't cut you a bit of slack after you rocked his world?" Max pushes my hair behind my ear. "It was good? He was good to you?"

"So good." I wink.

"I knew I liked him." Turning his attention back to my sister, he reaches for her purse. "We're on a tight schedule, Gina. We need to leave now if we're going to make it across town for nine."

"You'll call me later?" Gina moves to give me a hug. "I left a recipe for a tuna noodle bowl on the island. If you're feeling creative one night, maybe we can cook together and talk about your boss."

"I'll cook it for you soon." I pat her cheek. "Go knock the socks off of whoever is taking your picture today."

Leaning in, she whispers in my ear, "I'm not an expert, but I think you're in love, Bella."

Laughing softly, I whisper back, "I think you're mistaking great sex for love."

Pulling back just enough to look at my face, she keeps her voice lowered. "I'm not. Trust your heart."

Stunned, I watch her and my best friend walk out, leaving me with a million questions about what I'm feeling for Barrett and what that means for my future.

***

Nothing can break the bubble of a good sex hangover quite like walking into the middle of a heated conversation between your boss and one of your co-workers.

Dropping my coffee cup on my desk, I move toward the open door of Barrett's office.

He's face-to-face with Sonny Barusso, one of the executives who head up the IT department. Sonny has been with Garent Industries as long as it's been in existence. Word around the office is that he grew up next door to Ivan on Long Island.

"You can go straight to hell." Sonny pushes a finger into Barrett's chest. "I'm not going anywhere."

Barrett's hand fists at his side. "You're leaving today. You've been terminated."

Terminated? He fired Sonny?

Taking a step into the office, I look at my boss. "What's going on?"

The question is enough to shift Barrett's focus from Sonny to me. He shoots me a look that is meant to shut me up. "This doesn't concern you, Isabella. Close the door on your way out."

He can't understand what he's doing or the implications it will carry once Ivan finds out what's going on. Firing one of his closest friends may be grounds enough for Barrett to be the next one on the chopping block.

"If I could just have one moment in private, sir." I tack that on to the end to appease Barrett. I don't want him to think that I'm undermining his position.

He throws a hand in the air with a finger pointed at the door. "Out now."

It stings more than it should. It has nothing to do with the fact that Duke never ordered me around. What I'm feeling is based on what happened between Barrett and me last night. I can't expect the tenderness and passion we shared to take root in the office, but I did anticipate that he'd at least listen to what I had to say. I only wanted a minute to explain who Sonny is to Ivan.

Turning on my heel, I slam the door on my way out. I bypass my desk and head straight for the elevator. It's not my place to clue Mr. Garent into what Barrett is up to, but Greer in Human Resources will surely want to step in and defuse the situation.

If she doesn't, there will be hell to pay when Ivan gets back to New York. Regardless of what just happened in his office, I don't want Barrett to lose his job over this.

Punching a finger into the elevator call button, I release a heavy exhale. I need to learn how to separate business from pleasure because in his bed I'm Barrett's equal, but here, in the office, I still have to follow his direction and his orders regardless of how screwed up I think they are.

Chapter 43

Barrett

I wait patiently for my executive assistant to return from her journey two floors down to the Human Resources Department. The new head of HR gave me a heads-up that Isabella is there pleading for not only Sonny's job but Greer Delacorte's too.

Their careers at Garent are over. Ironically, I had to fire them for the same reason I fired Daphne Clegg. If you skim from the company coffers, you'll end up with nothing.

The auditor I hired to look over Garent Industries' books stumbled on a gold mine, or more specifically, an empty gold mine.

The scheme was foolproof under Duke's watch.

Daphne hired contractors who don't exist. Greer set up all the paperwork before forwarding that mess of lies to Sonny. His role was to take care of the technical side of payments. All the money was funneled into an offshore account that Daphne managed under a phony corporation she'd set up more than five years ago. That's when their scam first launched.

I shut it down. That trio of fools had close ties to Ivan so I had to let them go with the understanding that if they leave quietly they won't face criminal charges.

That was Ivan's call. I reached out after showing Daphne the door. Ivan's fine with eating the lost revenue. He's a better man than me.

The punishment should fit the crime. I know that first-hand. I've been paying my dues since I was fifteen-years-old. The time lost with my sisters was only part of the retribution. The guilt I'll carry until the day I die is my life sentence.

I perk when I hear Bella's heels on the polished concrete floor. She took the stairs. I've been waiting for the elevator to return since I watched the doors close with Sonny Barusso inside.

"Barrett?" she calls my name before she comes into view. "Are you here?"

"In here." I rise from my chair, buttoning my suit jacket.

She rounds the corner into my office. Dressed in a pink short-sleeve sweater and a black leather skirt, she looks incredible. Her hair is tied back in a messy bun. She's the perfect combination of business and casual.

She stops mid-step when she notices me approaching her. I stand tall, letting her drink in the sight of me in a navy suit with a light blue shirt and tie.

"Hi." A smile plays on her lips.

"Hi, yourself." I dive a hand into the pocket of my pants to adjust my erection.

She doesn't notice. She's scraping her bare thumbnail with all the might she has.

"Close the door," I direct her with a hand in the air.

She kicks it shut with her stiletto. It slams, pulling a laugh from me.

Her hands drop to her hips. "What's so funny? You're ruining people's lives, and you're laughing. It's as if you don't have a care in the world."

I wish to fuck that was true.

"They ruined their own lives, Bella." I lean against my desk, crossing my legs at the ankles. "They have no one to blame for their downfall but themselves."

She stares at me for a few seconds. "That makes no sense."

It doesn't to her because she's not aware of all the facts. Ivan asked me to keep this quiet. He went so far as to tell me pointedly not to share this with Bella. His exact words were, "Isabella needs to be out of the loop on this. Her bleeding heart won't be able to handle the news that not everyone at Garent is a saint."

I'm about to prove the man wrong.

"Sonny and Greer were stealing from Garent. Daphne was the ringleader."

Weighing my words, she steps closer. "For real?"

I nod. "For real."

"You caught them?" Her eyes bore into mine. "You're the one who caught them?"

I could show her the details. Letting her see the hard facts wouldn't hurt, but that's not what she's asking for. She wants reassurance from me that I'm confident that they screwed Garent over.

"I hired an auditor to run over the books. She noticed the discrepancies. I took it from there."

Swallowing hard, she moves closer to me. "You were right to fire them."

I don't expect an apology from her. She was defending her co-workers. To her, they were a team. The reality is that the three of them were looking out for themselves at the expense of everyone else.

"Garent Industries needed a housecleaning." I straighten my tie. "I'm the man for the job."

"So you do housecleaning?" She tilts her head. "May I request a session?"

I fucking love the playfulness. "It depends on how you'll be paying."

"With this." Her fingers run over her bottom lip. "I can give you a deposit now."

I've never been sucked off at the office before.

Her eyes are glued to my hands as I undo my belt before I unbutton my pants and lower the zipper. "Lock the door and get on your knees."

She handles that with deft ease, kicking off her heels and lowering herself to the floor in front of me.

Her hand dives in my pants. When she wraps her fingers around my already erect penis I groan.

"You're going to love this," she purrs.

Fuck.

I lean both hands back on the desk and watch as Bella tugs my boxer briefs down and circles the head of my cock with her sinfully red lips.

Chapter 44

Bella

My hand is wrapped around the root of his thick cock. My tongue is slowly driving Barrett crazy.

Every curse word in English has left his lips and a few in a language I don't recognize.

I know he's getting close. I can sense it in the way his hands are clawing at my hair. The bun I worked so hard on this morning was torn apart by his fingers as he set the pace.

"Jesus, Bella. I'm going to come."

A loud knock behind me sets me back on my heels.

His dick bobs in front of me. Swollen and stiff, it's wet from my eager mouth. I gaze up into his face. It's twisted in a combination of frustration and anger.

He grips the back of my head, pushing me closer to his cock. "Don't stop. They'll go away."

Before I can take him in my mouth again, another series of raps sounds through his office.

"For fuck's sake." He closes his eyes. "Go away."

He doesn't say it loud enough for anyone but me to hear it.

"Barrett?" A man's voice charges through the air just as the locked doorknob rattles. "Open this door. I need to see you now."

Darting up to my feet, I stare into his face. "Who is that?"

I know it's not Ivan. I'd recognize his voice anywhere. It can't be someone who works here because women outnumber men by at least five times at Garent, and I know every male voice with my eyes closed.

"It's your father." The man on the other side of the door unknowingly answers my question. "We need to talk now. Let me in."

"Oh my God." I whip around to grab my shoes. "Your dad is here."

Barrett grabs hold of my bicep, spinning me so I'm facing him. He plants a soft, wet kiss on my mouth. "We're not teenagers, Isabella. No one is getting in trouble for what we were just doing."

I glance down at his cock. "Put that away."

He laughs loud enough for his dad to hear him.

"Barrett?" Mr. Adler bangs on the door. "I'm not leaving until we talk."

Heaving out a sigh, Barrett tucks himself back into his pants before he fastens the belt. Running a hand over his hair, he flashes a smile. "That was fucking amazing, Bella."

Toeing into my heels, I smile. "I'm glad you approve, sir. Shall I show your visitor in?"

"If I say no will you send him back where he came from?"

Holding back a laugh, I shake my head. "The sooner you talk to him, the sooner I can interrupt and tell you that you have a meeting."

Closing the distance between us with two heavy steps, he cups my face in his hands and kisses me.

"I'm about to break this door down." Mr. Adler fumes.

Pulling away, Barrett sighs. "Better let the old man in before he hurts himself."

I smooth my hands over my skirt, move to the door and swing it open.

The man on the other side is frail with graying hair and a vacant expression on his face. He pushes past me, barreling into the room with the aid of a wooden cane. An oversized suit jacket is hanging from his shoulders.

I turn to see Barrett looking his dad over.

"You have some nerve," Mr. Adler wobbles closer to his son. "Thinking you could march back into her life like you did nothing wrong."

I know I should close the door and walk away, but I stand and stare at Barrett and his dad. This is what a fractured family looks like. These two men became strangers over something that happened a long time ago.

"I know what I did wrong." Barrett's arms cross over his chest. "You think I could forget that?"

"I think you're looking for salvation." Mr. Adler's hand clenches around the top of his cane.

"Salvation?" Barrett barks out a laugh. "I'm looking for ten seconds of peace. Just one fucking moment where this guilt doesn't eat me from the inside out."

Mr. Adler glances over his shoulder at me. "You can go."

"Don't order her to do anything." Barrett's shoulders fall back.

I don't need him to fight this battle for me. This is a private moment between a father and his only son.

"I'll go get a coffee." I step out of the office. "If you need me, you know how to reach me."

I lock eyes with Barrett before I close the door softly. All I see in his gaze is a sorrow so profound that it steals my breath.

***

I get back to my desk an hour later hoping that the Adler men aren't at each other's throats. I peer into Barrett's office. There's no one there.

I fall into my chair, dropping my purse in the bottom drawer of my desk.

A yellow sticky note catches my eye.

It's half-hidden beneath the file folder that serves as a cover for my crossword puzzle.

I slide the puzzle and the sticky note out and read the message handwritten in black ink.

I just checked my calendar. 6 meetings this afternoon? WTF? I'll be out for the rest of the day.

I laugh aloud. I scheduled all of those meetings to make up for the ones I had to cancel so he could spend time with his sisters.

My gaze drops to the crossword puzzle. It's new. I completed the other one when I filled in the blanks to form the word fear.

Only one clue is solved on this one. It's a five-letter word for fun. Written in bold black ink is my name. BELLA.

That's not the right answer. I'm more than just fun, but maybe that's all I am to Barrett. Maybe that's all I'll ever be.

Chapter 45

Barrett

"Dinner and a movie?" Dylan claps a hand in the center of my back. "I'm flattered, but you won't get to first base with me. Eden can set you up with someone. She's got a friend in her office. You'll be rounding third base by midnight if my fiancée makes the call right now."

"What?" I motion for him to step into my apartment. "How the hell would you know how far a woman is willing to go on the first date? You're engaged, Colt."

"Eden's a gossip. I get the goods on everyone she works with."

"I'm glad I'm not a prosecuting attorney working in the office next to her."

"You and me both," Dylan laughs. "You said dinner and a movie. I don't see food and the television is off."

"I have some leftover pizza in the fridge." I jerk a thumb over my shoulder toward the kitchen. "There's beer too."

"That covers the grub." He takes off in search of the days-old pizza. "What about the entertainment?"

I debated this all day. After seeing my dad, I needed a neutral ear to listen to me talk. Dylan's the guy who fits that bill. The problem is I have to confess sins from the past that he knows nothing about.

He'll give me hell for keeping things from him, but it's more than that. I've always been the one preaching to him about letting go of the past, but I've got a firm grasp on mine.

Shoving both hands in the front pocket of my jeans, I start at the place that makes the most sense to me. "I saw my dad today."

With a piece of pizza in one hand and a bottle of beer in the other, Dylan approaches. "Where? In the newspaper? Who even reads those anymore?"

"My office."

His chewing slows. He swallows hard. "You're bullshitting me."

I move past him to take a seat on a chair. "I swear he was in my office. Showed up out of nowhere."

With a thud, he drops onto his ass on the couch. "Jesus. If you're going to ride this penthouse thing out, you need a new couch. Do it for me. This is hard as a bag of rocks."

I huff out a laugh. "I'll work on that."

He places the bottle of beer on the table. "What did old Adler want?"

The only thing Dylan knows about what happened when I was fifteen in New York is that it set me on a month-long weed and beer bender.

It was the middle of summer, so I hung out at his place. He tried to pry the details about what happened out of me, but I always read from the same script. I told him I was drunk and that my dad caught me with a beer and sent me back to Chicago on the first available flight.

I was sent back on the first flight, but the damage I'd done far surpassed a few too many beers.

"Remember that summer when we were fifteen?"

He shoots me a look. "We smoked too much weed and plotted out the next big video game that would take the world by storm. That was supposed to be our ticket to fame and fortune."

Smiling, I nod. "That's the summer."

"He sent you back to Chicago three weeks early." He takes a pull from the bottle of beer. "Did he finally decide to apologize for being a dick?"

Sucking in a breath, I steady myself. "Is was more than beer that got me kicked back to Chicago."

Crossing his arms over his chest, he leans back on the couch. "It was Bizzy. The accident."

Stunned, I stare at him.

"Monica," he explains. "You think she could keep that shit to herself? She told my mom. Monica said we had to keep it hush-hush."

"Fuck." I rake both hands through my hair. "You knew all this time?"

"I knew you'd tell me when you were ready." He narrows his eyes. "I was hoping it would be before you fucked off to college in California, but I'm a patient man."

I shake my head. "Irving pushed for me to go to USC."

"Of course he fucking did." He laughs. "Ship the kid to the other side of the country. What the hell did that solve?"

Nothing. I would stay awake for hours each night rethinking what had happened on that street on the Upper West Side.

I'd close my eyes and see the cars, and the people. I'd hear the sounds and there was the silence from my sister. It's all etched in my memory.

"So he came to New York to warn you to stay away from Felicity and Bizzy?"

"Beatrice." I smile. "She outgrew Bizzy. She goes by Beatrice now."

"You saw her?" He inches forward on the couch. "Did you talk to her?"

I swallow past the lump in my throat. "Yesterday, for hours."

"Things are good?" He sips from the bottle. "You're good with her and with Felicity?"

"It's a work-in-progress to rebuild, but we're all committed to making it happen."

His gaze narrows. "Not all of you. I take it that Irving isn't on board? Monica can't be either."

"They keep reminding me that I can't swipe it all under the rug. That there are consequences I'll have to live with forever."

"You've put yourself through hell." He scrubs a hand over the back of his neck. "When I was torn up about what happened between Eden and me in high school, you'd always tell me to let the past go."

I did say that. It was advice I doled out freely but could never live by.

"Let it go, Barrett." He slides to his feet. "There's not one damn thing you can do today to change yesterday. Be a better man than you were then. That's the best you can do."

I wish it were that damn easy.

***

After polishing off the last piece of pizza in the box, Dylan picks up his phone. "I should head out soon. Do you want me to get Eden to set you up with that woman she works with? It sounds like you'd have a good time."

"No," I answer succinctly.

"No?" he parrots back. "Why not? You could use the exercise."

I let out a chuckle. "I'm getting all the exercise I need."

His eyebrows arch. "What the fuck? With who?"

He knows Bella. Not well enough to bring this up with her, but I want to protect her. I need to protect her. I ease into the answer with a warning. "You have to keep this to yourself."

"I miss the good old days when we would pinkie swear that we wouldn't tell a soul who we were banging in high school."

He wiggles his hand in the air, arcing his pinkie finger toward me. "I pinkie swear that I won't tell a soul who Barrett is dipping his dick into."

Batting his hand away, I throw my head back in laughter. "It's more than sex, Colt."

He takes a step closer to me. "Are you in love? How the hell did I miss that happening?"

I dart a hand in the air. "Not love. Deep like. Admiration. I fucking adore her."

"Sounds like love to me."

"It's not love," I say as much to convince him as myself.

How the fuck could I have fallen in love this quickly?

"Call it whatever the hell you want. I want to know who she is. Where did you meet her?"

"Keep this quiet." I tap a finger on his shoulder. "This stays here."

His eyes skim my face. "Holy hell. You're head over heels for Bella Calvetti, aren't you?"

I raise my brows in a silent question because how in the fuck did he figure that out?

Resting a hand on my shoulder, he laughs. "You spend all your time with her. She's beautiful, and there's a bag from Calvetti's in your kitchen. Great detective work on my part, I'd say."

"You're a regular Sherlock."

He pockets his phone. "I'm going home to my fiancée. Lock Bella down, Barrett. She comes from good people."

"You'll say hi to Eden for me?"

"Don't I always?" He taps my cheek. "I'll be in touch. Thanks for the old pizza and cheap beer."

I follow him as he makes his way to the door. "You brought the beer the last time you were here."

Glancing over his shoulder, he laughs. "That's how I know it's cheap. Grab the bull by the horns, Barrett and grab Bella before some asshole scoops her up."

There is no way in hell I'll let another man near her.

Chapter 46

Bella

Picking up another book with a torn cover, I look around the interior of Rusten's Reads. It's Saturday morning in Brooklyn. This is the time when foot traffic is at its peak. The store is in a prime location, yet the only other person in here is Misty Furst, one of the owners.

Barrett hasn't mentioned the business since we met with Ivan at Axel NY. I have no idea if he plans on following through with acquiring them as part of Garent Industries, or not.

"How are you making out, Bella?" Misty calls from where she's stacking children's books on a small circular table.

"Good." I smile, waving the two books I'm holding in the air. "I'll find another and then I'll be good to go."

I shift my gaze to the shelf in front of me. My reading tastes vary. One month I'm all about romance. The next I might be consumed with mystery novels. Today, I'm drawn to the science fiction section.

I peek around the bookshelf when I hear the bell above the entrance door ring. Hoping it's a crowd of at least twenty people; I take a step back when I realize who I'm looking at.

Barrett?

Dressed down in a pair of jeans and a dark blue sweater, he approaches Misty. "What have you got for me today, Misty?"

"You won't believe it." She shakes her head, sending her short gray curls bouncing. "We do have a copy of Pride and Prejudice tucked away on a shelf in the stockroom."

"I'll take it," he says, pulling his wallet out of his back pocket.

"Let me run and grab it." She moves, then pauses, turning back to him. "Next week won't be easy."

Straightening his shoulders, he rests a hand on the counter between them. "Change is always hard, but it's the right thing to do."

She blows out a breath. "I keep thinking about Monday morning and not coming here to open the doors."

What the hell?

I know the business isn't sustainable as is, but Ivan was clear about what he wanted. Rusten's Reads was supposed to get a second chance under Garent's umbrella.

I watch Misty walk away. Once she's out of view, I march across the store.

"Bella?" Barrett smiles when he sees me approaching. "How long have you been here?"

Dropping the books in my hand on the counter, I turn and face him head-on. "Long enough to know that you're not going to save this store."

"You're buying those books?"

The fact that he completely ignores what I just said sets my blood boiling. "Those and more if this is my last chance to shop here. I used to come here with Marti every Saturday morning when I was a little girl."

"I didn't know you were into sci-fi."

What is wrong with him?

Gazing around the quaint little shop, I bite back my emotion. I come here almost every Saturday morning. Sometimes, I buy books for myself. Other times, I'll pick up a few children's books to give to Palla for her kids. There have been days when I'll choose a handful of random books to donate to the community center around the corner.

This store is a piece of my childhood. I'd hold tight to Marti's hand when we'd come here. The moment we were in the store, I'd take off in search of one book that she'd buy for me. She told me it was our little secret. I was her only grandchild that she brought here. Rusten's Reads hold a special place in my heart.

"Here we go." Misty rounds the corner from the stockroom with a book in her hand. "I found it. It's a little worse for wear, but that means it's been read with love over and over again."

Barrett opens his wallet. He pushes a bill into Misty's hand. "This should cover it. Ring it up and bag it."

Misty glances at me. "I take it you know this kind gentleman, Bella, since you both work at Garent."

"He's not a kind gentleman. He's my boss," I quip.

Misty catches Barrett's eye. "Bella works for you? I assumed you brought your assistant from Chicago with you. Why wasn't Bella involved in our meetings?"

Because he knew that I'd fight tooth and nail to save this store.

Raking a hand through his hair, Barrett points at the bill in Misty's hand. The one hundred dollar bill in her hand. "That's for this book and the two that Bella wants. Keep the change."

Digging a hand into my bag, I shake my head. "No. I'll pay for my books."

Sliding the bill at Barrett, Misty smiles. "All three books are on the house. Consider it a thank you for going out of your way to save the store. I hope you'll both be here the day we reopen the doors as Velvet Bay Books."

Chapter 47

Barrett

Dammit.

This is not how I wanted Bella to find out about this. I have been working on this deal since I met Misty and Rusten over a coffee to discuss the future of their shop.

That was a couple of days after Ivan made it clear that he wanted me to follow in Duke's footsteps to save the bookstore from the fate that many of the mom and pop shops in Brooklyn have met. Businesses in this neighborhood stand a fighting chance if they appeal to the people who live here.

Park Slope is one of the prime locations in Brooklyn, so I decided after meeting the Fursts and hearing them talk about Bella, that it was worth the money and effort to take them under Garent's wing.

We signed an agreement that transfers majority ownership of the store from them to Garent. They'll get the makeover and rebranding they desperately need. With the ideas I'm implementing, they stand a good chance of turning their business around.

That is all thanks to the woman standing next to me with two sci-fi books clutched in her palm.

I'm holding a battered copy of Pride and Prejudice.

It's for her.

She's about to realize that if she hasn't connected the dots yet.

"I love the one idea so much," Misty says, oblivious to the strained silence between Bella and I. "The one about framing pictures of our customers over the years. I took so many photos with that old camera of mine. I have a box full of them."

Isabella's eyes widen. The lines between the dots are getting clearer.

"And the Saturday morning writing workshops for kids." Misty's smile is brighter than I've seen it since I met her. "Think about it. A couple of months from now on a Saturday morning just like this, there will be young writers gathered at a table. One might be writing the next great novel of our time."

The books in Bella's hands fall to the floor.

I reach for them, glancing over to see her rubbing the newly polished nail of her thumb. She went for light blue this time around. It matches the jeans and blue silk blouse she's wearing. Dressed like this with black leather boots on her feet and her hair in a messy bun on top of her head, she looks perfect.

I know her mind is racing. I know she's got to be wondering what the fuck is going on. I also suspect she's pissed as hell at me right about now.

"Barrett." My name escapes her in a trembling voice. "Can we talk in private?"

"Let me give you two some space." Misty picks up a stack of books from the edge of the counter. "I'll take these to the stockroom for when Velvet Bay Books opens. I could say that name all day. Whoever thought of it is a genius. It pays homage to Bay Ridge where we opened our first store before we moved here and our grumpy old cat."

Just as the words leave her lips, the gray-haired feline jumps up on the counter, parading across the worn wood.

"There's my girl." Misty scoops Velvet up in one hand. "Let's give these two some privacy. I sense they have something important to talk about."

That we do.

As soon as Misty disappears out of view, Isabella is in my arms with her hands in my hair. Her mouth finds mine in a kiss so tender that I feel my knees weaken.

I drop the books so I can tug her closer to steady myself and to feel more of her pressed against me. When I deepen the kiss, she lets out a moan of satisfaction.

Pulling away just far enough to speak, she presses her lips to the corner of my mouth. "I know what you did. Thank you. Thank you from the bottom of my heart."

***

We exit the store ten minutes later, after Bella promised Misty that she'd have a cup of tea with her soon.

I planned on surprising Bella late next week after construction had started on the interior of the store. I have the new exterior sign on a rush order. I wanted it in place before I brought her down here so she could see it and realize that this is her vision. All of this is Bella's vision.

"We should talk," she says, glancing down the sidewalk. "Are you hungry?"

I haven't eaten yet today. I got up early. After showering and dressing, I went down to the office. I put in a few hours there before I decided to make the trip to Brooklyn to check in on Misty.

Shutting down Rusten's Reads for a few weeks is an essential part of the rebranding process, but it's tough on her and Rusten. Before Bella and I left the store, I put Misty to task looking through the boxes of old pictures to find a dozen to frame. They'll be a reminder of what once was.

"I know a place." I hold tight to the copy of Pride and Prejudice in my hand. "You game to try something different?"

"Different for you or for me?" Her gaze drops to the book.

"Shit. I didn't think of that. You've probably already been to the place I want to take you."

Grabbing hold of the strap of the purse slung over her shoulder, she shrugs. "Try me."

"Crispy Biscuit."

"Jo is the best." She starts down the sidewalk. "I'll get her to make something from her secret menu."

I fall in place next to her, keeping up with her quick pace as she weaves seamlessly around the people headed toward us. "Who the fuck is Jo?"

A smile curves her lips. "The owner. I've been going to Crispy Biscuit for years."

Of course she has. This city owns a piece of Bella's heart.

I have no fucking idea what it feels like to give a piece of your heart away, but if this ache inside my chest and this desire to spend every goddamn second of my life with her is any indication, Isabella Calvetti owns all of my heart. She owns all of me.

Chapter 48

Bella

"Vegetable eggs benedict." Barrett pierces the perfectly cooked egg yolk with the fork in his hand, sending the bright yellow liquid cascading over the grilled portabella mushroom and roasted peppers. "You say this is delicious?"

I point at the avocado-lime hollandaise sauce. "That is the best part. I have to fight with myself not to lick the plate when I'm done."

"I'd love to watch that."

I contain a laugh as I slice my knife through the egg on my plate. "If this isn't pure satisfaction, I don't know what is."

Barrett lets out a chuckle. "I can think of a few other things I'd consider pure satisfaction."

That sets a blush up my cheeks. I take a sip of ice water to try and flush it away. "Take a bite and see for yourself."

He does. He scoops up a bit of everything on his plate onto his fork. I watch his face as he chews slowly. His eyes close briefly before his head bobs in a nod. "This is fucking amazing."

"I know, right?" I giggle. "I told Jo she should put it on the menu. It would sell like hotcakes, although the hotcakes here are amazing. We can try those the next time we come."

I curse silently for letting that slip. I want there to be a next time or a million more next times, but I don't know if he does.

"Sounds like a plan." Barrett washes down another bite of food with coffee. "Let's talk about the bookstore."

I've been processing everything since we left Rusten's Reads. At first, I was stunned that Barrett was saving the store, but when I realized where the ideas for the rebranding came from I was touched.

I should be pissed, but I'm feeling too grateful for that.

He looks down at the copy of Pride and Prejudice on the table. Patting his hand on the cover, he gazes at me. "This is how it all started."

"That book?" I raise a brow.

"It's the only Jane Austen novel you don't own." He slides the book across the table toward me.

I slide it back at him. "I already own it."

"You don't." He studies my face. "You keep all of Jane Austen's other novels in the bottom drawer of your desk. This is the only one you're missing."

With a push of his fingers, the book is next to my plate.

"I have two copies at home."

"I asked your sister if you did when I went there to find you the other night."

Gina wouldn't know a good book if it fell on her head. My sister is incredibly smart and innovative, but books have never been a big love for her. Not the way they've been for me.

"She told you I didn't?"

He nods slowly. "I even asked her to go to your room to check."

Since both of my copies of Pride and Prejudice are sitting on top of my nightstand, Gina must have had her eyes closed when she went on that search mission. Or she was looking at her phone's screen.

"She must have missed them." I smile. "I love the book, so I wouldn't mind having a copy for the office."

Placing his fork on the table, he studies my face. "Tell me why you love the book so much that you already own two copies of it."
I look into his handsome face that's so much more than a strong nose, and a chiseled jaw. It's the face of the man I'm falling in love with. "I've always had a literary crush on the main character. Mr. Darcy."

He flashes me a devilish grin as his hand hits the cover of the book. "Now I'm going to have to read this damn thing to find out what Mr. Darcy has that I don't."

I drop my hand on his. "Mr. Darcy has nothing on you."

***

Jo appeared at just the wrong moment in time. She refilled Barrett's cup with coffee and offered to bring us a piece of lemon meringue pie to share for dessert.

I didn't turn that down.

I'm still smiling about the conversation we were having before Jo interrupted us.

"What's the smile for?" Barrett yanks a few bills from his wallet and tosses them in the middle of the table to pay for brunch.

It's way more than the cost of the meal. He's more generous than I realized.

I inch the conversation forward because I want to talk about the ideas for Misty and Rusten's store. I know where he got them. "Is there anything in Garent's employee handbook that states that a boss can't go through his employee's desk whenever he damn well pleases?"

Leaning back in his chair, he raises his chin. "We're finally going there, are we?"

Resting my elbow on the table, I sigh. "You found the notebook in my desk drawer, didn't you? It was under the novels."

His eyes lock on mine. "You know I did."
I do know that. When Duke first told me that he was considering buying Rusten's Reads to rebrand it, I got straight to work making notes of all the changes I felt were necessary.

I was the one who sent him to the store when he was looking for a birthday gift for his mom. She loves to read, so it felt like the perfect suggestion.

He came back to the office from Brooklyn with a copy of Oliver Twist and a determination to save the corner bookstore. I was overjoyed.

I spent hours jotting down ideas for names, a color scheme for the revamped store and community events that would fill the shop with avid readers.

I never showed any of it to Duke because he didn't have a chance to move forward with the deal before he went to Fire Island.

When I heard Misty talk about the new name, I knew that Barrett had gotten a look at my notebook. I should be mad, but I can't be. My favorite bookstore is getting a second chance, just like the books inside of it.

I rest my chin on my hand. "Why didn't you tell me you were saving it?"

He scrapes his teeth over his bottom lip. "The truth?"

I nod. "The truth."

"You won't tell Ivan?"

I jut out my hand toward him. Wiggling my pinkie finger, I laugh. "I pinkie swear I won't."

He shakes his head. "Is that making a resurgence? Dylan tried to get me to pinkie swear last night."

I want to ask about what, but I'm way more curious about why he didn't tell me he stepped in as the savior of Rusten's Reads.

"Pinkie swearing has always been around." Dropping my hand, I grin. "Just tell me why all the secrecy about the store."

"Two reasons." He holds two fingers in the air. "The first is that it's got great potential. With your ideas and some smart marketing moves, I believe we can turn it into a hot spot in Park Slope."

I believe that too.

"What's the second reason?"

He waits for a beat before he leans forward. Lowering his voice, he says, "I did it for you, Isabella. I know how much it means to you."

Chapter 49

Bella

We held hands all the way back to his penthouse. I tried to pull away once we were on the subway, but Barrett only tightened his grip on me.

I whispered that a Garent employee might see us, but he shook his head telling me not to worry about that.

"I have to go back to Chicago for a few days." Barrett pulls the pins holding my bun in place. "It's Garent business. The new COO has hit a few roadblocks."

Shaking my hair loose, I smile. "You're going to go kick those roadblocks out of the way?"

"Something like that." He starts working on the buttons of my blouse. "You'll take care of things here?"

I can handle the office. I did it when Duke was out of town. "I'll keep things running smoothly."

He groans when the white lace bra I'm wearing comes into view beneath the blouse. "I'd ask you to go with me, but I don't trust anyone else to take over for me."

Pride blooms in my chest. My job is important to me and knowing that he feels I'm capable of filling his shoes is a huge compliment.

His hands drop to the waistband of my jeans. "You're mine for today. I'm not letting you leave until morning."

"I'll stay," I whisper as I watch him unbutton my jeans.

Kneeling, he removes my boots before sliding the jeans down my legs. I kick free of them.

Standing in his bedroom dressed only in my bra and panties, I don't feel exposed. I feel safe and cherished. I've never felt this comfortable with a man before. I trust him with my body and with my heart.

He yanks his sweater over his head in one fluid movement.

The sight of him, half-dressed with desire in his eyes, makes me want to strip bare and climb on him so I can wrap myself around his beautiful body and never let go.

"Feel this," he says, his voice low and filled with need.

Lifting my hand in his, he presses my palm against the center of his chest. I close my eyes. The rhythmic pounding of his heart is strong and rapid.

"You do that to me." He edges his cheek against mine, still holding my hand against his skin. "You make my heart race."

"You do that to my heart too," I whisper.

His free hand drops to my chest. Pressing two fingers between my breasts, he smiles. "I feel it. It's beating faster than mine."

Stealing a quick kiss, I laugh. "It's because you're so hot."

I expect at least a chuckle in return, but that's not what I get. He pulls back so he can look me in the eye. "It's more than that."

He's right. It's so much more than that, but I'm not ready to confess that to him. I'm not sure I'm ready to admit it to myself.

"You feel things in here." He presses his fingers harder on my skin.

"Do you feel things in here?" I respond with a push of my fingers into his muscled chest.

A faint nod dips his chin. "I've never met anyone like you before, Isabella."

Before I can tell him that he's the most incredible man I've ever met, his lips are on mine, and my words get lost in the passion of our kiss.

***

I writhe beneath him as he takes his time. I'm so close. His lips haven't descended beyond the skin right below my breasts, but my core is on fire. I'm aching for him to touch my clit. I want his lips on it, his tongue, and his teeth.

I groan out a protest when he inches back up to take my right nipple between his teeth again. When he nips me, the burst of pain sends a wave of need through me.

My hand drops to my mound.

"No." He yanks it away for the third time since we got into his bed. "I'll touch you when I'm ready."

"I'm ready now," I protest with a pout. "If you help me come, I'll help you."

The laugh that escapes him sends a vibration through my body. I try and push my legs apart, but he's pinned me to the bed. I can feel the weight of his heavy, thick cock on my thigh.

"Fuck me," I whisper.

For that, I'm rewarded with a harder bite of my nipple.

I yelp in pain. "Oh, God."

"You loved it." He looks up at me with his intensely blue eyes. "You love all of it."

I nod twice. "I'll love it more if you fuck me."

Without warning, Barrett moves back on his knees and flips me over. With an arm under my stomach, he scoops me up, until my ass is in the air. I breathe deep.

I'm exposed. I'm so exposed to him.

I feel him behind me. "Goddamn, this is beautiful. You are exquisite, my Bella."

Tears fill my eyes when his fingers part my tender flesh and his tongue trails over my cleft.

"This is what I want," he growls. "You are what I want. Always."

Chapter 50

Barrett

Wrapping Bella in my arms, I take a second to catch my breath.

I ate her to two orgasms before I crawled up her body and kissed her senseless. The need to be inside of her is driving me mad, but there's something I want more.

I want the peace that I feel when she's close to me. When we are like this, body-to-body with no barriers and nothing between us, my world feels settled in a way it never has before.

I feel like I'm home.

"You're so good at that," she whispers. "Like the best ever."

I've been tempted to ask about her past lovers. I know about Emil, but frankly, I don't give a shit about how many men she's been with or when any of that happened.

"I'm ready," she announces.

An uncontrollable laugh barrels through me. "What the fuck are you ready for?"

"You just said it." She plants a wet kiss on my jaw.

I cup the back of her head to tug her closer to me. "You're not shy about sex. I fucking love that."

"I fucking love sex." She enunciates each word with a tap of her fingers on my chest. "It's better than good food."

I would have disagreed before we met, but now I can't. Sex with her is on another level. It's not just about the physical release. With Bella, it's tied to my emotions.

Pulling away from her, I reach behind me for the condom package I tossed on the bed before I ate her out.

"Can I do it?" Her fingertips feather over my arm. "I've never done that."

I'm all for giving her every new experience she desires, even if it's rolling a condom onto my hard cock.

I hand it to her. "Be gentle."

A smile lights up her face. "I'm always gentle."

She is. Taking her time, she opens the package carefully before she sheathes me. "Is that good?"

"Perfect." I roll onto my back and tug her on top of me. "Like this. Ride me."

"Yes," she purrs, placing her hands in the center of my chest for leverage.

She crawls onto my body, straddling my stomach. The slickness of her pussy sets my hands on her waist.

"Slide back." I push her back. "I need to be inside of you."

Circling her hand around the base of my dick, she lowers herself slowly over the swollen head. I clench my teeth when her wet heat clasps around me, and when she takes all of me, I throw my head back on the bed.

"Yes, yes, yes," she chants with each slide of her body over mine.

I take control, gripping her hips to set the rhythm as I spear up into her over and over until I feel her clench around me before I come with an intensity that tears right through me.

***

I stand in the hallway and listen to Bella on the phone. I don't know a word of Italian, but I've got enough of a grasp of English to piece together what she's saying.

She was up and out of bed when her phone rang for the third time.

That was after we'd fucked twice. Dusk has settled over Manhattan now, so I thought I'd figure out what to feed my beautiful executive assistant. I think she's got that covered.

She's talking to her grandmother. I've heard her mention bruschetta and manicotti. I'm hopeful that we'll be dining on both within the hour.

"I'll be there, grandma." She sighs. "I'll come early to help with the food."

I walk into the kitchen to grab a glass of water, listening intently to her side of the conversation.

"Mom and dad are coming." She glances over her shoulder when she hears me open the cupboard door. "Gina has a work thing tomorrow, but Max will be there. He'll want to come early too so he can help clean the squid for the calamari. You know it's his favorite job in the kitchen."

She laughs in response to whatever her grandma says. A flurry of Italian words follow before she takes a breath.

"Tell Alfie I'll meet him in the lobby in thirty minutes," she says before pausing for a beat. "I love you too. See you tomorrow."

Ending the call, she drops her phone on the couch. "I'll need to get dressed before the food comes."

Approaching with the glass of water in my hand for, I nod. "I don't want Alfie seeing you in just your panties and bra."

Glancing down at her body, she laughs. "If I went anywhere looking like this, my grandma would lock me away for eternity."

Taking the glass from me, she swallows half of the water in one gulp. I wait for her to finish before I ask the obvious question. "What's going on tomorrow?"

Her gaze slides over my bare chest. I slipped on a pair of sweatpants before I left the bedroom. I would have been fine walking around with a naked ass, but I've yet to figure out how the hell to operate the blinds in this place.

The penthouse is wired to a home hub that controls virtually everything. I don't have the patience to sit down and program the thing.

"Tomorrow?" She tilts her head. "Who said anything was going on tomorrow?"

251

I hold back a smile. Isabella can't play dumb. It doesn't work for her. "What are you helping your grandmother with tomorrow?"

She hands the glass back to me. "Calvetti Sunday lunch. Any Calvetti in the five boroughs has to be at the restaurant at one o'clock so we can eat a meal together."

I wait for her to ask me to tag along, but she just stands in that sexy-as-fuck lingerie looking like every dream I've ever had.

She gazes down at her thumbnail before she starts rubbing at it. "My grandma started it forever ago. It happens every couple of months. She does it so she can see her children and grandchildren all in one place."

I've never met the family of any woman I've been involved with. Alyssa pushed for me to meet her parents, but I put it off until I broke things off between us. It's different with Bella. I want in on this and if I have to invite myself, I will.

"Does your last name have to be Calvetti to score an invite?"

"No." Her head shakes. "We don't all have the same last names. There will be Calvettis there and Joneses. And two of my cousins are Dalens."

"What about Adler?" I scratch my chin. "Can an Adler come?"

"You?" Both of her brows perk with the question.

I'd go for a joke here about my dad not being the life of the party, but I want to be at the Calvetti family gathering, so I stick to the serious approach. "I'd like to come with you."

Her gaze narrows. "You want to meet my family?"

"I do."

"There are a lot of us," she says simply. "Some of my family is overbearing. Are you sure you're comfortable with that?"

"Positive."

Her face lights up with a smile. "Lunch is at one at the restaurant. We can meet there."

The manners Monica instilled in me kick in. "Should I bring anything?"

"Peonies," she answers without hesitation.

I can handle picking up flowers on my way to Calvetti's. "Done."

"Marti's favorite is pink." She claps her hands together. "She'll love you forever if you bring her pink peonies."

It's a step in the right direction. I have a feeling Marti's approval means everything to Isabella, so I'll do whatever it takes to earn it.

Chapter 51

Bella

"You invited Hot Boss to meet the parents?" Max adjusts the hem of the dark blue sweater he's wearing. Underneath is a white dress shirt. "How do I look?"

I stand back to take him in. "You're killing it today."

"If I knew we were inviting boyfriends I would have asked Dr. Dan to join us."

I've failed miserably in the best friend department lately. I've devoted so much time to my job and my boss, that I haven't made time for Max. "Barrett kind of invited himself and he's not my boyfriend."

I hold up a red jumpsuit. "What about this?"

"Hard no." Max gazes past me to my closet. "Do you still have that wine-colored wrap dress? You need that and your nude heels."

I never put this much thought into what I'll wear to our family lunches, but today is different. Today my parents and Marti are going to meet the man I'm falling for.

I twist around so I can rummage through my closet in search of that dress.

"If he's not your boyfriend, what is he?" Max asks from behind me.

"My boss," I say with a laugh.

I glance over my shoulder to see him sorting through the long silver necklaces I tossed on my bed earlier.

"You're fucking him," he points out with a grin. "That widens the scope of what he is to you. It puts him in at least the lover zone. If your heart is invested in this, he's crossed over to the boyfriend zone."

Scratching my head, I turn my attention back to my overcrowded closet. "It's somewhere between lover and boyfriend."

"He thinks he's in the boyfriend zone."

I push my well-worn white robe over so I can peek in the back of my closet. "He doesn't think that."

"Who is the last guy who asked to meet your family?"

I spot a sliver of wine colored fabric. Leveraging my shoulder against the doorjamb, I tug on it hard. "No one has ever asked to meet my family. Emil didn't want to."

"Emil was a jackass." He laughs. "Your boss wants to meet your family because he's your boyfriend, Bella."

I stumble when the dress finally comes free. "I've got it."

Max tosses me a wink. "You've got a hot dress and a boyfriend. Admit that you can see a future with this guy."

I can see forever when I look at Barrett. Giving a voice to that scares me. It feels too good to be true.

"I admit that I can see having lunch with him," I counter. "We can talk about the future after Marti interrogates him."

"He'll pass with flying colors." He tosses a necklace at me. "Get ready, so we can go. I'm dying to see what your family thinks about boyfriend boss."

***

I stand and stare out the window of Calvetti's. At least half of my extended family is already here. I've opened a few bottles of red wine, and more than a dozen cans of soda for those who don't partake of alcohol.

Marti always makes up a batch of her fruit punch for my younger cousins.

The joyous laughter behind me fills me with a type of comfort I can only find with my family.

They've always been there for me.

I can't remember a time when they weren't.

Every time I see my Uncle Robbie, he reminds me that I was bald until my first birthday. My cousin Arlo always mentions that he was responsible for my Halloween costume when was I four. It was a combination of a princess and a pirate.

Cybil, my aunt, never tires of telling me about the time when Gina got hold of one of the red permanent markers Marti has always used to write on the brown paper take-out bags. My sister was eight at the time. I was five. I emerged from the kitchen of this restaurant with red cheeks, red eyelids, and a bright red nose.

I don't remember any of it.

Marti tells me that's because I've lived so much life since then that newer memories pushed out the old ones. Each memory I do have is a treasure to me.

I turn and face the people who love me the most in the world.

Soon my parents will arrive, and my grandma and then the man I'm falling in love with. This feels like a new beginning for me.

"Izzy C," my cousin, Luke Jones, approaches with a glass of water in his hand. "You look happy."

"I am happy," I tell him. "I'm really happy."

He wraps an arm around my shoulder to tug me closer. "No one deserves it more than you. I can't wait to meet whoever put that smile on your face." "You don't have to wait." I look up into his blue eyes. "He'll be here for lunch."

"He must be a brave man." He laughs. "Facing this many Calvettis at once isn't for the faint-hearted."

I scrub at the polish on my thumbnail. "Neither is running into burning buildings."

"I'm a fireman." He taps his finger in the center of the black T-shirt covering his chest. "I put on the gear and get the job done. Your guy is about to meet grandma for the first time. No gear. No backup."

"I think he can handle it."

"You're special to her, Bella." He kisses my forehead. "To all of us. He better be good to you, or he'll have to answer to Marti, and me, and every single person in this room."

My family is fiercely protective of me, but Barrett is too. I have a feeling that by the end of the afternoon, they'll be just as crazy about him as I am.

Chapter 52

Barrett

Just as I'm about to step into Calvetti's my phone rings again. I glance down at the screen. It's Monica. This is the third time she's called since I left my place. I ignore the call yet again before I slide the phone back in the front pocket of my pants.

I ditched the suit I was going to wear for gray pants and a black sweater. I don't know the dress code for a Calvetti family gathering, so I went with cleaned up, yet comfortable.

I glance through one of the windows at the front of the restaurant. There are at least sixty people inside. I know I want this, but damn if I'm not nervous as hell right now.

Looking down at the peonies in my hand, I take a deep breath and pull open the door.

The smells and sounds immediately strike me. The aroma of good Italian food wafts in the air. The voices in the room overpower a group of small children racing around with their sneakers squeaking against the tile floor.

People are talking in Italian, others in English, but it's the small group in the center of the room that I can't take my eyes off of.

Isabella is standing next to a man and a woman. The woman is her height. The man is taller. I watch their profiles as they carry on a conversation.

They're at least ten feet from where I am, and with the voices surrounding me, it would be impossible to hear them if they were speaking verbally to one another.

But they are talking. They're speaking in sign language.

I stare at them knowing I should approach, but I hang back. I don't move because I know they're talking about me.

Bella signs to both of them. I met him at a restaurant. I thought he was my date, but he wasn't. I sat down at his table by mistake.

How the fuck did I not realize that she knows sign language?

The woman laughs loudly. It's almost identical to Isabella's laugh. Her voice quiets once she starts talking. I'm too far way to hear what she's saying, but I can read the movements of her hands. And now he's your boss?

The man pats Bella's arm softly. You like this man, my girl? He makes you happy?

Bella's face lights up in a smile. I think I love him, dad. I haven't told him yet.

My heart races in my chest. I felt it. I sensed that she loved me too.

Her dad smiles back at her, his hands moving fluidly. He won't know unless you tell him. Your mom told me she loved me first.

The woman next to him turns her attention to Bella. I love you was the first sign your dad taught me. I think it was a hint about how he felt about me.

Watching her mom's hands, Bella laughs. Your love story is my favorite.

Until now. Your love story will be one for the ages. Her dad signs before he kisses her forehead.

Since no one has noticed me yet, I take a step to the side to give me more time to adjust to what I'm seeing. A woman to my left looks familiar to me. Her brown hair is cut short. Her eyes are bright blue.

A man calls her Cybil, but I've never met a Cybil.

Still, there's something about her, and many of the faces in here that makes me feel like I know them.

Suddenly, everyone parts and quiets down as an older woman emerges from the kitchen. Max, Bella's friend, is on her heel.

The woman wipes her hands on a white apron tied around her waist as she heads straight to Bella and her parents.

"Dolly," she calls out. "I need your help." Dolly?

I close my eyes against the memory of the last time I heard that name. It was the last time I heard that woman's voice.

When I look again, Bella is in the woman's arms. "I'm coming, grandma. I was just telling mom and dad about him."
Him? Me.

I'm the asshole who ran like a coward when I was fifteen-years-old. I left Bella's grandmother in tears on her knees in the middle of a street on the Upper West Side.

A rush of memories hits me. The sound of Martina Calvetti sobbing, the sight of blood, and the small motionless hand holding tightly to the stick of a red heart-shaped lollipop that was shattered into countless pieces on the street.

What my father said to me that day and in the days that followed makes no sense. None of this makes any fucking sense.

My phone starts up again in my pocket, sending glances my way. Bella and her mom turn to look, but not her dad.

Bella's face lights up like the goddamn Empire State Building when she sees me.

I'm the man she loves.

I'm also the jerk who didn't stick around to help her when she was a kid.

How the fuck is this happening?

I silence my phone again as she approaches.

"You're here." She stops just short of jumping in my arms.

She's so beautiful. Dammit, so fucking beautiful and so kind. After everything she's been through she still sees the good in the world. She saw the good in me.

"Are you alright?" I ask, my voice breaking.

I've wanted to ask her that question for nineteen years. I've thought about her every single fucking day for nineteen years.

Her blue eyes scan my face. "Are you okay, Barrett?"

My phone rings again. I shake my head.

"Should you get that?" she asks, her hand jumping to my forearm.

"It's Monica," I manage to say in a strangled tone.

"Your mom?" She steps closer. "It might be important."

The volume in the room rises when people burst out in laughter. I hang my head, needing quiet and time. Quiet so I can think and I need time to tell Bella who I am and how I wish I could go back to that day.

Moving past me, she pushes the handle on the door. "Let's go outside for a minute."

I'm grateful. I follow her out, stepping to the side until we're both out of viewing range of the people inside the restaurant.

The ringing of my phone quiets but starts again almost immediately.

Bella's gaze drops to the screen. "It's your mom again. I think you need to answer it."

It's the last thing in the world I want to do, but I give in because it will give me an extra thirty seconds to think about how I will tell the woman I love that I hurt her.

"Mother," I spit into my phone. "What is it?"

"Your father," she says through a sob. "He's in the hospital. It's not good."

The fear and sorrow that should be flooding me finds no room because I'm too fucking confused and numb. I can't feel anything but shame and regret right now.

It serves me right. This is my punishment for what happened years ago. I fell in love with the person I hurt most in the world.

Fuck you, fate.

"What hospital?" I bark back.

"Hospital?" Bella mumbles under her breath. "Your mom?"

I shake my head.

"Your dad?" she whispers.

I nod before I'm treated to another wailing sob from my mother who is putting on a show worthy of a nomination for worst actress ever. She's told me all too many times that she wished my father would drop dead. Today her wish may come true.

I need time with him first to understand his lies.

Handing off the peonies to Bella, I rake a hand through my hair. "What hospital, Mother?"

She manages to get out the name of a hospital in San Francisco.

I stumble through a civil goodbye to her after I repeat the hospital's name back to be sure I got it right.

"You need to go," Bella says before I can get out a word out after I pocket my phone. "I'll explain to everyone here about your dad. I can call Ivan too and let him know that you can't go to Chicago."

I cup my hands over her cheeks. Feathering kisses over her delicate forehead, I close my eyes. "I'm sorry, Bella. I am so sorry."

Pulling back, she looks into my eyes. "Don't be sorry. I understand."

Pressing a kiss to her mouth, I breathe in deeply. "Please try and forgive me."

"There's nothing to forgive you for." She glances down at the flowers in her hand. "Go see your dad."

With a final kiss to her lips, I walk away from the woman I love.

Chapter 53

Bella

I look down at my hand. The blue nail polish that was on my thumbnail is long gone thanks to my anxiety. A sinking feeling has taken root in my stomach. It's been there since Sunday when Barrett left me standing on the sidewalk outside of Calvetti's.

I've only heard from him twice since then.

The first time was on Monday morning when he texted me to say he was sorry again.

I sent him a message back telling him not to worry. My family understood why he had to rush off. Marti was most concerned. When she held the bouquet of peonies Barrett had brought to her nose, she asked if he needed anything.

She would have chased him down the street with a bag filled with food if I had let her.

When I asked how his dad was in my responding text, his answer was short and to the point – fine.

The second time he sent me a message was late on Wednesday night.

I had fallen asleep an hour before with the television blaring. I didn't hear the chime. I woke up at six a.m and read the message, but didn't reply right away because it was so early in California.

That message was all business.

He asked me if I could please reach out to Ivan again since they hadn't connected. He wanted to speak to him. I got in touch with Ivan once I was at the office. He agreed to call Barrett, so I texted my boss back to let him know.

That was over twenty-four hours ago, and I haven't heard a word since.

Taking a sip from the cup of coffee in my hand, I drop my eyes to the crossword puzzle in front of me.

The clue I'm stuck on is a four-letter word for when it's finished.

The chime of the elevator arriving draws my gaze up. When the doors fly open, I bolt up in my chair and slide the crossword under the folder on my desk.

Marching toward me with a grim look on his face is Ivan Garent.

"Isabella," he says my name somberly. "Come into Duke's office. We need to talk."

It's Barrett's office I want to say, but something tells me that everything is about to change.

***

"How's Duke?" That's my first question because it's one I know he needs to hear.

"It's a long process." He motions toward the door. "Please shut the door so we can have some privacy."

I do as he asks, skimming my hands over the skirt of my dark green dress. I'm a bundle of nerves. Something incredibly important must be going on if it took him away from his family.

When I turn back to face him, Ivan has settled in Barrett's office chair. He looks out of place. Nothing feels right anymore.

"Sit, please."

I lower myself onto of the two chairs that face the desk. Clearing my throat, I wait for him to say something.

With perked brows, he stares at me. "Is there something you'd like to say?"

For a brief moment, I wonder if he's here because he knows about Barrett and me. Did someone tell him that we're more than just boss and executive assistant? Maybe one of our co-workers saw us together on the subway or at Crispy Biscuit.

"No." I keep my answer simple. I won't confess to something I'm not sure he's aware of.

Clasping his hands together in front of him on the desk, he leans forward. "Barrett resigned this morning. He won't be coming back to Garent."

Time slows as I take in those words.

"His father is gravely ill," he goes on. "I offered him a leave of absence, but he assured me that wasn't what he wanted. He arranged for the removal of his personal items from the penthouse this morning."

Slow down. I try to spit those words out, but they catch in my throat.

"I assume he's moving to California to take over Adler Estates." He sighs. "We've lost one of the best, but if I understand one thing it's a strong commitment to family. Barrett is doing what he needs to for his father."

"I didn't think he was close to his dad," I whisper.

"He never spoke of him until he now." Ivan narrows his gaze. "Something like this puts everything into perspective. Illness, death, even addiction can rearrange a man's priorities."

What about love?

I thought Barrett loved me. I thought we had a future together here at Garent and in life.

Ivan pushes back from the desk to stand. "I'm sending Nellie Garlin from Chicago here as interim CEO. She'll arrive early next week. Bring her up to speed on everything, Isabella. I trust you'll handle the change in leadership as gracefully this time as you did when Barrett took over for Duke."

Still stunned, I rise to my feet. "I'll do my best, sir."

"Gather Barrett's things up." He opens one of the desk drawers before he slams it shut. "I'll contact him again to find out where to have it all sent."

I nod as he brushes past me. "Let's keep Garent moving forward, Isabella. That's what Duke would have wanted."

I follow him out of the office, plopping myself in my chair as he boards the waiting elevator.

Yanking my crossword puzzle out from its hiding spot, I read the clue I've been stuck on again.

A four-letter word for when it's finished.

I fill in the blanks. OVER

Just like Barrett and me.

Chapter 54

Bella

"You texted him how many times since you got here?" Max tries to steal a glimpse of the screen of my cell phone, but I press it against the center of my chest.

"Two text messages and one call that went straight to his voicemail," I answer without hesitation. "I haven't gotten a response yet."

When his eyes meet mine, I see pity. I don't want that from him. I want my best friend to tell me to forget about my boss and move on. I need Max to tell me that any man who ghosts a woman and slides out of her life without a word deserves to be placed in the run and done category.

You run away from him as fast as you can, and you stay done with him for eternity.

That's how I need to view Barrett. It's how I should view our short-lived relationship, but I can't.

I want an explanation. I deserve to know what happened.

"How many times did you text and call him before you got here?" he presses.

"Zero," I answer truthfully.

After Ivan left the office late this afternoon, I was in shock. I couldn't reach out to Barrett because I knew if I did, it would be coming from a place of raw emotion. I needed a few hours to collect my thoughts before I got in contact with him.

The text messages I sent him and the voicemail all contained the same four words: We need to talk.

"Are you going to text him again?" Max asks hesitantly.

"No." I toss my phone onto the couch next to me. "At least not tonight."

Max moves closer to me. Setting a hand on my jean-covered knee, he looks into my eyes. "You don't have to be strong, Bella. It's okay to cry."

I don't want to cry.

If I start, I'm not sure I'll stop.

"I want to keep my emotions in check, so when I do speak to Barrett, I can give him an earful."

Max leans back and clucks his tongue. "Oh, man. Hot Boss is in the direct line of the Calvetti wrath."

I try to suppress a laugh, but a giggle bubbles out of me.

"You've got this, Bella." He taps my knee. "You've lived through a lot worse."

He's not talking about my break-up with Emil. He's talking about the accident when I was a kid.

We were friends back then. Max remembers his mom crying when my mom called her with the news that I was in the hospital.

"I lived through the dinner you just cooked me," I joke. "So far. We'll see what the next few hours bring."

"That chicken did smell off, didn't it?" He plays along with me.

He knows full well that the dinner he prepared was delicious. I went straight home after work to shower the day away. I stood in the water until it ran cold. As I was toweling off, Max called to ask me to come to his place to help organize more of his family pictures. The lure was a dinner of maple glazed chicken and roasted sweet potatoes.

It was the first dish he ever cooked me when he moved into this apartment. I brought cheap wine that night. We got drunk and sang the songs we learned in grade school.

It was one of the best nights of my life.

"Why did I fall in love with him?" I ask in a voice too weary to be my own.

Once I'm home tonight in my bed, I'll let emotion overcome me. I'll cry myself to sleep wondering what could have been.

"Because he's your person," Max says matter-of-factly.

Confused, I glance at him. "If he were my person, he wouldn't have left me."

"Who says he left you?"

I take in his words, trying to make sense of them. "Ivan did. Barrett did without actually saying it to my face."

Max shakes his head. "Ivan said he quit his job and cleared out the penthouse."

I nod. "Exactly."

"That means nothing for you other than the fact that you have another new boss to get used to."

"It means he left Garent without telling me," I point out, slightly annoyed that Max is taking Barrett's side in this even though we have no clue what that is.

"You don't know why he did that." He leans back on his couch. "It may have everything to do with his dad or nothing to do with him."

Tired of arguing the point, I bring up the man himself. "Barrett didn't give me a warning, Max. He quit and moved without a word to me."

"He did make some major moves without your input," he acquiesces. "I think you need to consider the fact that he's in love with you too and knows that you can't take things to the next level if you're both working at Garent."

I huff out a laugh. "If he sacrificed the job he's wanted for years for me, you would think he'd tell me that."

"Love messes with a man's brain." He twirls a finger in front of his forehead. "Look at me."

I do. I stare at my best friend. "Are you in love?"

"Head over half-inch heels I am." He takes my hands in his. "Dr. Dan gets me, Bella. He gets all of this and loves it."

"I need to meet him." I smile. "Soon, Max."

Gathering me in his strong arms, he kisses the top of my head. "As soon as you work out your forever with your prince charming, I'll take you to meet mine."

I won't crush the fairytale ending he thinks I have coming my way. Right now, I'm holding onto the faintest sliver of hope that Barrett will burst back into my life with an explanation for everything that's happened since the last time I saw him.

Chapter 55

Barrett

Life can change in the blink of an eye.

That's what happened in this neighborhood nineteen years ago.

I look down at my phone to reread the messages that Bella sent me while I was in the air flying back here to start a new life.

With a trembling hand, I type out the most important text message I've ever sent.

Barrett: Please meet me at the corner of Amsterdam and 78th.

It's cruel to send Bella a message so early in the morning, but I've been anxious to talk to her since I got back to New York late last night.

It's Saturday.

The sun rose less than an hour ago.

I noticed it filling the bedroom of my new apartment. I wasn't woken by it. I had been up all night working on my future. It's a future that I want to spend with Isabella Calvetti, if she'll have me.

Once the clock hit seven, I headed to the stairs that took me three floors down to the ground level of my building.

From there, I set out on the pavement to the coffee shop at the corner of my block.

It may have been my first time walking through the door, but the people behind the counter made me feel welcome. They wanted to know my name and what I did for a living.

That's a work-in-progress, but I know I'll be fine.

As long as Bella loves me, I can face anything in this world.

When I finished the coffee, I made my way to the subway. I took it to the same stop that Bella had brought me.

The buzz of my phone in my hand twists my stomach upside down. I pray to God she'll come.

Bella: Right now?

Without hesitating, I reply.

Barrett: As soon as you can.

I glance around at this area of the city on a lazy Saturday morning. Some people are already up, jogging past me headed toward Central Park. Others are out looking for their first jolt of caffeine.

My eyes drop when I hear the sound of the chime and feel the buzz in my palm.

Bella: Are you okay?

My love is always worrying about everyone else. I've been through hell this week, but it's nothing compared to what she's lived through.

I answer truthfully.

Barrett: I'll be better when I see you.

Her response is instant.

Bella: I'm on my way.

I am too. I'm on my way to forgiveness and a path where I can cherish the woman that was meant for me if she'll have me.

Sliding my phone into the back pocket of my jeans, I take off on foot to make my way to the spot where my life changed forever.

***

I see her before she sees me. I take in how gorgeous she looks.

She's dressed in faded jeans, an oversized white sweater, and black low-heeled boots. Her hair is loose and in waves. She looks freshly woken.

She rushed here.

She stops at the corner and twirls in a circle. I raise a hand hoping she'll spot me, but her gaze darts past me.

I stand from where I've been resting my ass on a swing.

I'm in the playground of a public school. It's the same playground where I first met Isabella Calvetti.

She stormed into my life that day as a wide-eyed, smart-as-a-whip five-year-old kid wearing a baseball cap backward on her head.

She didn't care that I was older than her. She put me in my place. She urged me to do the right thing, and when she ran across the busy street right into the path of oncoming traffic, I tried my best to do right by her.

On her second spin, she notices me.

I hold up my hand to wave her over.

She points at the green light, silently telling me that she has to wait until the path is clear.

I'll wait as long as it takes if it means she's safe.

Chapter 56

Bella

I came because I want answers.

I was awake when he sent me a text message. I'd been up most of the night rehearsing what I wanted to say to him, but now that I'm looking at him, I only want to know why he's made such drastic changes in his life.

I walk slowly to where he's standing next to the swings I used to play on.

They've been spruced up since I was a child. The chains have been replaced and covered with plastic tubing so small fingers won't get pinched. The seats aren't wooden like they were back when I came here after school. Now, they're made from a pliable plastic, so they bend more easily to whoever is sitting on them.

I breeze past Barrett and take a seat on one, wrapping my fingers around the clear plastic tubing. "How are you?"

He answers quickly. "Sorry. I'm sorry, Isabella."

"For?" I leave the question open-ended for a reason. I want to hear him tell me what he's sorry for. I don't want to feed him anything.

"Everything," he spits out.

I finally gaze up into his face. His jaw is covered with a few days' growth of beard. His hair is uncombed. The black T-shirt he's wearing is wrinkled.

He looks like he hasn't slept in days.

"I asked you to come here for a reason." He scrubs a hand over the back of his neck. "I chose this spot because I needed to see you here."

My eyes dart from his face to the street that I just crossed. "Why here?"

He crouches in front of me. His feet are inside shoes that are too expensive for the matted brown grass they're touching. "We met here, Bella. We met right in this spot nineteen years ago."

I shake my head. Maybe he's delusional from lack of sleep or grief over his dad's condition. "We met at Atlas 22."

His hands move quickly in front of him. You played with my sister that day. You played with Bizzy.

It takes me a second to realize that Barrett knows sign language.

Confusion rushes through me. Shaking my head, I get up off the swing and walk around him, headed out of the playground.

He can't be that boy. He can't be Bizzy's brother.

I don't really remember him. All I know is what my grandmother told me about him and small flashes of memories that only come to me when I'm asleep.

He was the boy who came to the park with his eight-year-old sister. She was deaf. He couldn't sign.

Marti told me that I gave him hell for not learning how to talk to her.

I schooled him on how to say hi, and bye, and most importantly I love you.

"Bella," he says my name as his hand falls on my shoulder to stop me. "Please let me explain. I've waited nineteen years to explain."

"You're not him," I say with my back to him.

"I'm him," he insists. "You had a baseball cap on your head. Mets, I think."

"Yankees." I turn to face him.

My brother loves the Yankees. The cap was a hand-me-down from him. I'm wearing it in many of the pictures my mom took of me when I was a kid. After the accident, I never saw it again.

I've never mentioned the cap to Barrett.

"You gave me shit for not knowing how to sign." His hands move in unison with his words as he signs.

I wish I could remember every detail of that day.

"I don't remember that."

"I had to take care of Bizzy that day. I couldn't communicate with her." He bows his head. "She couldn't read lips. I couldn't sign."

I've always known how to sign. My dad is deaf. In our family, you learn sign language at the same pace as you learn how to talk.

"Your grandma gave her candy." He smiles. "It was a red heart-shaped lollipop. She gave you one too."

My grandma always kept a bunch of candies in her purse for her grandkids and any kids who came into the restaurant.

"That sounds like my grandma," I whisper.

"Bizzy signed something to her...thank you, I think." He gazes at my face. "You jumped right into the middle of that, and you two hit it off. She must have told you I didn't know how to talk to her because you turned to me and asked what kind of big brother I was."

I fight to hold back a smile. "I was taught it's always best to say what you feel."

"Oh, you did." He laughs. "I learned sign language after that day. I wanted to talk to my sister. I needed to talk to her after what happened on that street."

***

I can't relive that day because I don't remember it.

All I know is what Marti told me.

We all left the playground together. Bizzy had a ball she found at the park in her hands. I was still working on the lollipop my grandma had given me.

Marti stood at the corner talking to Bizzy's brother, or maybe it was at him.

Whenever she tells me the story of that day, she says that he was quiet. In her eyes, he was embarrassed that he was taking care of someone he couldn't talk to.

Bizzy was bouncing her ball, harder with each slap of it in the pavement on the sidewalk.

My grandma's not sure of what happened next, but the ball flew into the street, and I took off after it to get it back for Bizzy.

"Isabella?"

I glance at Barrett before my eyes wander to a family that just arrived at the park. The parents are cradling large cups of coffee in their hands while their two little girls squeal in delight at the unoccupied play equipment.

"Will you come with me to my apartment so we can talk more?"

I study his face. "You have an apartment? Here in the city?"

I thought he was moving across the country. If he's not, how did he rent a place in New York this quickly? He just moved out of the penthouse yesterday.

Holding a hand out, he nods. "I found the perfect place. I'd like to show you."

I drop my hand in his, trusting that this is a journey I need to take with him.

Chapter 57

Barrett

A million questions are running through her head. I see it in her eyes.

We didn't speak on the subway, and the words we've exchanged since have been mostly about the neighborhood that I'm now calling home.

Park Slope in Brooklyn.

I open the weathered white wooden door of my apartment with the key in my hand. Swinging it open, I motion for her to step inside.

She does so silently.

I stand behind her watching as she glances around the two-bedroom apartment. It's slightly bigger than the place I had in Chicago.

The furniture is modest but functional.

A simple black leather sofa sits in the middle of the room. In front of it is a rectangular glass coffee table.

Near the window there's a small circular table and two chairs.

The extra bedroom has a double bed and a dresser. In the master, there's a queen-size bed and one nightstand.

I'll donate all of it once my furniture from Chicago gets here.

"You live here?" she asks with a glance over her shoulder.

I nod in reply. "I moved in late last night."

Her eye catches on a note pinned to the wall near the door. "Is this a short term rental?"

"Was." I tug the note free of the pin. Crumbling it in my hand, I go on, "Felicity mentioned that she was renting out the apartment she lived in before she got married last year. I'm buying the place. We'll start getting the details sorted on Monday."

"Your sister lived here?" She watches as I toss the paper into a wastebasket near the door.

"I live here now."

The corners of her mouth tug up. "I like it."

"Me too."

Her gaze finally settles on my face. "You're Bizzy's brother?"

I can't imagine what's running through her mind. We dove into a relationship oblivious to the fact that we shared a horrific experience in the past.

Our future will make up for it. I'll make sure of that each day I get to have on this earth with her.

"Beatrice's nickname when she was a kid was Bizzy," I explain. "Your nickname was Dolly?"

"Is." She lets out a laugh. "Marti is the only one who calls me that. She says that I'm her little doll. Her Dolly."

Of course she is. They must share an unbreakable bond.

"I'm sorry, Bella." I choke back a rush of emotion. "I'm sorry I took off that day."

Her eyes narrow as she studies my face. "Please don't say sorry."

"I wanted to find you after I took Bizzy home." I exhale harshly.

"My dad stopped me cold. He said he would call every hospital until he found you. He told me he spoke to your dad on the phone."

She shakes her head softly. "No. That didn't happen. It couldn't have happened."

I know that now. He finally admitted it this past week when he was trapped in a hospital bed with tubes attached to him.

When I ran into his apartment with Bizzy in my arms, my father lost it. He screamed at me about responsibility and trust. Once my sister was calmed down, he left the room to check on the girl who had been hurt.

He came back with a tale about the girl's prognosis. He told me she'd never fully recover from her head injury, and her life was forever changed. He went on about all the anger that family felt toward me. I demanded to know their names so I could find them and get on my knees and beg for forgiveness, but he told me to shut up about it. With a wag of his finger in my face, he told me her father wished I had died on that street. They wanted to be left alone, so he shipped me back to Chicago thinking that I had ruined lives.

The lie was to protect the only thing he valued in me. That was the promise of a future in football.

He told me that he didn't want me to ruin my chances of a scholarship to Michigan State by admitting my part in the girl's injuries. It turned out my game wasn't good enough to get me anywhere without him footing the entire bill for my education.

"I'm sorry I didn't find you sooner, Bella." I hang my head. "I should have done more. I could have hired a private investigator. I checked the archives of the newspaper, but there was nothing about the accident."

She moves closer to me. "Barrett?"

When I look up, tears are clouding her beautiful blue eyes. I reach for her face, cradling it in my hands.

"Thank you."

I wipe a tear from her cheek. "For what, Bella?"

Her hands move to cover mine. "For saving my life. The doctor told my parents if you hadn't pushed me out of the way, I wouldn't have survived."

I stare at her, trying to process what she just said.

"I'm sorry we didn't find each other sooner too." Her eyes lock on mine. "Marti looks for you everywhere. Whenever she passes a man with brown hair, or one walks into the restaurant, she studies his face. There's been something she's wanted to say to you since that day."

"What?" I croak out the word.

"I'll let her tell you." She springs up on her tiptoes to kiss the corner of my mouth. "Whenever you're ready, we'll go see her."

Glancing down at the watch on my wrist, I realize it's still morning. "Today?"

"Today."

Chapter 58

Bella

The Saturday lunch service at Calvetti's is always a treat. New people wander in as they scour this area of the city looking for a special place to eat.

My grandma takes time to stand at the door to greet diners. With a shake of her hand, they're welcomed into her restaurant as if it's her home. She's never turned anyone away even if they didn't have enough money to pay for their meal.

In those cases, she'd find something for them to do around the restaurant.

Her heart is the most beautiful I've ever known.

I walk in first with Barrett trailing behind me. He changed into a blue dress shirt that's not tucked into his jeans. He shaved and combed his hair while I waited in his new apartment.

It felt comfortable in a way the penthouse never did.

I haven't asked him about work yet, but that will come later.

Now, it's all about reuniting him with my grandma.

"Marti," I call out to her as she speaks to a table surrounded by people with graying hair.

I know that crew. She plays poker with them one night a month. Rocco taught her everything she knows. She's used her winnings to spruce up the kitchen.

She turns to face me. The apron around her waist is spotted with red sauce. Her cheeks are pink from the heat in the kitchen. The smile that takes over her mouth warms me through and through.

I'm about to give her the greatest gift in the world.

"I have a surprise," I say as she approaches.

Taking me in her arms, she pats the center of my back. "Sit, Dolly. There's lasagna. I made it myself."

"Grandma." I take a step back, reaching for her hands. "There's someone here to see you."

Her gaze flits across my face before it settles on the man standing behind me.

I feel her hands stiffen in mine just as her breath catches.

Tilting her head, she furrows her brow. "Dolly."

I let her go when I feel her tug away. Rounding me, she walks shakily toward Barrett. I turn to watch them.

"Mrs. Calvetti," he says her name with a tremor in his deep voice. "I'm so pleased to meet you."

She stops short of taking the hand he's offering. Instead, she leans back on her heels.

I move to stand next to Barrett so I can see the expression on her face.

The tears flowing down her cheeks give it away. She knows.

I have no idea what he looked like when she met him in nineteen years ago, but she recognizes him.

Stumbling forward she falls into his arms. "My boy. It's you. It's finally you."

With his shoulders rocking from the sobs running through him, he holds tight to her. "It's me. I'm here."

***

Once they parted, Barrett went to use the washroom. Marti took me in her arms as she watched him walk away.

We're seated now, at a table in the corner of the restaurant. My grandmother's hands are holding tight to the hands of the man I love.

"How did you find him?" She looks over at me. "Who helped you find him?"

I smile at Barrett. "Do you remember that man I told you about? The one I met at the restaurant when I thought he was my blind date?"

"Your boss?" Her nose scrunches. "The man you love?"

"That man loves her," Barrett interjects. "I'm that man."

Marti's gaze volleys from Barrett's face to mine and back again. "No."

"Yes," we say in unison.

"The boy who saved my Dolly will marry my Dolly?"

"Woah." I hold up a hand. "Grandma, slow it down."

"I'll marry her," Barrett says in a serious tone. "I want nothing more in this world than to be her husband."

That sets me back in my seat. "Barrett."

"Isabella." He turns to face me. "I love you. I damn well know you love me because I saw you sign it to your parents last week."

"You know sign language?" Marti gives him her full attention again. "You didn't know any back then."

"Your granddaughter gave me hell for that." He reaches to take one of my hands in his, all while still holding tight to Marti's hand. "I went home to Chicago and I studied. I needed to know how to talk to my sister."

"Bizzy." Marti's voice perks. "How is little Bizzy?"

"Beatrice," I correct her. "She goes by Beatrice now."

Ignoring me completely, Marti looks to Barrett. "How is she?"

"She's happy." He beams. "She's a teacher at a school in Brooklyn."

"You'll bring her for lunch one day," my grandma states. "I'll cook something special for her."

"She'll like that," Barrett says without reservation. "I think she'll like that."

A tear streams down Marti's face again. Drawing in a deep breath, she swallows hard. "You risked your life to save Bella. If you hadn't pushed her out of the path of that taxi, she would have…"

"I'm fine, grandma," I interrupt when I see emotion overtaking her. "I'm perfectly fine."

"Your head." Barrett nods his chin toward me. "You hit your head hard, Bella. Your nose was bleeding. You were knocked out cold."

Marti moves to cover his hand with hers. "It was a concussion. That's all. Some scrapes and bruises, but she was home two days later."

"I thought her injuries were more serious," Barrett confesses with a sigh. "I was told that she'd never be the same again."

"This girl," Marti begins before she turns to wink at me. "This girl of ours is one tough cookie. We were scared, but she showed us that she could handle anything."

I sit back and take in the moment. The man I love, and my grandma already share such a strong bond.

"What about Bizzy?" Marti asks. "She ran onto the street after you. I saw her fall on her knees."

Barrett explained that to me on the way here. After he ran into the street to save me, Bizzy took off after him. She only made it a few inches before one of her sandals flew off and she tumbled onto her knees on the hard pavement.

My grandma watched as Barrett grabbed my hand and swung me out of the way of the oncoming traffic. We fell to the street together, with his body shielding mine from the asphalt. My head hit, but the blow was softened because his arm was under my neck.

Barrett said it happened so fast that by the time Marti was on the street, he was on his feet rushing to help his sister.

"It was just a cut knee." Barrett turns to face me. "It scared her though. She knew Bella was bleeding from her nose. That's what she told my father when I got her back home."

Sorrow pools inside of me over what she must have felt and what Barrett's been through since that day.

"Everyone is good." Marti brings her hands together to join mine with Barrett's. "You two are in love. One day I'll have a grandbaby to love, and I'll tell him or her about how brave their daddy and mommy are."

"Grandma," I bite out her name with a smile. "This is very new."

"It's not new," she scoffs. "You met almost twenty years ago. You were meant to be together. Fate knows. I know. What more is there to know?"

Chapter 59

Bella

I roll onto my back. "I love this bed."

"I love you," Barrett reaches for my bare hip. "I love every inch of you, Isabella."

I snuggle closer to him.

We stripped naked once we got back to his new apartment after sharing a plate of lasagna and a glass of wine. Marti wanted us to stay, but I told her we needed time alone.

That brought her eyebrows up to her hairline. She whispered that I shouldn't play it safe since she wants a grandson who looks like Barrett.

I kissed her goodbye, and for the first time that I can remember, she didn't tell me to look both ways before I crossed the street.

Today, she told me to be happy.

I can't remember a time when I was this happy. I feel like my heart is going to explode out of my chest.

If this is love, I want to experience it forever.

"Tell me you love me, Bella." Barrett runs a fingertip over my chin. "I've only watched you sign it. I want to hear it."

Turning to face him, I kiss him softly before I whisper the three words. "I love you."

"Louder."

"I love you," I say with more volume.

"Fucking scream it." He laughs.

"I love you," I shout as loud as I can.

He closes his eyes. "Who knew those words could feed a man's soul?"

I slide over his body, gripping his shoulders for leverage. "I thought you had left me."

His gaze locks on mine. "Never. I swear to you that will never happen. My heart is joined to yours for eternity. This is my forever."

I steal a tender kiss from his mouth. "I want this to be forever."

"You're done, Bella." He tangles his hand in my hair. "I'm the one. You're done looking."

"I knew you were the one when I sat down at Atlas 22."

His chin lifts. "You did?"

"I felt something that night I'd never felt before," I confess. "I felt comfortable and complete."

Cupping a hand under my ass, he flips us over until he's hovering above me.

His thick cock rests against my inner thigh. "I always want you to feel that way with me. "

I want that too.

"You'll marry me," he says, inching his body closer to mine. "You'll be my bride one day."

Nodding, I let out a small moan. "I will, and you'll be my lover every day."

"For the rest of my goddamn life."

I suck in a breath when the tip of his cock slides over my slick cleft. "I'm on the pill. I'm clean if you want to…"

I cry out when he enters me without warning.

"Jesus," he bites out the word between clenched teeth. "I've never done this."

I haven't either.

The feeling of his bare flesh inside of me almost sets me over the edge. "I could come already."

"You will."

He pumps deep, and again. Each thrust is more exquisite than the last.

We make love with slow strokes with the sun hitting our skin as the world slips away.

***

Hours later, we're sitting on his bed with the sheets tangled around us.

"I spoke to Ivan when you fell asleep."

I had drifted off after we made love. Barrett had offered to clean me, but I wanted to feel his release. Once I woke, we showered in the tiny stall with his elbows hitting the walls and my laughter filling the small room.

I run a hand through my wet hair. "About coming back to Garent?"

"No," he answers quickly. "I have other plans."

"Adler Estates?"

"Hell, no." He laughs. "Irving will recover. He'll go back to barking out orders. I'll stay clear of that and him for now."

I arch an eyebrow. "There's hope for you two?"

He shrugs. "I have no fucking idea. Time will tell."

I move past the discussion about his dad. "What are your plans for work?"

"We'll get to that." He circles his fingertip over my bare thumbnail. "First, I want to tell you about my agreement with Ivan."

I move back slightly. "What agreement?"

"You're in charge of the rebranding of the bookstore." He jerks a thumb over his shoulder. "We're four blocks from there so on your way home from work every day you can stop in and check progress. You're taking the lead on this. It's hands-off for the interim CEO of Garent. This is all you."

I hone in on the one thing he just said that caused my heart to skip a beat. "On my way home?"

"Move in here, Bella." He rests a hand on my bare thigh. "Live with me. Love me. Let me spoil you with backrubs, and good food, and great sex."

"Yes," I say because I want nothing more. "I'll move in."

He kisses me softly on the mouth. "We'll bring your things over whenever you're ready."

Soon. I have to tell Gina. I know she'll be happy for me.

"I'm looking at office space a few blocks from Garent's building next week."

A smile curves my lips. "For?"

He kicks himself free of the tangled bed coverings before he stalks toward his clothes.

I stare at his body. "You're beautiful."

That rewards me with a dimpled grin. "Said the most beautiful person in the world."

I laugh off his comment. "What are you doing?"

He scoops his jeans off the floor and tugs something from the back pocket. "I made some mock-ups of my new business cards."

He hands his business card from Garent to me.

I question him silently with a perk of my brows.

"Turn it over."

I flip it and read what's written in his handwriting.

Adler Consulting

I look over at him when he settles next to me again. "You're starting your own business?"

With a curt nod, he answers. "I've been batting the idea around for years. I've saved a lot of money. It gives me enough of a cushion that I can take the plunge. Now seems like the perfect time."

With skepticism edging my tone, I ask the obvious question. "Did you quit Garent because of us?"

"I don't want to sneak around town with you." He tucks a lock of my hair behind my ear. "That factored into it, but there's more. Ivan planned to bring Duke back as CEO eventually. He told me as much when I called him from California. To stay with the company long-term, I would have had to move back to Chicago for a job there. I wanted out and Ivan let me go without a fight. I've considered starting my own venture for some time. This is the push I needed to do that."

I cock my head. "Tell me more about the business."

"There's value in helping people rework their visions. I saw that in what we started to do for Misty and Rusten. I saw it with Empire Soaks. I want to do more. Business management consulting, rebranding, corporate reorganization, you name it."

"Wow." I stare down at the card.

"This is your dream too, Bella." He reaches for my hand. "I saw it in that notebook you had in your desk drawer."

It is. This is what I'm working toward. I want my own firm, so I can help people achieve their dreams. I've been keeping notes for years about my vision. Working at Garent is giving me the hands-on knowledge that I need.

Another business card lands in my hand.

I glance up at him. "What is this?"

"Flip it over." He directs me with a spin of his fingers in the air.

I do.

Calvetti & Adler Consulting

My hand shakes as I read the words over and over. "Barrett."

"I know you're tied to Garent until your current contract is done." He runs a hand over my hair. "I'll get us off the ground and maybe by then, we'll be looking at this."

He pushes another card at me.

I flip it over immediately.

Adler & Adler Consulting

He taps a finger on the card. "You're the first Adler in that equation. I want to make that clear. You always come first."

Tossing the cards on the bed, I crawl on top of him. "You're going to make every one of my dreams come true, aren't you?"

With a slide of his hips against mine, he kisses me. "I am. Starting right now."

Epilogue

Six Months Later

Barrett

"This is our second wedding in three months," I point out to Isabella as I adjust the collar of the white button-down shirt I'm wearing. "First, Max and Dan, and now this vow renewal."

"Max eloped." She shrugs a little. "You had a good time in Vegas."

I had a fucking blast. Isabella and I did the strip right. We ate well, she gambled her way to a thirty thousand dollar windfall at a poker table, and we spent a hell of a lot of time in bed.

We've been enjoying as much time as we can together since I left Garent Industries and she moved in with me. She's working side-by-side with Nellie Garlin. Duke will return to his post next month. My business is flourishing and when Bella's contract with Garent runs out, she'll join me full-time. I left that decision in her hands, where it belongs.

Her first meeting with Beatrice was rough. There were a lot of tears and questions. Bizzy is still Team Irving, so it was hard for her to grasp that the things our father said back then weren't true.

We took Beatrice, Felicity, and her husband to meet Marti and Bella's parents at Calvetti's for dinner one night. The food was good. The conversation was even better.

Beatrice was happy to sit at a table where every person present could engage her in conversation. I kept up with everyone else. Learning sign language cemented my new bond with my sister. Time and healing will help us grow even stronger.

We don't have to see eye-to-eye on everything, but we love each other. That's what matters when you put your head on your pillow at night.

Monica's learning that lesson too. A new gray-haired actor at the community theater she's been directing at in Chicago has become an important part of her life. I'm happy for my mom. The drama he brings to her life is exactly the type she needed.

"I happen to think it's very romantic that Misty and Rusten want to renew their vows inside their store." She skims her palm over the front of the little black dress she's wearing. "A candlelit ceremony. Old books. What could be better than that?"

This is it.

I tug the small ring box out of the front pocket of my pants and drop to a knee on our bedroom floor.

"This is better."

That turns her right around.

Her mouth drops open.

"Isabella Calvetti." I look up into her beautiful blue eyes. "You were made for me."

"Are you asking me to marry you?" she interrupts.

Her bare feet pad across the hardwood floor until she's right in front of me.

"Let me get through this."

"May I?" She points at my leg.

May she what? I nod because I'm curious as hell.

Draping an arm around my neck, she sets her sweet ass down on my thigh as if it's a chair. "You go first."

"First?" I wrap my arm around her waist to balance her weight on my leg.

"I want to propose too."

Jesus, this woman. I love the unpredictably she's brought into my life. "Why don't you go first?"

"You're sure?" she asks with a smile.

I press a kiss to her mouth. "Go for it, beautiful."

Her fingers skim over my eyebrow. "I didn't know that a piece of my heart was missing until I found you."

Shit. This is going to rip me in two.

"You make me happy in ways I didn't know existed." Her fingertips run down my cheek. "If you marry me, I promise I'll make you that happy too."

"We'll conquer the world together, my Bella. We're a great team."

"Our baby is going to be so badass." She laughs.

My heart skips a beat. "When we have a baby it will be so badass."

We agreed to start trying a month ago. We both know how quickly life can change so we're going full throttle. We want to experience as much as we can together.

She darts to her feet. "I don't have a ring. I have something else to give you instead."

I stay where I am because I'm pretty fucking sure that I'll fall over if I try to stand. I sense what's coming. My heart is hammering inside the wall of my chest.

She scurries over to her purse. Reaching inside, she clasps something between her palms.

Once she's back in front of me, she taps on my shoulder. "Open your hand, Barrett."

I do. I take the card that she's been shielding from my view.

It's one of my old business cards from Garent.

"Flip it over," she says in a voice that's barely more than a whisper. "Flip it over now."

I do.

I fall back on my ass when I read what she's written.

Adler & Adler & Adler Consulting

"Bella." I look at her face and then her flat belly beneath the dress. "What is this?"

She drops to her knees. "We're having a baby."

I tug the pear-shaped diamond ring out of the box and slide it onto her finger.

"I'll marry you, Bella."

Staring down at the ring, her eyes fill with tears. "I'll marry you too."

She flies into my arms, and as I hold her against me, I take it all in. This is my life. This is my future. This woman is everything I've wished for, and we're about to make all of our dreams come true.

THANK YOU

Thank you for purchasing my book. I can't even begin to put to words what it means to me. If you enjoyed it, please remember to write a review for it. Let me know your thoughts! I want to keep my readers happy.

For more information on new series and standalones, please visit my website, **www.deborahbladon.com**. There are book trailers and other goodies to check out.

If you want to chat with me personally, please LIKE my page on Facebook. I love connecting with all of my readers because without you, none of this would be possible.
www.facebook.com/authordeborahbladon

Thank you, for everything.

Preview of BLOOM

BLOOM, a hot new standalone from New York Times, USA Today and Wall Street Journal bestselling author, Deborah Bladon.

Liam Wolf should come with a warning.

The man is all kinds of hot.

He's nailed down the tall, tattooed, gorgeous-as-sin look.

I shouldn't be swooning over him.

He's in my floral shop to order a bouquet for the woman of his dreams.

I swallow the bitter taste of envy and design a to die for arrangement.

I offer to deliver the flowers personally because I'm a glutton for punishment.

The delivery should go off without a hitch.

It doesn't.

I end up at Liam's office with the bouquet in one hand and a *no thank you* note from his ex-girlfriend in the other.

I walk away. Liam follows me.

What blooms between us is based on a rebound.

We agree to a simple no-strings-attached fling, but I soon discover that nothing in Liam's world is simple.

Chapter 1

Athena

My floral shop, Wild Lilac, seems to be the place for all the hot guys in Manhattan to come when they want to buy their girlfriends flowers.

Today is a perfect example of that. One of my first customers this morning was a hotshot NHL hockey player. I only know that because I saw his face on a billboard in Times Square during the playoffs last season.

After he bought and paid for the perfect bouquet for his special lady, a looker in a suit walked through the door.

It took him over an hour to choose the arrangement he wanted. I was happy to oblige since it turned out to cost a small fortune. It will be delivered tomorrow right before he goes to the yoga studio she owns to drop to one knee to ask her to spend her life with him.

I look over at the man who walked in less than a minute ago.

He's hot-as-sin.

His dark blond hair is pushed back from his face and skimming the collar of his black button-down shirt. The sleeves are rolled up to his elbows, so the black and gray tattoos that cover his muscular forearms are visible.

He looks semi-corporate since he's dressed in black pants and shoes.

I turn to the side to stop myself from staring at him.

"Excuse me?"

If there ever was a perfect voice for phone sex, it belongs to this man.

I look over at his face. His jaw is covered with a trimmed beard. His blue eyes pierce through me as he stares at me.

The man is a gorgeous giant. He must be at least six-foot-five.

"Can I help you?" I ask cheerily from behind my checkout counter because swooning over the clientele will not pay the rent on this place.

"I need some flowers." He huffs out a laugh. "Nice flowers. I want something extra special for a woman I'm seeing."

Something deflates inside of me. It's not as though I was expecting him to be in here buying flowers for his mom. That mad rush happens in May. It's late September. The bulk of my orders right now are gestures of undying devotion, new baby arrivals, birthdays or sadly, red rose heavy arrangements to honor the recently departed.

His eyes skim the front of the black sweater I'm wearing. "What's your name?"

That's not a question I'm asked often since I usually have a nametag pinned to my chest, but this sweater and sharp objects don't play well together.

"I'm Athena."

"Nice." He flashes me a smile. "I'm Wolf."

"Wolf?" I question back because that's got to be a nickname. "Your name is Wolf?"

His hand jumps to his chin. Smoothing his fingertips over his beard, he huffs out a laugh. "It is. I'm Liam Wolf."

"Liam," I repeat his first name because it suits him in some abstract, unexplainable way.

The breadth of his shoulders and his height make him intimidating to look at, but his eyes and the tone of his voice tell a different story.

I'm running a business, so I go to the heart of the matter. "What kind of flowers are you thinking of?"

"Whatever takes your breath away," he says.

Never mind the flowers; that statement did the trick.

Speechless, I stare at him.

He bows his chin. "I'm looking for an arrangement that will surprise the hell out my girlfriend. It has to be unique. Do you think you can handle that, Athena?"

I can handle anything, even creating beautiful bouquets for men like him to give to other women.

"I'm up for the job." I smile.

Sliding a credit card and a sealed envelope toward me, he takes a pause. "Her name and address are written on there. I need you to take that to her with the flowers today."

All of my deliveries have already gone out, and it's nearing five now.

"My delivery cut-off is at two o'clock." I glance down at the large silver watch on his wrist. "I can have this in her hands tomorrow."

"It has to be today." He leans both hands on the counter. "I'll pay extra if you can get it to her before seven."

Who am I to stand in the way of true love? I have nothing planned for tonight, so I do my good deed for the day. "I can take it to her personally. No extra charge."

His eyes scan my face. "If you can make that happen, I'll be forever in your debt, Athena."

I set to work writing out an invoice for an elaborate arrangement of the most expensive flowers I have in stock. If I'm going to do this tonight, I might as well do it right. I hope the woman on the receiving end of the bouquet and the note realizes just how lucky she is.

ABOUT THE AUTHOR

Deborah Bladon has never read a romance hero she didn't like. Her love for romance novels began when she was old enough to board the bus, library card in hand to check out the newest Harlequin paperbacks. She's a Canadian by heart, and by passport, but you can often spot her in New York City sipping a latte and looking for inspiration for her next story. Manhattan is definitely her second home.

She cherishes her family and believes that each day is a gift for writing, for reading, and for loving.

Printed in Great Britain
by Amazon